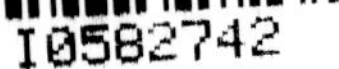

Beasts & Blades

by

Amanda Kaye

To hear about the next exciting release from Amanda Kaye
sign up for her newsletter at
www.amandakayebooks.com/subscribe-now/

1

Book or dagger? Dagger or book?

I survey the two items on my bed as though I don't already have every line and detail memorized from countless hours of use. Really, I'm stalling because parting with either is going to be like losing a piece of myself. But if Papa and I want to eat this week, something else has to be sold off. My heart yearns to keep the faery tale book, but the Guild won't give me another contract if I don't have my weapons. And without a contract, we'll never climb out of this hole.

With a sigh, I return the dagger to the empty shelf, then hold up the collection of stories, taking a deep breath. The scent of old parchment and warm leather brings a flood of memories with it. Reading tales to the kids I've protected over the years, or enjoying the stories on my own during one of my few lazy afternoons. The gold lettering that once graced the cover rubbed off long ago, and the pages are soft from countless perusals. *I'll be lucky to sell it for two pennies.* I rub a hand over the aching knot growing in my chest. It hurts to think of letting it go for so little, that something so treasured is worthless to others.

My steps are heavy as I descend to the lower floor in the snug cottage I share with Papa. It feels spacious now that the pianoforte and the grandfather clock are gone. All that's left are the simple wooden table and three chairs sitting on the threadbare green rug near the fireplace. The sunny kitchen holds more memories than pots, but I wouldn't change a thing.

The clomping outside the front door heralds Papa's return. "Julietta? Where are you, my darling girl?"

I set the book on the table, then open the door with a grin. "Right here. Did you slay any dragons today?" I kiss him on the cheek, his whiskers scratchy against my face.

"Only three or four. They get craftier every day." Papa peers at me through his spectacles, his brown eyes owlish behind the thick lenses. Everyone, including Papa, loves to say how much I look like my mother, with my button nose and straight brown hair, but my eyes are undeniably my father's. His bushy white hair is half-stuffed under a blue wool cap, his jacket buttons misaligned. Crushed violets fall out of his coat pockets, joining the others already scattered around the dirt.

Papa stomps the last of the mud off his boots, sending another bunch of squashed flowers tumbling to the ground. "I couldn't wait to tell you about it. It's stupendous. It'll change everything." He partly unbuttons his coat, then gets distracted by a bird flying overhead.

When he doesn't continue, I prompt him, "Tell me about what?"

"What? Oh!" His eyes light up. "My new invention."

He undoes the last few buttons and wanders into the house, ambling around the sparse living room with a faraway look on his face. The next time he passes close by, I snatch his coat and hat away, hanging them on the back of the door.

Papa doesn't notice the loss, his mind elsewhere. "The spiderwebs across the trails today got me thinking. There has to be a way to take the mechanics of a spinning wheel and apply it to general sewing. Think about it! Perfectly even stitches in seconds. We'll start with simple things like curtains and table coverings and such, then shirts and trousers. There might even be a way to do fancy stitching eventually."

I beam at him. "That sounds amazing. I'll make us some tea while you tell me more about it."

"None for me, dear. I'm still warm from my walk." He squints at the book I left on the table, turning it around to better examine the cover. "I don't recall seeing this one before."

"It was a gift from one of my employers. That family with the two little girls." Those girls were the definition of mischief until I got them to settle down for a story, their faces full of wonder as I read to them each night before bed. I swallow down the lump in my throat and force a smile. "I thought I'd sell it. After all, I'm a bit too old for faery tales. It's time for someone else to enjoy it."

He gives a deep sigh, his shoulders slumping as he drops into a chair. "I'm sorry, Julietta. This is all my fault."

I grab his hand. "Don't say that! The Fates have sent us a string of bad luck, but everything will change soon, you'll see. The Guild will have a contract for me any day now."

As he shakes his head, the lines in his face deepen. "It's not your job to take care of me."

"We take care of each other. It's you and me, Papa. We'll figure things out like always. It's just taking a little longer this time." I squeeze his hand, wishing I could take all his worries away.

Papa nods, his good mood returning. "You're right. It's far past time for our luck to change. I'll go to Lyvon next week to see if *The Belle* has docked."

I bite my lip. *Not this again.* "It's been almost two years …"

"Luck, like love, only comes with faith. You'll see, my dear girl. The ship will come back and then everything will be fine again. No more Guild jobs for you. We'll get you a new pianoforte and so many books you'll need three lifetimes to read them all."

"I don't need those things, Papa. All I need is you."

"Nonetheless, I need to check on the ship again, and there's some friends I'd like to visit. Why don't you come with me this time? I worry about you being here all alone, and mayhap you'll meet a nice young man that catches your fancy."

I chuckle. "Nobles hire me to root out assassins and protect their children. I think I can manage staying on my own for a few weeks."

"Yes, yes, but you always have a partner on those assignments. And it doesn't stop me from worrying about you. I know you've been impatient to get another contract, but I'm glad you're home. It's been a gift to spend so much time with you."

I shift in my seat, ignoring the twinge of guilt. "I'm happy to be home with you, too."

He smiles knowingly. "But you can't help also wanting to do something else, be somewhere else." A hint of sadness shines in his eyes. "You get it from your mother, Fates protect her. She was constantly planning another adventure for us, even though she always longed for home when we traveled. It was hard being torn between two desires, but we found happiness. That's all I want for you."

"I am happy." *So why am I always looking for something I can't describe ...?* I shake my head, clearing the silly thought away. "Like I said, all I need is you. But I confess, it's nice to take a break from the village occasionally."

"Then come with me to Lyvon next week."

"It's tempting, but I should stay here in case the Guild needs to contact me." I stand and smooth out my patched gray skirt. "Speaking of the village, I better go before it gets too late. Do you want me to pick up anything for you while I'm there?"

Papa fumbles for something in his pockets, his face taking on that preoccupied look he gets when he's thinking over a new idea. "Nothing for me, my dear. But please let Monsieur Gerrard know I'll stop by tomorrow afternoon if he's free. Don't tell him, but I've finally figured out how to counter his chess opening."

"Your secret is safe with me." I drop a kiss on top of his shaggy white hair, then duck out the door with my book in hand.

The sunshine chases the faint chill from my skin as I walk down the dusty road to the village. The houses and shops are placed haphazardly, creating a maze of narrow alleys and wide roads between the thatch-roofed buildings. I wave to the people who call out greetings, but don't stop, wanting to get my unhappy errand over with as soon as possible. Monsieur Gerrard's shop is on the far side of town, a neat structure tucked between two homes. The weight in my stomach grows heavy as I approach it, and I cross my fingers he's closed so I can put off selling my treasured book for another day.

Unfortunately, the Fates have other plans, as the shopkeeper's off-key singing can be heard through the bright red door. One deep breath, then I tuck the loose strands of my brown hair under my kerchief and go inside. A few minutes later, I emerge with empty hands and the promise of a small bag of barley to be delivered later today. I swallow hard as I hurry around the corner of the shop, fleeing the pity Monsieur Gerrard couldn't completely hide.

Safe in the shadows, I wrap my arms around my waist and press my lips together, tears stinging my eyes. *It's just a book.* I swallow down the lump, blinking rapidly. *That barley will keep us going for another two weeks if we're careful. It'll be fine. I'll buy my book back as soon as the Guild sends me another contract. Everything will be all right as long as Papa and I have each other.*

With a quick swipe at my eyes, I paste a smile on my face and step back into the sunshine. I wander aimlessly, seeking a distraction. Everything is pleasant and simple, just as it was yesterday, and the day before that, and the day before that. Some people spend their whole lives here, never leaving Cassia. While my home is beautiful, I can't imagine that kind of life for myself.

Never mind. Gloomy thoughts have no place on a beautiful day like today. Instead, I focus on enjoying my visit to town. While it's not far from our home, I never come here as often as I'd like. The scent of fresh-baked bread tickles my nose as I admire the pink peonies tumbling from Suzette's window boxes, reminding me of the crushed flowers forgotten in Papa's coat pockets. Children roll hoops down the road while two women gossip by a water barrel. Yes, life here is serene and uneventful.

There's nothing wrong with living in a peaceful town. I'm used to keeping my guard up when I'm out on a job, but I could get used to this. I swing my arms with a little extra gusto as I walk down the alley, the tension falling out of my body. *Time to stop worrying and let the Fates handle things.*

A knife presses into my side. I gasp, my heart leaping into my throat.

The man growls, "Look what I caught."

My pulse pounds as my body reacts on instinct. I elbow my attacker in the stomach, then spin out of reach, keeping a grip on his wrist. As he hunches over with a grunt, I twist the assailant's arm until the knife clatters in the dirt. My foot kicks the back of his knees and he crashes down in a cloud of dust.

I pounce on the man, ready to teach him a lesson about attacking women in the street, when my mind catches up with my eyes. I barely stop my punch in time. "Marcel! What are you doing here?"

The Guild member curls up on the ground, his fine blond hair flopping across his forehead. Marcel's handsome face reddens as he struggles to catch his breath between chuckles. "You're losing your touch, Julietta. You didn't even pull your dagger."

"Keeping my guard up around here is dangerous. Normal people don't expect to be stabbed when they tap you on the shoulder." I offer him a hand up. "Did you come all this way because you enjoy attacking me in the streets, or are you here on business?" *Have the Fates finally answered my pleas? Will it be enough? Why did Marcel come instead of sending a messenger? Please, please, please be here with a contract.* My heart races as I swallow down all the questions fighting to break free.

He straightens with a groan. "Can't I just want to see you? I treasure these moments together, poppet. Everyone knows you're my favorite." Marcel retrieves his giant black hat from the road and beats the dust off it.

So, he wants to play it that way. Fine. I can humor him— or shake it out of him if he takes too long. I raise an eyebrow. "And that's why you haven't come to see me in over a year?"

"Shove off. It's only been three months." At my face, he grins. "Mayhap a bit longer. You know how things are in the Guild."

I smirk. "Or you're still mad about that thing with Ysabel."

"Ysabel who? I only have eyes for you, my beauty." Marcel casts a critical eye over me, delicately wrinkling his nose. "Darling, why do you insist on dressing like a drab little sparrow? Between that kerchief and the dress, it's a wonder I noticed you at all. Are you trying to blend into the dirt?"

"Not all of us need to call attention to ourselves. Besides, how could I possibly compete with your good looks?"

"Very true. I am exceptional." He straightens his favorite blue jacket with the oversized brass buttons, then links his arm through mine. "Where can a gentleman buy a lady a drink around here? Or do we have to forage in the forest for food and wine?"

I laugh as I steer him toward the common house. "You're welcome to stay in Lyvon if my village isn't to your taste."

"But then I wouldn't have the pleasure of your company. And I wanted to bring this contract to you personally."

My drumming heart skips a beat as I fight to keep my face serene. *Thank the Fates!* I nudge his side, keeping my voice steady. "I'm intrigued. You never play the messenger. What's so special about this job that you'd come all the way to Cassia?"

"Patience, poppet. First, I need whatever passes for a good glass of wine in this part of the kingdom. Traveling is a dusty business and I'm parched."

He's enjoying this too much. It must be big. Really big. I bite the inside of my cheek to keep from grinning. *Let him have his fun. No point in rushing him or he'll just draw it out longer to torture me.*

Marcel's rich clothing and handsome face draw a number of curious glances and questioning looks as we make our way down the main road. He leers and winks at anyone who looks his way, relishing the attention while I smother a groan. I can already feel the rumors circulating about me and my mysterious friend. It'll take months for the villagers to move on to some other piece of gossip.

The common house won't be busy until this evening, but there are a few people scattered around the tables in the room. Lyle pours two glasses of red wine, which we take to a table in the corner. By silent agreement, Marcel sets his chair against the wall so he can watch the rest of the room while I position mine toward the windows so we can't be ambushed from behind. He's already noted the escape routes through the window next to us and the kitchen doorway, but

I'd wager he hasn't noticed the small door tucked beneath the stairs that leads to the back alley.

Marcel raises his glass in a toast, then takes a sip. He winces dramatically. "What is that, vinegar? It can't be wine."

I swirl the ruby liquid around my glass, letting it breathe. "It has to be better than that dishwater you claimed was cider."

He presses a hand over his heart. "You wound me, Julietta. And after I came all this way to bring you a present. You should thank me, not insult me."

I snort. "Like last time? I'm not going to travel two weeks just to learn they terminated the contract while I was on the road and I have to come home again."

He gives me a wounded look. "That only happened the one time, and you know I sent a messenger to stop you. It's not my fault you travel so quickly."

"It was payback. You need to learn to let go of your grudges."

"How could I ever be mad at you, darling?" Marcel chuckles. "But if I was, we're even now. Which leads me to our current business." He leans forward, his eyes gleaming. "This is it. The one you've been waiting for."

My mouth goes dry as my pulse kicks into a gallop. *Keep calm. He's baiting me. Don't act desperate or he'll pounce.* I force my fingers to stop drumming on the table, pressing my hand flat against the stained surface. "That's what you said about the last one."

"No, no, I'm serious. Even after the Guild's cut, you'll be a very rich woman."

More games. Given that Marcel came out here himself and how much he's drawing this out, I can't even imagine what he has. Pushing down my growing excitement, I lean back in my chair like he doesn't hold my future in his hands. *I need to think about this like any other contract. Details first, then decide if the pay is worth it.* "Who's being targeted?"

"Prince Devereaux Saint-Veil of Fallian Province."

I stare into my wineglass, trying to recall what I know about him. I've heard the name and a few things about the kingdom, but nothing else. "Who's my partner?"

"Good news, poppet. This is a solo contract, so you won't be splitting the fee with anyone."

My eyebrows fly up. "Alone? How can they possibly expect me to protect the prince and search out the threat at the same time?" I shake my head, my heart growing heavy as the answer to my prayers slips out of my reach. "You know even the most mundane contracts can turn dangerous without warning. I'm a passable fighter, but not the best. You need someone who can defend him if needed."

"Nonsense. You can bury a dagger in someone's eye from twenty paces. Not to mention what you did to that brute in Vinail—"

I hiss, "Keep your voice down! I need to maintain a respectable reputation around here." Thank the Fates, nobody seems to have heard him. The tables closest to us are empty, and the few people in the room aren't paying any attention to us, aside from an occasional passing glance.

He widens his eyes innocently. "Of course, darling. Can't let the peasants know you can kill a man ten different ways with your hands. They'd burn you at the stake."

I give him my sweetest smile. "Perhaps I should demonstrate some of those techniques on you."

He raises his hands and grins. "Peace, poppet. Just a

small jest. People in our line of work need to find their fun wherever they can." Marcel smooths an imaginary wrinkle on his sleeve. "I'm sure you won't be expected to stand watch all day by yourself. They probably have their own guards and just want you to do what you do best: find out who's behind the threat. And nobody is better at rooting out a conspiracy than you."

A knot of uneasiness grows in my chest. *Something's wrong.* My eyes narrow as I study him. "Why are you selling me so hard on this contract? What's the catch? What aren't you telling me?"

"So suspicious, darling." He gives a languid wave of his hand. "No catch."

The alarm bells ring louder. "You're losing your touch, Marcel. You used to be a better liar."

His smile loses a fraction of its brilliance. "You were specifically requested. If you don't agree, then they'll go elsewhere."

I stare at him.

He shifts in his chair, the charming grin disappearing. "It's for a year."

"A year?" I sit back hard in my seat, my mind buzzing. *I can't leave Papa for a year. But if I turn down this contract, Fates only knows when the next one will come. The Guild will be annoyed at losing out on a commission, so they won't be eager to send another one my way. And in another few weeks I'll have to take a job in Lyvon or one of the other big cities. Papa would be crushed if I had to find that kind of work to support us. He already feels so guilty over our bad luck.*

But a year ...

Marcel's voice breaks through my whirling thoughts.

"They're at La Sailles—their little hunting lodge deep in the mountains. I'm told the blizzards in that area block the pass for most of the year. The Guild members familiar with those conditions confirmed there's usually only a brief window to travel through the mountains safely."

No letters or visits home, either. I'd be completely on my own. I take a long sip of wine to give myself time to get my dismay under control. *Focus on getting the details first, then decide what to do.* "Why La Sailles? Why aren't they staying at the main palace in Charistel?"

Marcel rolls his eyes. "Why do nobles do anything? You can ask his sister, Lady Isabeau, when you get there. She's the one who contracted with the Guild."

His sister? "That's rather unusual. Is she his guardian?"

"His parents are alive and currently ruling the kingdom. And as far as anyone can recall, Lord Devereaux is of age."

Nothing about this makes any sense. Why wouldn't his parents make the arrangements? Or the prince himself? "And what age is that, exactly?"

He shrugs.

I massage my temples, trying to relieve the building pressure. "Does Lady Isabeau know I work with children? That I usually do the research and interviews while my partner provides the protection?"

"She asked for you. That's all I know." He twirls the glass by its stem, studying the dark wine like it's the most fascinating thing in the room.

My teeth grind together as I drum my fingers on the wood. "Do you know anything useful? Where's the briefing package?"

A sick feeling fills my stomach as Marcel pulls a single piece of rolled parchment from his jacket. My frown deepens to scowl when I find a scant paragraph of hastily scribbled notes. There's little more than the facts I already knew and a few wild conjectures. "Haha, Marcel. Very funny. Where's the real background?"

He has the decency to look chagrined. "That's all I could scrape together before I left. We've never had a contract with Fallian Province. Never even had a contract with anyone who had a problem with Fallian Province." Marcel straightens, his usual carefree charm returning. "Which is a gap you'll be able to fill in for us once you finish your job."

"But—but—" I shake my head, the sickening feeling growing. "This doesn't have anything about the prince aside from his name and that he's the heir. Why can't his guards handle this? What exactly is the threat? Have there been any assassination attempts? Who are their enemies? Strengths, weaknesses, anything?"

Marcel shrugs one shoulder while admiring his reflection in a windowpane.

I grab his chin and swing his face back to mine. "Marcel. Focus. You're sending me to protect a prince. Alone. For almost a year. With no idea what I'm walking into, or what's going to be thrown at me. This isn't how the Guild operates. It's how people get killed in our line of work."

He brushes off my hand and gives me a lazy grin. "How much trouble could they possibly be in when Fallian Province is so insignificant? Lady Isabeau is probably one of those hysterical nobles who confuses a sneeze with the plague. And I bet that lordling is the type to faint at the sight of blood and spends all day wailing about smelling salts. You know the sort. Plus, think of the money, darling." He pauses, drawing out the moment, relishing my impatience.

When Marcel names the figure, I can't stop my jaw from

dropping. *Fates! That would solve all our problems. Papa could fund every invention he can ever imagine!*

Marcel leans back in his chair. "Of course, I would've thought of you for this job even if you weren't specifically requested. But if you want me to offer it to someone else, I'm sure I could convince the lady to accept a replacement …" His eyes twinkle as he takes a sip of wine.

The money makes me want to leap at the offer, but it doesn't silence the warning bells ringing in my mind. "I can't collect a payment if I'm dead."

"Don't be so dramatic. You'll be snowbound in a cozy little hunting lodge, babysitting a feeble prince who lays in bed all day. No visitors coming and going. The worse thing that'll happen is you'll catch a sniffle." Marcel plops a heavy purse on the table, the coins inside clinking loudly. "You get ten percent upfront. But you have to leave in the next few days if you want to make it there before the pass closes for the year."

I eye the pouch, my heart racing. *That alone would let Papa live comfortably for a year. Spend a year trapped in a mountain palace with a bunch of whining nobles and solve all our problems, or keep selling off our remaining things one by one and hope the Fates send something else my way before it's too late?*

I pick up the purse. "If you'll excuse me, there's a book I need to buy."

3

"A little hunting lodge," I mutter to myself. "Hilarious, Marcel."

From my viewpoint on the cliff's edge, the land spreads out before me, revealing the hidden secrets below. The forest is a wave of shadows lapping against the outer stone wall that rises at least twenty feet into the air. Set far behind the barrier, in the middle of the valley, is the palace. A small palace compared to some of the monstrosities I've seen, true, but still a palace. Even in the deepening twilight, the white stones glow against the black mountains, drawing the eye to it. My village could fit within its walls with room to spare. The castle boasts at least five stories with six tall towers dotting the night sky, and wide, arching walkways connecting them. Behind the castle are more outbuildings—barns, storehouses, and the like. It's impossible to see how far the grounds go in the fading light.

Another blast of wind threatens to send me tumbling over the cliff. I yank the edges of my cloak closed, wondering why I bother. My skin is the same temperature as the frozen air, and the frigid gales trying to knock me over snatch away what little body heat I generate. What I really need is a roaring fire and a strong cup of tea to thaw out. My horse stomps his foot and gives an unhappy whinny, his breath coming out in a puff of white smoke.

I pat the stallion's golden neck. "You're right, Henri. We'd better get to the palace before the storm hits."

The terrain is rough going as we wind our way down from the pass and into the valley. I study the landscape for strengths and weaknesses, trusting the horse's eagerness for a cozy barn and warm mash to keep us on the road.

Every step closer to the palace increases the tightness in my chest. There's always a glimmer of nervousness going into a new job, but the weight of this task sits heavier than my normal contracts. No matter how many plans I run through my mind, or how many times I try to convince myself I'm overreacting, I can't shake the nagging worry I'm forgetting something critical. Not having a partner to back me up and compensate for my weaknesses makes me vulnerable, and by extension, that makes the prince an easier target. I'm going to have to be extra diligent without a second set of eyes and hands.

An uneasiness creeps through my bones and a chill that has nothing to do with the cold runs through me. *Mayhap I should've listened to that last innkeeper and waited to see if the storm would clear first.* I shake my head. *No. If their stories are right, it might be months before the pass is open again. There's no turning back now. Better to press on and get to shelter before the full force reaches us.*

The horse picks up the pace when we reach the valley floor. The wind gains strength, howling its fury at the mountains. A thick blanket of snow falls, joining the mounds already smothering the ground. Ice clings to the stallion's straw-colored mane. I hunch over Henri's neck, holding my cloak over his sides so we can share our heat.

Even with all their stories about how travel is impossible after a storm, I can't rely on the snowed-in pass to keep people out. The storm may close up the route for a normal traveler, but a determined assassin might still get through. I'll check the pass myself once this blizzard is over. Item three hundred and twenty-four on the to-do list.

Both Henri and I heave a sigh of relief when the huge outer walls come into view. I cringe at the wide opening and absent gates even while thanking the Fates nothing will delay us. No challenge rings out as I ride through the stone archway, no guards or gatehouse in sight. *Item three hundred and twenty-five.*

The wind shrieks in my ears. A wall of steely gray clouds rolls down the mountain, blotting out the sky. Fear squeezes my heart as I urge Henri into a gallop, racing to beat the growing storm pounding on our heels, pleading with the Fates to protect the horse from a stumble that could mean death for both of us. I can't help but keep glancing over my shoulder, shuddering as the clouds seem to gain on us second by second. Despite Henri's heroic efforts, the storm swallows us before the palace is in sight.

It's impossible to see any shapes or even determine what's around us as the gales whip snow and ice through the air in a blinding maelstrom. I've read about storms like this, but my imagination fell far short of reality. The air is stolen from my lungs with each breath. I press my face against Henri's neck, gasping. My legs are frozen in place, my fingers insensible. The dropped reins crack through the air, flung around by the squall. The stallion valiantly pushes on, though I can't tell if we're heading in the right direction. I cling to his mane, squeezing my eyes shut. My racing heart and panicked wheezes gradually fade into the background as my mind goes numb from the cold. Every minute blends into the next. It's impossible to tell how long we've been slogging through the endless storm that's determined to kill us.

When the palace finally appears like a shining beacon of safety, I want to weep from relief. Henri stumbles to a stop at the entrance. I slide off the horse and fall face first into the snow piled against the stairs. My limbs refuse to move. The small part of my brain that's still working screams at me to stand up before we freeze to death.

My numb fingers search overhead until I bump against something solid. Teeth gritted, I grab the stirrup and force my body up, using poor Henri for leverage until I'm standing. My unfeeling legs stumble through the snow and up the stairs, tugging the stallion to follow. I shoulder the door open, falling onto the marbled granite floor as the wind shoves me forward. Not bothering to get up, I manage to kick the door closed, my ears popping as the rage of the storm is abruptly cutoff.

I close my eyes and concentrate on breathing. The entryway would be chilly by anyone else's standards, but to me, it's a sauna. My teeth chatter as warmth creeps into my body, making the frozen parts of me go from numb to painful. The cool air scorches my icy skin, the cold inside me intensifies to an agonizing degree until it feels like my muscles are burning. Each breath scrapes my lungs raw. All I can do is stare blankly between shuddering gasps.

Henri whoofs in my hair, his warmth thawing my thoughts for a moment. I yank off my icy glove and rub the white stripe on his nose. "Looks like we made it here alive—or half-alive, at least. Thanks, Henri. I couldn't have done this without you."

The stallion nudges me encouragingly as I struggle to sit up. Slowly, the haze in my vision drops away, and the room comes into focus. My jaw drops. I've been in some spectacular palaces, but this one stands out for its grandness. The entrance is a marvel of gleaming white granite soaring up four stories to a stained-glass roof that must be dazzling in the daylight. Statues of graceful forest creatures stand guard along the walls. The stone archways are decorated with carvings of vines, roses, and small birds peeping out between the flowers.

It's fantastical, and stunning, and … cold. Lifeless. For all its beauty, I can't imagine anyone calling this place home. *Why would the prince choose to come here for winter? He must have a dozen other homes he could pick from if he doesn't want to stay at the main palace in Charistel. Why come here?*

I shake my head. *Enough lollygagging. His motivations aren't my concern. I need to get myself and Henri settled, then focus on my job.*

"Hello? Is anyone here?" My voice echoes off the stone. "Hello?"

No point in sitting here and freezing until someone finds me. I point at Henri. "Stay here and guard the front door."

The stallion wanders away, hooves clicking loudly on the floor.

"Great job." Wrapping my cloak tighter, I pick a random hallway and shuffle down it as fast as my numb legs will move.

The extraordinary beauty of the entryway continues in

the passage. The decorations and stonework make me feel like I'm walking through a frozen enchanted forest, its occupants encased in ice. Carved ebony doors featuring meadows, trees, and peaceful forest lakes hint at hidden secrets I long to explore another day. Right now, all I want is to let Lady Isabeau know I've arrived and then sleep for a day or three. After that, she can tell me what's really going on with her brother and why she hired me.

"Stop right there! Who are you? What are you doing here?"

I wince at the angry tone, cursing the cold and fatigue for dulling my mind and allowing someone to catch me unawares.

The man glaring at me has noble written all over him, from the haughty expression to the richly tailored clothes. Even without the finery, the easy confidence he exudes would make it impossible for anyone to mistake him for a commoner. Someone used to being obeyed without question.

Despite the scowl, my frozen heart can't help but skip a beat at that handsome face. It's as if he stepped out of the pages of my faery tale book. He shares that annoyingly attractive combination of features implying both hard edges and softer possibilities. His brown hair is closer to honey, making his dark brown eyes a captivating contrast. The bulky coat can't disguise the wide, muscular shoulders. Rougher hands than expected for a noble. Someone who isn't afraid of labor—or a spoiled aristocrat who doesn't like riding with gloves.

Still, I imagine most women find that edge of ruggedness irresistible, especially compared to the layabouts so often found at court. Someone as striking as this man would have everything in life handed to them, even without an aristocratic title. Only the tightness around his eyes makes me hesitate to write him off as another pompous rogue. It's a feature I've noticed in the few nobles who realize their positions carry more responsibilities than hosting a good party.

I can't imagine a better setting for this unwelcoming man. Only someone with his perfect features could stand out from the breathtaking beauty of La Sailles. *A granite noble in a granite palace. Perhaps everything here is made of stone.* Stifling a hysterical giggle, I shake my head, trying in vain to restore my wits. *Fates save me, my mind has gone completely loony.*

I twist my numb face into what I hope is a smile. "Hello, I'm Julietta Dantes. I was—"

He stalks toward me, eyes flinty. "You're going to be very sorry you came here."

"If you would—"

"Did you think I wouldn't find out? This is treason."

Things are getting out of hand. Why is he determined to pick a fight with me? I hold out my hands in a placating gesture, speaking in a soothing tone. "I honestly have no idea what you're talking about. I'm here to talk to Lady Isa—"

He closes the short distance between us, his fingers curling into fists, muscles tensed to attack. "It's in your best interest to come quietly to the dungeon. I won't hesitate to use force if I have to."

Normally it'd be refreshing to find someone who doesn't dismiss a fight with me just because I'm a woman, but tonight I'm in no mood for anything except finding Lady Isabeau and then my bed. I back up a step, trying to give him one last out. "I don't know who you think I am, but you're mistaken. Lady Isabeau hired me for a job here. If you could just point me in her direction, I'll be on my way. No fighting necessary."

He narrows his eyes. "Do you honestly think that'll work? I'm not letting you get away this time."

Arrogant beast. If he wants a fight, I'll give him one. I shrug. "If you insist. Just remember, I tried to stop you."

While the hallway would be considered wide by normal standards, it still constricts maneuvering in a fight. Thank the Fates most of my weapons training focused on tight spaces. My area of expertise may not be combat, but the Guild won't accept anyone who can't protect themselves or their charges.

He probably thinks his height and weight are advantages, but I'm going to show him how they—not to mention that arrogance—can be used against him. *No weapons. Lady Isabeau isn't likely to welcome me with open arms if I stab one of her friends on my first night, even if he deserves it.*

I bounce on my toes, readying my muscles.

He raises an eyebrow. "Are you quite finished?"

"Not yet." *I can't let him corner me or he'll overpower me in seconds. Keep moving, make him work for it. If he's tired, he's clumsy.* I toss my cloak behind me, shivering at the loss of its meager warmth. "All right. Whenever you're ready."

He smirks. "Don't worry, I won't damage that pretty face."

I flip my braid over my shoulder and give him an angelic smile. "Funny, I was about to say the same thing to you."

He lunges forward and I spin away. I let my instincts and training take over, moving without thought to block and duck his strikes. Always on the defensive, not taking advantage of the openings he gives me as we travel down the hallway.

The impression of a granite man falls away as he moves gracefully and swiftly from attack to attack, though his expression remains stony. Most men like to roar and yell when they fight, but he's deathly silent. His fighting style is more akin to a panther: fluid speed combined with precision, all while making it look effortless.

A kick aimed at my knee misses, but carries him far enough forward to grab my wrist. I twist my arm, forcing him to release me before leaping out of reach.

We circle each other, wary after tasting the other's skills.

He wipes his forehead with the back of his arm and grimaces. "At least they didn't insult me by sending some helpless damsel." The noble sheds his coat and pushes his sleeves up, revealing muscled arms.

I pretend to be concerned. "Tired already? Do you need a nap before we continue?"

"On the contrary, I'm just getting warmed up. But I'll be happy to accept your surrender if this is too grueling for you."

"Very considerate, but I'd rather put you flat on your back."

He grins. "I don't go down easily."

I arch my eyebrow, smothering my smile. "We'll see about that."

The nobleman watches me carefully, but makes no move to attack first this time.

The man has patience, I'll grant him that. But he's used the last of mine. Time to put an end to this.

Feinting to the right, I round on his left side and drive my elbow into his ribs. He tries to grab me, but I skip away, luring him after me.

He's quick, but I'm quicker.

I spring forward, sweeping my foot out. The man backpedals. I follow, not giving him time to reclaim his rhythm. Kick. Kick. Duck. Punch. Strike. Each blow lands with a satisfying thump.

Ugh, I wish I could use my dagger. I need to finish this fight before I collapse. I slam against his shoulder, fatigue making the move sloppy, hitting too high. The noble grunts, but stays upright. The unexpected resistance throws me off balance, and I stagger back a half-step.

He chuckles. "I told you."

The smirk stokes my anger, energizing my tired muscles. The exhaustion is gone in an instant. I use the small space to my advantage, leaping sideways and pushing my feet off against the wall, tackling him. We crash to the ground. I roll out of his reach, using the momentum to push to my feet.

He glowers at me as he stands. "I slipped."

"Sure, you did. When I knocked you over." I smile sweetly.

He charges with a roar. I trip him, using his momentum against him, and he smashes to the floor with a grunt. This time, I put my foot on his chest to prevent him from rising again. The man scowls at me, but doesn't put up any resistance. I'd expected anger, but all I see in his expression is annoyance.

He presses his lips together. "You need to leave."

Even now he's trying to order me around! I've dealt with a lot of snotty nobles in my time, but this one is ruder than most. I pull out the knife hidden in my sleeve and tap the point against his chest. "If you promise to stop attacking me, I'll let you up. Otherwise, I'm going to put an end to your miserable existence. Which would you prefer?"

He holds up his hands. "Truce."

Watching him warily, I lift my foot off him and offer my hand. He ignores it, swinging to his feet with ease. I retrieve my cloak, yanking it on to trap the body heat generated by the exercise. *At least the chill is finally gone from my bones.*

Exhaustion is quickly draining the energy that sustained me through the fight. "Since we've established I won't be going to the dungeon tonight, please tell Lady Isabeau Saint-Veil that Julietta Dantes of Rauleg is here to see her."

He doesn't bother looking at me as he straightens his clothes. "She's not in residence. Isa hardly ever leaves Charistel, and never in winter. So, Julietta Dantes of Rauleg, what business do you have with my sister?"

Fates take her, she was supposed to be here. Wait, sister? Did he say sister? Iciness fills my veins. "Are—are you—Devereaux Saint-Veil?" *Please say no, please say no, please say no.*

A hint of amusement sparks in his brown eyes. "Of Fallian Province. At your service." He gives me a mocking bow.

I suck in a breath as my mouth goes dry. *It's him. The prince. This is bad. Really, really bad. Fates help me, I was expecting someone too ill to defend himself, or mayhap someone barely out of short pants who can't use a sword without cutting off his finger. Not this intimidating man. Did Marcel know? He must've known.*

There's nothing I can do about it now. *Move on and kill Marcel later.* My lips move, but no words come out. I swallow hard, heat creeping up my neck as I try again. "My lord." I bow, my movements jerky. "Lady Isabeau Saint-Veil—"

"Of Fallian Province." His lips twitch.

I narrow my eyes. *I should've stabbed him when I had the chance.* "Your sister hired me to provide security during your stay here." After a moment of fumbling, I hand him the bundle of documents from my cloak.

He barely glances at the first page before tucking them away in his pocket. "Ridiculous. I'm perfectly safe."

She didn't tell him about the threat? Or does he prefer to stick his head in the sand and pretend nothing's wrong? "Your sister disagrees. She says you're in danger."

He folds his arms. "And she thought one woman would be sufficient to protect me from this imagined threat?"

I lift my eyebrow. "Do you need me to knock you down again?"

"I was referring to the number of defenders, not the skill." He tilts his head back and stares at the ceiling. After a moment, he shakes his head. "No, I can't tolerate your presence here. You have to leave."

Tolerate? He can't be serious. "Tolerable or not, I have a contract. And you can use my help." I gesture around me. "Where are your guards? Nobody stopped me at any point as I crossed the grounds and came into your home. And I've already proven an assassin could easily kill you and flee. Face it, you need me." I fold my arms and stare him down, daring him to disagree.

Lord Devereaux's jaw tightens. "Once the storm closes the pass, I won't need guards. The only people with access to La Sailles will be my staff. Besides, guards are a distraction. You're dismissed. Go home."

I struggle to keep my expression friendly while fighting the urge to strangle him. "I have a contract."

"Not with me. This is my kingdom and my home. I

won't have strangers poking their noses in where they don't belong." He leans forward, crowding me, his eyes hard. "Get out. Now."

He's really going to do it. He's going to throw me out without a second thought. A fist squeezes my heart as I feel Papa and my future slipping away. I hate that my fate is in the hands of this cold-hearted man. I fight to keep my voice steady as I choke out, "My lord, I swear I won't be in your way. You'll never know I'm here." Softer, "My family needs this." My cheeks burn with humiliation, despising myself for practically begging this despicable man to let me stay and protect him.

"Why am I wasting my time?" Lord Devereaux looks past me and shouts, "Helene! Where are you? Helene!"

"Here, milord." A tall, wiry woman hovers in the doorway to the left. Her dark blue dress is neatly pressed, her black hair pulled back into a tight bun. There's a curl to lip and her nose wrinkles unpleasantly. I can't tell if it's her reaction to seeing me, or if she always looks like she smells something offensive.

"There you are. Take care of this hellion." He waves in my direction.

The nose wrinkling doubles. "What do you wish me to do with it?"

Definitely me.

"Send her home."

"My lord, there's a blizzard outside." The housekeeper's tone is apologetic.

"Fine. Give her a coin, then send her home."

There must be a way to fix this. I've traveled too far to be sent away now. Papa and I need this. I lick my lips, then fix him with a determined stare. "Lady Isabeau Saint-Veil hired me—"

"I don't have time to deal with my blasted sister's meddling."

"If I could—"

"You need to leave immediately."

"I wanted—"

He turns and walks away. "My housekeeper will escort you out."

I clamp my lips shut, determined not to demean myself further in front of this arrogant beast.

Helene clasps her hands in front of her and grimaces. "Milord, it's not safe for anyone to travel to the village right now. She can't leave until the storm is over."

Lord Devereaux waves over his shoulder. "Just keep her out of my sight until you send her home. Until then, make sure she doesn't leave her room without an escort." With that last declaration, he disappears around the corner.

"As you wish, my lord." The housekeeper takes my arm in a bruising grip. She drags me in the opposite direction, muttering under her breath.

My steps are heavy as Helene steers me through the palace. *How can this be happening? This job was the answer to all my prayers. Now, I'm being sent home in disgrace. No payment. The Guild will never give me another contract. What will Papa and I do now?*

A spark of anger ignites in my chest and I shake my head. *What am I doing? I won't let them boss me around like this. I've worked for kings. I know my value and my skills. Devereaux Saint-Veil isn't going to chase me off without a fight. My contract is with his sister. And until his sister says otherwise, I'm going to fulfill my side of the deal, and then collect my pay for a job well done.*

I yank my arm from the housekeeper's grasp. "You'll have to show me to my room later. Right now, I have work to do."

I can't wait to see the look on his face ...

The housekeeper stalks my steps as I make my way back to the entryway, where Henri is lipping the antlers on a stone deer. Smirking at Helene's gasp of outrage, I take the stallion's reins and ask for directions to the stables. Her thin face turns red as she struggles to contain her fury, but she silently points the way.

I pat Henri's soft cheek. "One more time through the snow, and then you can have a nice long rest." I brace myself, then pry the door open, instantly chilled by the wind. My horse gives an unhappy sigh as he follows me out into the storm. Thankfully, the stable isn't far and I quickly get him housed in a snug stall with a large meal.

Rubbing my hands together, I stand in the middle of the building, plotting my next move. *Where to start, where to start ... The staff. I'm going to need a few allies if I want to survive Lord Grumpy's wrath when he figures out I'm still here. The quicker I can get on their good side before that cranky housekeeper turns them against me, the better. I squint into the dark of the storm. If this household's like all the others, the staff will gather in the kitchen to stay warm and gossip about my arrival.* The well-trodden trail in the snow between the stable and the palace should take me straight to the kitchen. Or at the very least, it'll take me to another door and away from that annoying housekeeper.

The exhaustion tugging at me warns me this won't be a long visit. Best to go in and make my greetings quickly before I fall asleep on my feet. I follow the path to a small door set in the side of the palace and dive inside, spilling light and heat into the chilly night air. The quiet chatter in the room cuts off abruptly.

Here in the kitchen are the first signs of warmth. A cheery fire burns in the fireplace, casting a lovely glow on the stone walls. There's the delectable scent of roasting meats that always seems to linger in the air long after the meal is served. The copper pots and pans hanging from the ceiling are shiny and dented from repeated scrubbing. Off to one side of the room is a long trestle table that was long ago worn to a smooth finish, the deep golden color inviting everyone to gather around it. The small staff is settled on the benches with cups of steaming tea in front of them.

My heart speeds up as my mouth goes dry. *Why am I nervous? I've done this a hundred times. There's nothing to be anxious about.* "Hello." I try to smile as their faces swivel my direction, making my stomach jump. "I'm Julietta Dantes. Pleased to meet you."

Helene's voice comes from across the room. "Our lord's unintended guest for the duration of the storm."

I keep the smile fixed on my face as my heart sinks. That dratted housekeeper must have watched me from a window and guessed my plans. I should've expected that. My mind must still be dragging from my travels.

Helene's lips are a thin line. "No need to introduce you to everyone. You won't be here long." She turns and addresses the rest of the staff. "Lord Saint-Veil has ordered Miss Dantes to depart as soon as it's safe to travel."

An older, red-faced woman in a stained blue dress snorts. "Then she'll be stuck here for at least a week, the way the storm's blowing."

I quickly run a hand over my tangled hair as I move closer to the group. "Oh, I plan to be here a lot longer than that." *No matter what Lord Grouch thinks.*

Helene ignores me. "Until then, she'll be escorted by myself or Orvil at all times. Mind your mouths don't run away with you around her or any of the villagers. Remember, our lord frowns on gossip. His business is his own."

The same woman rolls her eyes. "You'll be there to make sure we don't chat her up, so why do you need to remind us?" She turns to me. "What brings you here, miss?"

Fates, what should I tell them? I can't tell them the truth in case one of them is working with the enemy. My usual story that I'm a tutor for whoever I'm guarding clearly won't work. Why, oh why, didn't I wait until morning when my mind would be clever? What excuse can I give them for keeping watch on Lord Crankypants?

I blurt out, "I'm his matchmaker." *What? Why did I say that? It's totally ridiculous. Matchmaker? Princes don't need matchmakers. They're married off based on political alliances and negotiations. Who's going to believe—*

The youngest girl squeals, her red curls bouncing as she leans forward. "That's so romantic. Can I help? What princesses are you considering? Are noblewomen also in the running? This is so exciting!"

Helene snaps, "Shush, Caitlin. As I said, our lord's business is his own and we'll stay out of it. Miss Dantes will be gone before you know it." She glares at me. "I'll show you to your room now."

The warmth in the kitchen seeps into my bones, releasing the tension from my muscles as I grin at the enthusiastic Caitlin. "I'd appreciate any help you or anyone else here can give me. You all obviously know Lord Devereaux well. Lady Isabeau is the one who hired me. Such a loving sister. She's concerned he's buried himself in work, and she wants to look out for her big brother's happiness."

Caitlin and another girl sigh dreamily. Despite the housekeeper seething behind me, everyone leans forward, watching me with rapt expressions.

I definitely have their interest now. Hopefully, their curiosity will overcome any more warnings from Helene. I stifle a yawn, then another. *Better to leave them wanting more and let their curiosity grow.* "I'm really looking forward to getting to know all of you. Now, if you'll excuse me, I had a long day of traveling. I better go to bed before I fall asleep on my feet. Good night."

The group murmurs their goodbyes as the housekeeper marches me away from the kitchen. Excited whispers break out behind us. *At least they bought it. Now nobody will question it when I spend time with Lord Sourpuss. And if he wants to contradict my story, he'll have to tell everyone his sister actually hired me to babysit him. His enormous ego won't allow such an indignity.*

Imagining the prince's face when he hears my cover story adds an extra bounce to my step. I have at least a week before the storm is over. More than enough time to assess the situation and see what I'm up against—from enemies within the palace and outside it. The staff seems more than willing to welcome me if I can keep Prince Curmudgeon and his housekeeper from scaring them off.

This is going to be fun.

5

New day, new plan.

I'm determined Lord Crabapple and his housekeeper won't drive me away without a fight. He may be in charge here, but Lady Isabeau is my employer. I'm going to do my job to the best of my ability, whether he likes it or not.

I'm sure Helene was tempted to shove me in a broom closet, but good manners and hospitality overrode her desire to torture me. Last night I was too tired to see anything around me except the bed, so it's a pleasant surprise to find myself in a beautifully appointed room with a small sitting area and a private bath. Here's the reminder of spring I crave. The painted cream silk on the walls depict a lovely meadow full of colorful flowers. A fireplace on the far wall keeps the room at a cozy temperature, while the thick comforter and multitude of pillows tempt me to stay in bed all day. It's the most comfortable thing I've ever slept in, with a down-stuffed mattress below me and a billowy yellow lace canopy overhead. I may not be wanted here, but it seems the rules of courtesy still apply. *Good. I'll use every one of them to my advantage.*

Someone left my saddlebags inside my door, saving me the trouble of hunting them down. I carry them over to the wardrobe and unpack, my lips pressed together as I shake out each dress before hanging it up. *I don't care what Prince Pompous says, I'm staying. And that starts with claiming this as my room.*

After stretching out my aching muscles and rubbing a salve into the deeper bruises from my unfortunate sparring match with Lord Devereaux, I'm ready to face whatever today will throw at me. I select my outfit with more care than normal. Usually, my goal is to blend into the background as much as possible and not call any attention to myself, but this job is different. The palace may be huge, but the staff appears relatively small—likely twenty or thirty at the most. No way to avoid attention in that group. Besides, I want to bring a little cheer to this place, if only to remind myself that not everything is as joyless as this palace. *And I need to do it without freezing to death.*

I shake my head at the shawls and linen dresses I naively thought would be good enough for a winter in the mountains. *If I can't feel warm, at least I can look warm.* I add a second layer of underclothes, then grab a light gray dress and my favorite green shawl with embroidered blue butterflies. An extra set of stockings makes my boots snug, but will probably let me keep all my toes. Instead of my custom braid, I use a blue ribbon to tie my hair loosely away from my face, letting it tumble down my back. *A fitting look for the prince's matchmaker—as long as they don't spot the knives hidden in my clothes.*

The housekeeper thought locking me in my room would keep me confined, but a couple of hairpins spring the door open in seconds. I seek out the kitchen again, determined to get better acquainted with the staff. They may have orders to be unhelpful, but I still need to be able to identify them and know them well enough to spot any strange behavior. A good assassin will use any tool at their disposal, and the staff is always a weak point in protecting a noble. Because they have access to the house and information, they're likely targets for bribery and blackmail.

But despite all the logical reasons I should get to know the staff, really I'm searching them out because I want to make a few friends, otherwise this is going to be a lonely job. Months on end with nobody to talk to, no friends to share a laugh with … No, it would not be pleasant.

The route to my room last night was a blur, so I use my best guess to find my way back. My impression of a lovely but cold palace is reaffirmed as I go down stairs and through passageways. It's an indifferent beauty that does nothing to warm the spirit. Delicate carvings and exquisite statues catch my eye, but there's no soul in the designs, no passion to chase the chill emanating from the stone.

As I approach the kitchen, I peek around the corner, trying to anticipate my reception. *The housekeeper probably came back and gave them another talking to. They'll be wary after that. But mayhap … curious? I'm a stranger from another kingdom, and they have a long, boring winter ahead of them. Anything new to break the routine should be welcome. I'll start with one of the younger girls, since they'll feel the most comfortable with me and we'll hopefully have some things in common.*

It's always awkward being the only outsider in a group, but I've done it before. Too many times. *Sigh.* It would be nice not to move around so much, to make friends just to lose them a few months later. I always feel like the outsider, even in Cassia. The villagers think I'm odd because I work for the Guild, so I never quite fit in with them.

Mayhap this time will be different since I'll be here for so long. They could be real friends, not just acquaintances I say goodbye to as soon as I've started feeling comfortable around them. I love my work for the Guild, but it's disheartening knowing I have to start over some place new every few months. Even when I'm home with Papa, I can't forget I might have to leave for a job at a moment's notice. Knowing I'm here for the long-term is oddly comforting.

Laughter comes from the kitchen, and I slow my steps. A fluttery feeling takes up residence in my stomach and I bury my hands in my skirt. Another loud burst of laughter. I lick my lips, shuffling back a step. *Perhaps I should come back another time ...*

I shake my head. *Stop stalling!* It's like I tell the kids I protect—it's perfectly acceptable to be afraid, just don't let it stop you. I lift my chin and march over to the open kitchen door.

The scene is a mirror image of last night. The fire crackles cheerily in the fireplace, bathing the room in a warm light. A large pot sits over the flame, simmering, casting a delicious scent of beef and roasted vegetables through the air. A dozen or so staff members are gathered at the long trestle table, the scattered remains of a devoured meal in front of them. The Fates are smiling on me today, as there's no sign of the bad-tempered housekeeper.

The bald man spots me in the doorway and sets his teacup down with a loud *clink,* cutting off the conversation. Everyone twists to stare at me.

The man stands, his face stern but still managing to look

deferential. "Good morning, milady. Are you lost?"

"Good morning." I give them my brightest smile. "Call me Julietta, please. It's so nice to see everyone again. My apologies for being so late for breakfast. I'll be happy to have anything that's left, or I can whip up something."

The man's spine gets impossibly straighter. "Milady, such measures will not be necessary. We're happy to serve your meal to you in the sunroom."

Through long hours of practice, I hold my smile in place and keep my tone even. "I'm not a lady. Just another member of the staff, like all of you."

My heart sinks as he shakes his head. "Not like us, Miss Dantes. The staff eats in the kitchen. You'll take your meals with Lord Saint-Veil. Now, if you're ready, we'll be delighted to serve you breakfast. In the sunroom."

My stomach gives a loud growl. A few nervous giggles squeak out around the table as I try to ignore the heat climbing in my cheeks.

The man looks to the far end of the table. "Lacee, please show Miss Dantes the way."

A sweet-faced girl with blue eyes and long brown hair twisted into a loose bun starts, then quickly gets up from the table. She bobs a curtsy and gestures to the doorway. "This way, milady, if you please."

I glance around the room, searching for an ally. Someone willing to speak up and help me change the man's mind. If they can't see me as one of them, if they try to keep me separate, then my job will be ten times harder. *And I'll be alone ...*

Everyone avoids my eyes, even the outspoken woman from last night. Despite the sinking feeling in my stomach, I keep my expression pleasant and my chin up as I step out of the room. *Never let them see you hurt. Besides, it's not their fault. That housekeeper must've scared them. This will just take a little longer than I thought.*

The girl leads me through several passageways to the other side of the palace, far from the warmth of the kitchen. I hurry my step to match her pace. "Lacee, was it? I'm Julietta. It's nice to meet you."

She darts a quick look at me before dipping her head down.

"Have you worked for Lord Devereaux for long?"

She bites her lip, her blue eyes wide.

"Where are you from?"

The maid wrings her hands, stealing another glance at me from the corner of her eye.

I suppress a sigh. The girl wants to chat, but her fear of the housekeeper is keeping her silent. A little time and the right circumstances will get her to open up, but this isn't it. Instead, I use our trip to admire the exquisite craftmanship around me while adding details to my mental map of the palace. I'll need to know every inch of this place if I want to protect the prince.

The sunroom does little to resemble its name. A few candles on the table provide the sole illumination, failing to fight back the darkness. Long windows line the wall, showing the storm raging outside. The only landscape that's visible is the snow beating against the glass, with dark clouds looming behind the snowflakes and hail. The walls and floor are more of the ever-present white granite with a dark blue carpet beneath the black table. There are two place settings, but no sign of the lord of the manor. Two footmen stand next to a sideboard loaded with covered dishes.

When I turn around, Lacee has disappeared.

I smile at the young men. "Hello."

They don't react.

"Lovely weather we're having, don't you think?"

Blank stares.

"Why don't we all strip down to our underclothes and make snow angels on the lawn?"

Not even a twitch.

I slump into a chair and scowl at the table as the silent footmen scoop eggs, sausages, spiced apples, and two warm cinnamon rolls onto my plate. *They're determined to keep me at arm's length. But it's all right. I have months to change their minds. Today is a fresh start and I'm not going to waste a minute.*

The scent of cinnamon calls my attention back to the cooling food. *At least I won't starve. This looks amazing.* I can't remember the last time I had a huge breakfast. Probably when I finished my most recent contract and was home with Papa. We always celebrate with breakfast, whether it's me completing a job, or him closing a successful business deal. And there haven't been too many of either to celebrate lately …

But there's no time like the present. The first bite of flakey pastry melts in my mouth in a blissful, buttery haze that leaves me groaning in ecstasy. *As Mama always said, nothing solves a problem like sugar.* I happily dig in, devouring the food.

A throat clears behind me, making me jump in my seat. "You're still here."

Lord Devereaux pauses in the doorway, fixing me with a frown. He's striving for unaffected, but his shoulders are tense. Still, there's a fluid grace to his movements that I remember from yesterday's bout as he walks across the room. When he passes me, I catch a whiff of something familiar, like books and leather mixed into a heady combination.

"And in your presence, without an escort. Seeing your orders so thoroughly disobeyed must be a terrible way to start your morning." I take a long sip of tea, smirking at him over the rim of the cup. "I'm staying."

The prince takes the seat at the head of the table, then nods to the two footmen, who jump into action. "You're only here until the storm is over. Which should be another day or two at most." He turns to his plate, attacking the food with a methodical, single-minded focus.

"I'll be here until my contract is over. Which means I'm not leaving until—" my eyes dart to the two other men. *There are ears everywhere. Anyone could work for whoever is targeting the prince.* "You're settled." *Good. Nice and vague.* "If you have a problem with that, you can take it up with Lady Isabeau." *What are you going to do about that, Lord Sulkiness?*

His mouth presses into a thin line, his brown eyes flashing. "I'm going to give my sister an earful the next time I see her. Unfortunately, that won't be until the spring."

I give him an angelic smile. "I guess you're stuck with me then. I'm sure we'll enjoy our long, long visit together." I take another sip of my tea, savoring the cinnamon warmth.

"Hardly. But until the storm stops, there's no purpose to this conversation. I have business to attend to." He pushes away from the table, his plate already empty. Lord Devereaux adjusts his jacket, looking everywhere in the room except at me. "I trust your room is satisfactory."

The random change in topic leaves me blinking in surprise. "Uh, yes. It's quite lovely, thank you."

"If you require anything, let Madame Deneuve know." He glances out the window at the storm, then brushes some imaginary lint off his sleeve. "I have business to attend to this afternoon."

He said that already. "Madame Deneuve?"

"Helene, my housekeeper. She can provide anything you need. Just ask her." His eyes, so intent, snap to mine, making my stomach jump. "Good day, Miss Julietta." Lord Devereaux abruptly turns away and strides out of the room.

Ignoring the footmen, I pick at my food, my mind whirling as I try to figure out the implications of this sudden crack in the granite. This considerate side of Lord Crabby has me off-balance. I'd never have guessed the stoic, unfeeling man from last night would be concerned if my room was acceptable. More likely he'd have a foot shoving me out the door, or merrily waving goodbye as Helene threw me in a snowbank. This—this is odd. Nice odd, but still odd. *What is he up to? For all I know, he might be trying to get me to relax before tries to get rid of me again.* I vow to keep my guard up around him until I figure out what game he's playing.

I shrug and return to my breakfast. *This doesn't change anything. I'm here to do a job, so I better get on with it.*

There may be a long winter ahead, but that doesn't mean the threat—whatever it is—to Lord Devereaux will wait. Without knowing the nature of the danger, I have to assume the worst: an assassin is after him. And no matter what Prince Grouchy wants, I'm going to protect him to the best of my ability. Having traveled through the blizzard, I'm reasonably sure an assassin can't get to the palace now. And even if they're already onsite, a careful assassin won't strike until the storm slows so they can escape before they're caught. That gives me time to get familiar with La Sailles and the staff before I need to glue myself to Lord Cranky's side. *I'll start with confirming the layout of the palace's ground floor and noting all the entrances and exits…*

The scent of books and leather lingers in the air, distracting me as I work out my plans for the day.

Helene is posted outside when I exit the sunroom.

I grin at her. "Ready for a fun-filled day of traipsing around the palace?"

"I'll escort you back to your room now," is her dry reply.

"Sure, but first I want to check on Henri." Whistling, I waltz toward the palace entrance.

She mutters a few choice curses under her breath, following close behind before abandoning me at the front doors. Henri gives a happy whinny when I look into his stall. His coat shines from a recent brushing and fresh hay covers the floor.

I rub the white stripe down his nose. "I guess I don't have to worry about how you're doing. Looks like the stableboys are treating you like a king."

He butts his head against my chest, then returns to crunching the remains of a withered apple. I give him a final pat, then duck out of the stables through the back entrance and make my way to a random window on the side of the palace, counting on the storm to cover my movements.

It's a matter of moments to pry the window open and climb inside—a security weakness, but not worth addressing.

While I need to be aware of all the potential ways an assassin could get into the palace, I can't monitor them all alone. And the endless rows of ground-floor windows make posting people to watch the doors pointless. Better to focus on securing a smaller area I can control than to guard every inch of this monstrous chateau by myself.

I spend an hour exploring the rooms in the hallway until I'm sure Helene has given up hope of me returning to the entryway or the kitchen. My guess is she will try to search me out somewhere else rather than ignore Lord Devereaux's orders to have me escorted. She'll probably stay close to him so she can ambush me when I try to find him. But I have as much desire to see him again today as he does to see me.

It would be smarter to prowl the upper floors, where I can scout without fear of discovery, but something draws me back to the kitchen. I can pretend it's because I want to study the staff and their movements as part of my research, but really I want some comradery. Henri is a sweet horse, but he's not a great conversationalist, and he has a terrible sense of humor.

Walking back into the quiet kitchen is like stepping into a memory from home. For a moment, I swear I can feel my mother's arms around me, showing me how to stir the batter. My muscles relax as I breathe in the heavenly scent. Dough is rising on the counter and that wonderful stew is bubbling over the fire.

The red-faced woman from last night is chopping vegetables at a furious pace. She mutters, "Filching buns and loaves, thinking I won't notice. Jar of peaches here and raspberry preserves there. When I find out which one of them is responsible, I'm going to take a wooden spoon to their hide."

I hold up my hands. "I swear it wasn't me."

She holds a hand to her chest. "Fallen frogs, you startled me."

"My apologies. May I help?" I nod to the pile of turnips ready to be washed. Without waiting for her reply, I grab an apron off the peg, then push up my sleeves and start dunking and scrubbing.

The cook returns to her chopping, casting a wary eye at me as she moves through the pile. The looks grow less frequent as time passes. After I finish with the turnips, I move on to scouring the pots soaking in the sink.

The woman doesn't look up as she asks, "What's that you're humming?"

"Was I?" I laugh. "Sorry, I tend to do that when I'm working. It's a song my mother used to sing when she was cooking."

"Nothing wrong with a little music in the kitchen. I'm partial to a good lullaby." She winks at me. "It makes the bread rise faster."

I smile back at her. "Good tip. I'll remember that."

We continue working in companionable silence, moving from task to task, until the woman closes the oven door and wipes her forehead. "That's it, milady. Thanks for all your help."

"It's Julietta, please. And are you sure? I could help you decorate the cakes for dessert tonight." I walk my fingers toward the bowl of icing on the table, giving her a mischievous grin.

She laughs and swats my hand away with a rag. "You're worse than the prince. And call me Rosemarie."

"The prince? Really?" I lean my elbows on the table and gaze up at her. "He's so stiff and proper. I can't imagine him getting into any trouble."

"Don't get the wrong impression, he's a good lord and he'll be a great king one day."

"Of course. But …?" I raise my eyebrows, encouraging her to continue.

She shakes her head with a chuckle. "He and his sister used to get into such mischief. One year when he was, oh, six or seven, Lord Devereaux and Lady Isabeau snuck into the kitchen in the middle of the night and ate an entire cake."

I tilt my head. "That doesn't sound so bad."

"It was the birthday cake for the Floren ambassador."

My hand flies up to my mouth as I giggle. "Oh, no! They didn't."

She nods, her lips twitching. "They did. Eight tiers of cake and preserves and fruit covered in frosting. I came into the kitchen that morning to put the final decorations on it before the banquet, only to find an empty platter smeared with icing. We had no idea what happened until their nurse found them asleep in their beds, covered head to toe in frosting."

I burst into laughter, imagining them happily snoozing away after their sugar rush wore off. "I bet they weren't even sorry."

"Not one bit."

"I can't blame them for sneaking treats. Everything is delicious, especially those cinnamon rolls at breakfast. You must give me your recipe."

"Thank you, dear. But I know you're a captive audience."

"In that case, I would just say it was good. I only say delicious when I mean it." I wink.

She chuckles. "Flatterer. Now you go off and enjoy the

rest of your day. I'm going to check the pantry and see if anything else is missing."

I skip out of the kitchen with a laugh, leaving Rosemarie to her inventory.

Spirits restored, I turn my mind back to business. The next few hours are spent searching the bowels of the palace. I'm about to leave yet another storeroom when the back of my neck prickles. Trusting my instincts has saved my life more than once over the years. I freeze in place, trying to figure out what alarmed my senses.

The room is empty except for a few small crates lined against the left wall. They're barely large enough to hide a cat, but I inspect them anyway. No pry marks, no sign they've been moved recently. I pace the perimeter, finding nothing but stirred up dust.

Shrugging, I relock the door behind me and move to the next room. When you're looking for assassins, you see them in every shadow. *But better to be paranoid than dead.*

Just when I've pushed the uneasy feeling from my mind, a faint scratch comes from outside the door.

Blood pounds in my ears. I do my best not to react as I stare blankly ahead. *There—they're watching behind that open door.* My muscles burn from the effort of not leaping into action. Every nerve screams that I can end this now, but my Guild training wins out. *Patience. This might be the only chance to trap the assassin, so I can't risk letting them slip through my fingers because I'm sloppy. Figure out a plan first, then pounce.*

Fifteen, no, sixteen feet. If I try to rush them from here, they'll have time to flee. Can I get closer and trap them inside? If I do, will they be able to escape before I get help, or should I restrain them and then look for someone? I work through my options carefully as I pretend to continue the inspection. I settle on locking the assassin inside the room and calling until someone finds me. No chance for them to escape, and the worst case is I'll spend a few hours sitting on the cold floor. *Helene will have everyone searching for me by nightfall.*

I keep my movements as casual as possible so I don't

startle the hidden trespasser, going as far as to throw in a few yawns. The open door is always in the corner of my eye in case they try to slip out. Each step brings me closer to the spy, but also increases the intruder's need to flee before I spot them.

When I reach the room two doors down from their hiding spot, I leap over and slam the door shut. "Yes! I've got you now." I crouch and insert my hairpins to flip the lock, using my shoulder to keep the door closed.

A blow from behind sends me reeling. I crash into the door, smashing my head against the wood. Bitter iron floods my mouth from my bit tongue. *How did they get behind me?* Cursing, I roll to my feet, ready to trounce the attacker. Footsteps slap against the stone. I sprint after them, determined to put an end to this now.

My assailant knows the palace, ducking through corridors and around corners without hesitation, never getting trapped by a locked door or dead end. I follow, always chasing, never gaining. The glimpses I catch are of a bulky shape. I can't even tell if I'm chasing a man or woman.

They escape outside through a small side door. My lungs burn as I plunge into the snowstorm. Slush fills my boots as I wade through the snow after them. They beeline for the stables.

You won't escape me! I fly into the building moments behind them, my eyes darting around the dim structure. *Where are they? Where did they go?* I hold completely still, my heartbeat pounding in my ears. No noises, aside from the howling storm and the horses moving around their enclosures.

I prowl down the row, peering into the stalls, listening

for any rustle to give away the assassin's position. A few animals poke their heads out to watch my progress. When I reach the far side, I check for fresh footprints outside the door to confirm they didn't sneak out the back. *Still inside.* I spin back around with narrowed eyes.

They're in here somewhere ... My eyes land on the ladder. *The hayloft.*

I'm almost to the top when the ladder shudders. My foot slips and I cling to the rungs. The intruder shoves the bottom, pushing the ladder away from the hayloft and into the open air. Another shimmy loosens my grip. A split second of terror, then I'm falling through the air.

And into a horse trough.

The shock of being dunked into an ice bath makes me gasp, sucking in a lungful of water. I pop my head out, sputtering. Shaking with cold and anger, I climb out, sloshing water everywhere. *I'm going to find them and drag them to the dungeons if it's the last thing I do!*

A flash of black disappears out of the barn, heading back toward the palace.

With an inarticulate roar, I chase them. My world shrinks to the back of their cloak as my rage gives me an extra burst of speed. I close the gap just as they burst through the kitchen door. I leap, wrestling them to the ground.

Crashes and smashing glass can't distract me from overpowering the thrashing bundle of clothes in my arms. Screams and shrieks erupt as we roll around the floor, knocking people about. The intruder kicks out, missing my head and shattering a large jar. Everything turns wet and slippery. Snarling, I scratch and yank at their clothes, at their limbs, at anything I can reach.

Someone grabs my arm, allowing the invader to escape

my hold. I writhe in their grip as the assailant slips and slides on the damp floor, shoes scrabbling for grip. With a snarl, I yank free and dive across the floor, tackling the prowler, sending us both tumbling headlong into a sack of flour.

"Enough!" a woman shouts.

I keep a firm grip on the intruder as I shake the flour out of my eyes. A soft whimper comes from under the cloak. My reason slowly returns, bringing with it a sinking feeling in my stomach. *Something's wrong.* The shape is too small, the voice too high. *What ...?* My breath catches in my throat as I peel back the caked fabric.

Large, tear-filled eyes stare back. The boy's lower lip quivers as he ducks away from me, stopped by my firm hold. *He can't be more than ten.* My lungs compress as I snatch my hands away like they're burned. I stare in disbelief as a woman breaks through the group and pulls him to his feet.

The woman hugs him, her voice filled with concern. "Ty, what are you doing? Are you all right?" She glares accusingly at me. "What were you doing to my son?"

"I ... I ... Um ..." I swallow hard, my ears and neck impossibly hot. "I thought he was spying on me?"

A young girl pushes her way through the crowd, her shrill voice bouncing off the kitchen tiles. "We just wanted to see what she was doing. We didn't hurt anything! She tried to lock Ty in a storeroom! And she chased me into the barn!"

The glaring faces swing back to me.

"No, I—that's not what—" I start to stand. My feet slide out from under me, dumping me back on the ground. Nobody moves. Wishing I could crawl under the table and disappear, I grab the edge of the counter and haul myself up. "That's not exactly what happened."

Rosemarie flaps a towel at the gaping group. "The story will have to wait. Everyone out except Nancey and Caitlin. I need to get this mess cleaned up and a new supper prepared for Lord Devereaux right away. You'll have to eat late tonight."

There are a few grumbles and a lot of angry stares directed my way as everyone reluctantly shuffles out of the room. The destruction in the kitchen is more obvious without the spectators. Stew and vegetables splattered on the floor and the walls, while broken glass and metal trays litter the floor. Soaking through it all is oil from the broken jar against the wall. Flour in the air mixes with the oil, creating a clumpy paste that's smeared everywhere.

I cringe, wringing my flour-crusted hands. "Rosemarie, I …"

She gives me a sympathetic look. "You too, Miss Julietta. The best thing you can do right now is take a bath."

I want to argue, but she's right. "I'm so sorry for the trouble I caused." I dip into a quick curtsy, then wrap my arms around my waist and hurry out of the kitchen, ignoring the eyes following me down the hallway and the trail of oily footprints behind me.

I pound my fists into the dough, sending puffs of flour flying through the air. "Stupid, stupid, stupid." *Why did I think things would go smoothly today? Everything about this job has been a disaster since I left Cassia. Weeks of travel to get to this burning kingdom, dealing with lice-ridden beds and lecherous innkeepers. Getting into a fight with the prince the moment I arrive. And today's mess ...* I grimace.

Could I be making a bigger fool of myself? Misstep after misstep. Perhaps the storm is a blessing from the Fates. Without it, I'd be out on my ear, heading home in disgrace. At least it buys me a few more days to make it clear I'm here to stay. I have to—for Papa. And for myself. My pride would never let me do less than my best on any contract. I'm not going to botch this one. But after this is over, I'm taking a leave from the Guild. I'll find something to amuse myself far away from sneaky children and arrogant princes.

I take a deep breath, letting the scent of icing and spices waft over me, soothing my hurts. *Sugar cures everything.* The dough rolls out perfectly. I add another layer of butter, folding the pastry over, then sprinkle in the mixture of cinnamon and sugar. My hands work automatically as I hum a lullaby from my childhood. Memories of my mother's soft laughter and gentle hands guiding mine wash over me. Baking always makes me feel closer to her, although I usually only have a chance to do it when I'm home.

The air shifts and a shadow flickers by the doorway. Someone is watching me.

My nerves jump to attention, but I beat them back down. *No more chasing intruders today. With my luck, I might end up burning down the palace.* I debate ignoring the lurker, then shrug. *Today can't get any worse.* "Hello there. I'm baking sticky buns for breakfast to bribe everyone into forgiving me. Would you like to join me?"

There's a shuffling of feet, then my observer moves into the light. The sight of a disheveled Lord Devereaux has me fumbling the spoon I'm holding. Rumpled and exhausted, he still manages to look disarmingly handsome. His sleeves are rolled up, revealing those muscled arms again. The shadow of a beard gives him a roguish air which is enhanced by the unruly hair falling over his forehead.

I quickly cover my clumsiness by dropping into a curtsy. "Milord! I, uh, didn't expect you to be up at this hour."

He runs a hand through his tousled hair, only increasing the mess. "My apologies. I didn't mean to disturb you. I didn't think anyone else was awake, so when I saw the light, I was curious."

"No apologies necessary. It's your palace. You can go wherever you want."

His back stiffens. "Yes. Well. I'll leave you to it. Good evening."

I wince, my spirits sinking. *Wonderful. I'm supposed to*

be making friends, not alienating everyone I see. Well, there's no point in tiptoeing around him. It's not like he could have a lower opinion of me at this point. I might as well treat him like I treat my other protectees. "Where do you think you're going?" I push a bowl in his direction. "Start stirring."

"Me?" He hesitates in the doorway, looking around like there might be someone standing behind him. "You want me to help you?"

"There's a spoon right over there."

I spread another layer of butter on the dough, watching the prince out of the corner of my eye. He wavers, taking a half-step toward the exit, then nods to himself and strides over to the table.

As he dutifully stirs the honey mixture, Lord Devereaux clears his throat. "I reviewed your documents. Everything appears in order, although I still don't understand why my sister bothered to hire you. That aside … based on your association with the Guild, and your contract terms … I've determined you don't need an escort while you're here."

It's oh so hard not to smirk. "Is admitting you're wrong making you uncomfortable, or is it the bruises from our fight?"

Lord Devereaux's smile flashes so quickly, I'm half-convinced I imagined it. "Both."

Could it be? A glimmer of humor? Mayhap that crack in the granite is bigger than I thought. "I'll bring my salve to breakfast tomorrow. It'll help with the bruises. I'm afraid the pride is a little harder to soothe."

"Have no fear, it heals quickly. Though I haven't been trounced so thoroughly since I trained with a wooden sword instead of steel. I'd like to think it's because of your skill, and not my lack of practice."

"You held your own for most of it. But the offer still stands. I'll happily knock you down again if you need me to." I grin.

"Thanks," he says drily. "Perhaps another time. But for now, I'll buy out your contract. There's no reason for you to leave here empty-handed when the storm ends. After all, it's not your fault my sister had the ridiculous idea I needed protection. It's only fair that I pay you what you were promised."

Squashing my instinct to snap at him, I take a deep breath before responding. *He's trying to do what he thinks is right. From his perspective, it's a nice gesture and very generous. No reason to take offense when he didn't intend any.* "Thank you, but I'm not leaving here until the pass opens and my contract ends. And I'm not looking for a handout. I'm being paid to protect you while you're here, and that's what I'm going to do."

He straightens, pulling his indignation around him like armor. "I'm not in danger."

Just when I thought we were making progress … "Your sister disagrees."

He snorts. "Isa thinks overcooked eggs are an assassination attempt. You can't take her seriously."

I lift a shoulder. "Forgive me if I side with her, but it's my job to be suspicious. And it was foolish of you to come to the chateau with no guards. You're inviting an attack."

"I don't care how much training they have. Nobody's going to make it to La Sailles through this blizzard. They'll freeze to death before they get through the pass."

"Today, mayhap. But what about when the storm lets up?" I shake my head. "Why do we need to argue about this?

Can we agree to disagree? Let me do my job and I'll stay out of your way as much as I can, so everyone gets what they want."

He mutters, "And you think I'm stubborn." Louder, "How did you become a bodyguard? It seems like an unusual line of work for a young woman."

Ah, the inevitable misunderstanding about my job. "I'm not a bodyguard. A bodyguard's job is to stop the knife from stabbing you. My job is to figure out who wants to stab you before they try."

"Shouldn't a bodyguard do that too?"

He seems genuinely interested, so I answer him. "Not necessarily. A bodyguard typically acts as another set of eyes and ears in the moment. I do that as well, but I spend most of my talking to people and researching and looking for things out of the ordinary. Things that could signal a threat." I sigh. "Not that I'm doing a great job of that lately."

He raises an eyebrow. "Aren't the elite Guild members supposed to keep up an aloof and confident appearance at all times? Aren't you afraid they'll kick you out if you admit you're human?"

"I'm too tired to keep up appearances. Besides, honesty is always the best policy."

He chuckles. "You wouldn't last long in politics with that mindset."

It's my turn to raise an eyebrow. "I disagree. In my experience, a little honesty can accomplish more than false flattery and manipulation. People usually do their best, and most know they have to compromise to get what they want." I sigh again. "I apologize. The long day has loosened my tongue."

That disarming smile makes another appearance, making

my heart skip a beat. "No apologies necessary. Though it puts me in terrible danger of conceding your point, I find your honesty refreshing. Now, what was so terrible you feel the need to bribe my staff with treats?"

"You don't know? I'm surprised Helene didn't run straight to you and tell you everything."

"I've been locked in my study, working all day. I'm sure she'll have a very dry, factual recounting to serve me with breakfast."

Another joke? Perhaps there's hope for him after all. Ignoring the lightness in my chest, I consider his request. *Should I ...? Why not. It's not like things could get any worse.* I quickly fill him in on the misadventures from earlier today. Watching his eyes light up and listening as his laughter fills the room eases the humiliation weighing me down. Soon, I'm telling the story between giggles. "You can see why I need to do something special."

"Don't be too hard on yourself. Faye and Ty are always causing trouble, even though Jolee's convinced they're innocent little angels." Lord Devereaux surveys the collection of jars and the flour dusting the tabletop. "But I think you have another scolding coming when Rosemarie sees what you've done to her kitchen."

"Nonsense. We have a few more hours before she shows up to start the morning bake, and these sticky buns will win anyone over. Just wait until you try one." I blow a strand of hair out of my eye. "Here, help me shape them."

I cut a strip off the dough, then demonstrate how to roll it into a loose circle. He watches me intently, his lips moving as he silently repeats my instructions.

"Your turn." I slide some dough over to him. "And remember, this isn't a test. It's supposed to be fun! Enjoy yourself."

He grumbles, "It feels like a test."

I throw a chunk of pastry at him and laugh. "You're worse than the kids I deal with. You might enjoy it if you let yourself. It'll remind you of your cake-thieving days."

Devereaux freezes. To my everlasting amusement, his ears turn red. "Who told you about that?"

His face! He can't decide if he's mortified, amused, or insulted. Haha! "Doesn't every kid steal cake?" I ask innocently, squashing the giggles threatening to erupt.

His shoulders relax. "Yes. Yes, they do." As he studies his strip of dough with a critical eye, he says, "I'd be a poor host if I didn't concern myself with my guest's wellbeing."

That's an odd change in subject. Where's he going with this?

"Your outfit is entirely unsuitable."

I bite back a sharp retort. *Wait until he finishes before you smack him.*

"The storm will continue for a few more days and you clearly weren't prepared for the weather here at La Sailles. My sister sent some winter clothing when she was under the delusion she'd join me for a few weeks. They're in her suite." At my blank look, he adds, "You should avail yourself of them. You're of a size, I think. And I would hate for you to lose a toe to frostbite."

"It would definitely throw off my balance." Warmth spreads through me, and I smile at him. "That's very kind, thank you. And here I thought you didn't care."

He leans closer and whispers, "Don't tell anyone. I have a reputation to maintain."

"Your secret is safe with me." I make a crossing motion across my heart.

We're silent for a few minutes as we work to shape the buns. Devereaux tackles every one like the fate of the kingdom rests on his ability to roll the dough, his forehead crinkled in fierce concentration. He's terrible at it. Really, really terrible. Each one is lopsided with the sides squashed in and the filling oozing out the top. I bite my lip to keep from laughing as his scowl deepens with each monstrosity.

When the sixth one is almost recognizable, his forehead finally smooths. He beams at me, his brown eyes crinkling in the corners. "I'm getting the hang of this."

"Excellent." I hide my smile as I rub the back of my arm across my forehead. "If this prince thing doesn't work out, you can always get a job as a baker."

He clears his throat. "You, um, have flour … right there." Devereaux points to my face.

"Oh." I wipe my face again. "Did I get it?"

His lips twitch. "You made it worse. Here, let me."

Devereaux slides around the edge of the table, stopping in front of me before I realize his intentions. He's a hairsbreadth away, the warmth from his skin washing over me, bringing along the scent of books and leather I noticed this morning mixed with sugar and cinnamon in a mesmerizing combination. I freeze, the air rushing out of my lungs. This close, I can see the tiny green flecks swimming in those dark depths. His fingers brush my cheek, leaving a trail of heat behind.

"There. All taken care of."

I suck in a breath. "Thank you." Self-conscious of how shaky my voice sounds, I spin around and grip the counter. *Don't act like a ninny. He was just helping you. Nothing happened.* I shake my head, trying to clear the odd tension and busy myself setting the rolls on a baking tray and spooning the honey mixture over them. "Can you stir the icing?"

He silently retreats to the other side of the table.

"These look like they'll come out perfect. Sticky buns are delicious anytime, but I like them best warm. Most people really like these. It's my great-great-grandmama's recipe. My mother taught it to me when I was barely big enough to hold a spoon. The kids I work with seem to enjoy it, too, though they mostly like eating the icing." I pop a piece of sugary dough into my mouth to cut off the flow of nonsense. *I was wrong. This day can get worse. He's going to think I'm a halfwit if I keep babbling. Fates save me, I need to pull it together—or find a hole to crawl into until spring.*

"So, I'm not your first?" At my startled look, Lord Devereaux nods to the bowl. "You make these with the children you protect?"

"Oh." My laugh is too loud. My hands flutter over the rolls, making unnecessary adjustments before sliding the tray into the oven. "I try to make them with all the kids if I can. They need to learn to have more fun in life. But most royal cooks are fiercely protective of their kitchens, guarding it twenty-four hours a day. Luckily, the staff here is too small to do that, otherwise they would've barred me after today."

He tilts his head to the side, studying me. "Why does it matter if the children you work with have fun or not? You're there to protect them, not entertain them."

I look at him in surprise. "It's the most important gift I can give them. Everything in their life is always so serious, and everyone is constantly reminding them about their responsibilities. The never-ending weight of expectations can be crushing, especially at that age."

The prince stares down at the bowl, stirring the icing slowly. "It wasn't that bad." His hand stops. "Actually, it was. But it helped prepare me for what was coming."

My heart squeezes, wondering how much it cost him to admit that to me. "I understand the need for seriousness most of the time. But having fun doesn't mean it's useless. They play and learn to protect themselves at the same time. I use games like Fox and Hare to teach them how to hide from their enemies, or Seekers to be observant and look for discrepancies in their surroundings. I try to make it exciting instead of scary."

He mulls over the information while I check the buns in the oven. *Just a few more minutes.*

"How long do I need to keep doing this?"

"Switch arms if you're getting tired." I silently giggle as he grumbles and keeps stirring.

Some magical mixture of the late hour and cozy companionship prompts me to blurt out, "I don't envy you. I know most people think your life is easy as a prince, but I've seen the other side. The sleepless nights. Fending off threats to the kingdom that most people won't ever hear about. Always guessing at the motivations of the people around you. People only seeing the title and not a person."

Lord Devereaux clutches the spoon in a white-knuckled grip, frozen in place. His dark eyes burn into mine, something vulnerable flickering in their depths. I take a step toward him, reaching out, before catching myself and stumbling to a stop. Something slams shut behind his eyes and the emotions disappear, leaving me wondering if I'd imagined the whole thing.

My face heats up as I force out a chuckle. "My apologies. There goes my mouth running off again. I really am a fluff brain tonight."

Lord Devereaux glances away and clears his throat. "Yes. Well. You appear to have everything in order here. Good night."

He drops the spoon into the bowl with a loud *clank,* icing splattering across the table. The prince bolts out of the kitchen, leaving me staring after him.

What just happened?

The acrid scent of smoke wrenches me from my bewilderment. I race to the oven, but the sticky buns are a blackened mess. With a sigh, I yank them out and dump them in the waste bin before grabbing the sack of flour to start over.

After shivering through a lonely breakfast where Lord Devereaux fails to make an appearance, I decide to take him up on his offer and find Lady Isabeau's suite with the promised wardrobe. I keep a wary eye out for the prince, reluctant to have another encounter this early in the day when I still haven't puzzled out what happened between us in the kitchen. One minute we finally seemed to have reached some kind of truce, the next there was … whatever that was. *Best not to think too much about it. I'm just off-balance because I don't have a partner and everything keeps going wrong. Once I figure out a good routine and make friends with some of the staff, everything will go back to normal.*

Directions from Rosemarie let me locate Lady Isabeau's room with ease. The suite is probably fit for a princess, but it's hard to tell with the furniture covered in protective sheeting and all the tapestries and draperies absent. I creep through the suite, feeling like an intruder despite having Lord Devereaux's permission. With a last glance over my shoulder, I locate the closet door and pull it open.

And gasp.

A rainbow of colors is spread out before me. Yellows, blues, greens, purples, reds. Dresses with bold designs and delicate embroidery. Silks and velvets and satins and wools. Lovely cloaks and shawls and wraps. It's a delight to browse through the beautifully designed dresses. It's probably only a tiny fraction of Lady Isabeau's wardrobe from Charistel, but choosing between the two dozen dresses stuffed inside makes me feel like a princess. On the job, I usually dress to blend into the background and not call attention to myself, but Lady Isabeau's clothing is designed to stand out. Her dresses are a little tight in the bust and loose in the waist, but they're leagues prettier than the brown and gray outfits I brought with me—and more importantly, they're warmer.

Sadly, her delicate, fur-lined boots are too small, so I double up on my stockings and resign myself to chilly toes. At least the rest of me will be comfortable, and I can get better boots in the village if the road is ever deemed safe. Unfortunately, there's nowhere to hide most of my weapons in her dresses. Since I'm unwilling to permanently alter them, I have to make do with a few of my thinner knives tucked up the sleeves. Funny how they don't design a princess's wardrobe to conceal daggers.

My first task accomplished, I set out to find Lacee. After my success with Rosemarie in the kitchen, she seems like the next person most likely to talk to me … if I can catch her alone.

I take my best guess where she'd be this time of day, scouting down passageways until there's a whiff of soap and warm water in the air. I follow the scent, hoping it'll lead me to the maid. After several corridors, I stumble across a room filled with dripping linens drying on the lines. Quiet singing guides me through a maze of laundry to where Lacee's folding towels in the corner with nobody else in sight.

Her blue eyes are huge as she takes in my burgundy gown trimmed with black lace and the matching shawl. "Miss Julietta, you look beautiful."

It's hard not to preen under her admiring gaze. I finally look like the lady the staff mistook me for. I brush my hand against the velvet, relishing the soft, textured feeling of the fabric. "Lord Devereaux kindly offered to let me use his sister's wardrobe, since I'll probably freeze in my clothes. I wasn't expecting it to be this cold all the time."

"They're definitely more fitting to your station, if you don't mind me saying so. And I'd be willing to wager Lord Devereaux is going to be more eager to talk to you once he sees you in that dress." She winks.

Heat rushes to my cheeks. "Nonsense. I'm sure he'll find me just as vexing as he did yesterday." *The last thing I want is for my protectee to look at or think of me that way. This dress is just a matter of survival, that's all.* I quickly change the subject. "How long have you worked for Lord Devereaux?"

She purses her lips. "What does that have to do with finding the prince a bride?"

I wave my hand through the air. "It's all part of the process. I do extensive background on all the people I work with so I know who will suit each other. I'm a very good matchmaker."

Her grin turns sly. "And does matchmaking normally include dousing people in oil and rolling around on the kitchen floor?"

I groan and drop onto an empty stool near her. "I'm

never going to live that down. It was all a big misunderstanding. How was I supposed to know they were children?" I pick up a sheet from the pile, deftly keeping it out of Lacee's reach when she tries to snatch it back.

Her eyes widen with alarm. "Miss Julietta, you shouldn't be doing my chores. It isn't proper." Lacee reaches out again.

I roll my eyes. "Fates, you're all very set on propriety around here. There's, what, twelve of us here, including myself and Lord Devereaux?"

"Twenty-two."

"There you go. Barely enough staff to open a handful of rooms in the chateau. The least I can do is help where I can." I expertly fold the sheet while I talk, the edges crisp and even. I add it to her stack, then take a towel. "Now, you were going to tell me about working for Lord Devereaux."

Lacee tilts her head to the side. "You're an odd one, my lady."

"Julietta, please."

She smiles. "Julietta. Well, I started at the palace as a kitchen girl and worked my way above stairs. That's why I was selected to come here. Most upstairs maids would refuse to deal with the laundry because it's below their station, but I'm not afraid to roll up my sleeves and dive in."

"All alone? But you're too young to be away from your family for so long."

She gives a delightful giggle. "You must be country-bred if you believe that. I'll probably get engaged in a year or two if I find a lad who catches my eye."

I shake my head in disbelief. "You marry young here in Fallian Province. Back in Rauleg, we typically don't wed until our mid-twenties."

She gasps. "So old! How can you stand it?"

Thinking over all the oafs I've had to deal with over the years, I mutter, "Easily." Shaking my head, I smile at the girl. "So, what do you like best about working in a palace?"

Lacee chatters throughout the afternoon, telling me about her life back in Charistel, her family, and the other staff here. There's a simple goodness and innocence about her I can't help but be drawn to. I find myself hoping we'll become fast friends for the time that I'm here.

But not too close. After all, anyone here could work for the assassin. I mentally sigh. While I love my job, there are definite drawbacks. Except for Papa, I can never fully trust anyone's motives or information. Anyone can become an enemy, given the right circumstances. *Mayhap it's time I consider a new line of work. Something where I can make real friends.*

My time with Lacee, besides being an enjoyable afternoon, gives me critical information about the staff, the palace, and the nearby village. From her comments, I surmise this winter trip is out of character for Lord Devereaux, adding another layer to the mystery of why he's here. Unfortunately, nothing she tells me gives me any idea who might target the prince. There's a shocking lack of gossip about him in the court and among the staff. Nobody is universally liked, but the prince seems to have earned enough respect that he's avoided even the normal silly rumors around secret dalliances or hidden vices. And there are no conflicts or any animosity with nearby kingdoms, aside from the typical spats and rivalries that come from being neighbors.

What brought him here in the middle of winter? Why not stay in Charistel where he's protected? The prince is proving to be as big a mystery as who wants to harm him.

The next morning, I take my time choosing a beautiful hunter green dress embroidered with gold flowers on the hem and gold threads shot through the fabric. I waltz down the hallway toward the entrance, humming a jaunty dance tune to myself. *Should I try to spend more time with Rosemarie today? She probably knows the most about the staff out of anyone, except for Helene. There's no point in trying to talk to Madame Stick-In-The-Mud. Or perhaps I should visit with a different maid. It'd be nice to make another friend today.*

I drift toward a window. The blizzard has finally let up for the moment, creating a winter faery land outside. The sky is a blinding, perfect blue. A blanket of white covers everything, giving the world a fresh and clean look, untouched by man. A gentle, rolling landscape of sparkling snow stretches to the horizon. Trees and buildings poke through, creating small splashes of color.

Hmm, I should probably survey the grounds while I have the chance. Everyone's probably right about the storms keeping any ordinary spies away, but if there's enough days like today, an assassin could break through. Better to look around now before the blizzard starts again. I glance down at the beautiful dress with regret. *No point in ruining Lady Isabeau's finery. I'll wear my clothes to tramp around the snow, then change back into this gorgeous gown when I'm finished.*

Before returning to my room to change, I take a moment

to enjoy the scene outside, memories tugging at me of the last time it snowed at home with Papa. It was an ordinary day, with no festivities or holidays planned. We were gathered around the fire while I worked on some mending and he reviewed a business proposal—the ill-fated one that rendered us penniless, but we had no way of knowing that at the time. Papa noticed the first flakes sticking to the window and declared we needed to celebrate. We made gingerbread and sang carols while sipping chocolate. It's one of the happiest days I can remember, especially with everything that came after. The notices of the ship being delayed and then declared lost. Creditors cleaning out our savings, then taking the furniture and anything else valuable from the house.

I rub my chest. The hollow ache there only goes away when I'm home. The first few weeks after I leave Papa are the worst. Not that I miss him any less as time goes on. The homesickness and worries are always there; I just get used to them until they're a normal part of my daily existence. *I hope Papa isn't too lonely.*

I wipe away a tear threatening to spill over, then shake my head to chase away the lingering shadows. All the talk yesterday with Lacee has me feeling extra nostalgic. Being busy is the best distraction.

My mind stays occupied with mapping out the best route to tour the grounds as I hurry toward my room. Hopefully, the next storm will hold off for a few days, but in case it doesn't, I need to get the higher priority targets inspected first. *And if the storms don't start again soon, I'll need to stay near Lord Devereaux as much as possible, in case there's an attack.* Not for the first time I wish I had a partner to help carry all the duties. It's a struggle to manage everything on my own.

Lacee appears in the hallway ahead of me, distracting me from my mental checklist. I raise my hand, smiling. She abruptly spins, darting around the corner and out of sight. My stomach tenses as I speed up. I follow her footsteps through the palace as she dashes from hallway to hallway. I quickly review our visit yesterday as I pursue her through the chateau. *We had a good time, didn't we? I thought it was fun. She even told me about chasing that piglet through the marketplace and falling into the fountain in her festival dress. You don't share stories like that if you don't want to be friends with someone. No, I'm sure we left on good terms. What's happened since then?*

Dropping any pretense of dignity, I sprint through the castle, closing the distance between us.

"Lacee, wait." I tug her sleeve, pulling her to a stop near the palace entrance. "What's going on? Why are you running away from me?"

She keeps her eyes downcast. "I'm sorry if I gave you that impression, my lady. Did you need something from me?" The dull tone is a startling contrast to yesterday's laughter.

A sickening feeling washes over me. "Please don't call me 'my lady.' It's Julietta."

"It would be inappropriate for me to address you by your name, my lady." Her red-rimmed eyes dart to mine, then back to the floor. "If you don't need me for anything, I have to get back to my duties."

I don't try to stop her as she scampers away, my stomach twisting. *Lord Devereaux or Helene must've threatened her job if she continued to be friendly to me. They probably threatened Rosemarie, too. They have all the power here. No matter what I do, they can make my life miserable. And worse, they'll make the lives of everyone around me miserable. Everyone will go from avoiding me to outright hatred. And I can't blame them. If they're dismissed from their jobs here, they'll never find another good position. I'd be putting them out on the streets to starve. If Lord Devereaux and Helene are determined to get me out of the palace, they'll eventually succeed. I'll go down fighting, but I'll lose in the end.*

But ... I thought Lord Devereaux and I had come to an understanding. I chew on my lip. *Perhaps he didn't have time to tell Helene about his change of heart? Or does he still want me gone?*

The prince bellows, "Miss Dantes!"

I spin around, my hand covering my racing heart. "Lord Devereaux, you startled—"

He stalks toward me, his face stormy. "What have you done?"

A knot forms in my chest as I bury my hands in the fabric of my skirt. "The dress? You said I could borrow some clothes since—"

"I don't care about the burning dress." He towers over me, his eyes flashing. "You went through my papers! Those are not for your eyes, or anyone else's."

"I didn't!" My mind races, trying to figure out where these accusations are coming from. "I—"

The prince rages on, ignoring my protests. "Those documents contain sensitive information. I could have you brought up on treason. Do you know the harm you've caused? This, on top of upsetting the staff and causing chaos everywhere you go. I've tolerated your presence here long enough."

Heat creeps up my neck as my fists clench. I fight to keep my temper in check, knowing where this could end. "We should sit down and discuss this. There's been a misunderstanding."

He leans closer, his voice laced with venom. "The only misunderstanding is trusting you to stay out of my way."

I shove him back, yelling, "You're not listening! I haven't been anywhere near your burning papers. Fates save me, are you determined to ignore everything I say? Listen for a moment!"

"I'd never believe the word of a liar and a thief. I'll be contacting the Guild and telling them exactly what you've done."

Ice fills my veins. *They'll have me blacklisted. Papa and I will never survive.* "No, wait! I didn't do anything! Lord Devereaux, you must believe me. Please!"

I grab his arm, but he shakes me off, his face twisted in disgust.

"You're confined to your room until I can ship you off to the village. Just be thankful I don't throw you in the dungeon for what you've done." He storms off, shouting, "Helene, where are you?"

My legs threaten to collapse as he disappears around the corner, his yells echoing off the walls. *He's going to get me thrown out of the Guild. I'll never get another contract. It doesn't matter he's delusional and has no proof. The Guild won't risk it. I'm not worth tainting their reputation. Even if I plead my case, they'll have to take his side.*

A fire sparks in my belly, chasing away the ice. My hands shake. *Lord Devereaux's going to ruin my life over nothing. Less than nothing. He won't take a moment to hear any explanations. He believes he's right, and that's all that matters. He doesn't care that, with a word, he can destroy lives. And if he did, he'd probably be happy about it. Would think it's his right as a prince or some other hogwash. As though he's more important than anyone else.*

His accusations whirl around my mind, feeding the fire. *He dares call me a liar! The self-righteous arrogance! Every time I start to think there's a human underneath that insufferable ego, I'm proven wrong. Enough. He doesn't want me here. The staff doesn't want me here. I don't want to be here. What am I fighting for? Lady Isabeau is going to fire me as soon as her brother fills her ears with his lies. She'll never pay me. Lord Devereaux thinks I'm going to cower in my room until he can kick me out? He doesn't know who he's dealing with. I'm not going to spend another moment here!*

I race through the hallways, swiping angrily at the tears streaming down my cheeks. I fling open the door to my room and frantically throw my belongings into the saddlebags, not bothering with any organization. *The village isn't that far. I can get there before nightfall and then wait until the pass opens. Better the village than being trapped here with that beast.*

I rip off the borrowed dress throw it on the bed. *Thief indeed. He may call me a thief, but I know I'm not. I'm not going to give him the satisfaction of taking a single thing from his Royal Repulsiveness.*

Before I bolt out the door, my annoying conscience prompts me to write a quick note stating I've left the palace so they don't search for me. *Besides, I don't want any more unjust accusations thrown at me. If they don't know I'm gone, he'll blame me for burning tomorrow's breakfast.*

The hallways are blessedly empty as I run to the

entrance, avoiding the kitchen and anybody who might be there. When I open the door, a blast of cold air steals the breath from my lungs. The world is a harsh glare of sunlight reflecting off the white landscape. I push on, wading through the snow to the stables. Henri gives a happy whuff when he sees me, twisting to sniff my hair and clothes as I saddle him. I rub his cheek, then wrap my arms around his thick neck. "Sorry for dragging you out of your nice, warm stall. But I promise I'll spoil you properly when we reach the village."

I lead my horse out of the stable, vowing to leave Lord Devereaux and his accusations far behind.

9

"Only a little further, Henri. The village is just over that hill." I reach back and pat his cheek.

The weary stallion huffs heavily as he trudges behind me. I don't blame him; even I don't believe it. The trees are thick overhead and gathering clouds darken the horizon, making it difficult to tell how much time is left until sunset. There's a heaviness in the air that makes my skin crawl. I was sure we'd have reached the village by now. Lacee said it was only a few hours of travel in normal weather, so we must be getting close, even with the snow and cold slowing us down. There were a few moments of panic when I thought we'd strayed deep into the forest, but the route we're following through the woods is wide enough that I have to believe we haven't lost the road.

Branches creak overhead. I wrap my cloak tighter around me, thankful the trees have prevented the snow from piling up. Wading our way through the hip-high drifts on the palace grounds soaked my clothing and sapped most of my energy, even with Henri doing most of the work and breaking our trail. Here in the forest, there's a few scant inches of icy slush coating most of the ground, with some hidden pockets of deeper piles. Feet and hooves squeak on the snow. Ahead, there's a *crack* followed by a *whoomph* and a series of loud crashes. My horse spooks, dancing sideways at the noise. I shush Henri, running my hands along his neck and murmuring reassuring nonsense.

A wolf howls off to the right. I snap my head around, scanning the trees, my heart leaping into my throat. Keeping my eyes locked on the forest, I slide to Henri's side and root around in my saddlebag until I locate one of my longer knives.

"Don't try me, wolf. I'm in no mood to deal with you." I tug the stallion into a quicker walk, staying close to his side.

I keep talking, trying to keep myself and Henri calm. "You're probably wondering why you have such a silly master to take you out here in the cold with nothing but trees and snow in sight. But I know you understand why I couldn't stay at the palace after he accused me like that. And I'm going to take care of you and keep you safe. After all, that's my job. And I don't care what Lord Temper Tantrum thinks. I'm good at it, especially when stubborn people don't get in my way."

A branch snaps, making me jump. Henri nudges my shoulder. I pat his back, glad I'm not out here alone.

I peer into the trees, watching the shadows for movement. "Mayhap I can use the time at the village to find a new job. Marcel won't help me. He'll never go against the Guild. But Papa and I will figure it out. We always do. Now I won't have to be away from him for so long. And he worries about me getting hurt when I'm on a contract. So really, this is a good thing."

The heaviness in my chest reveals the lies behind my cheery tone, but I shove down the desperation threatening to overwhelm me. I'll have a good cry when I'm settled in a room tonight. Right now, I need to make sure Henri and I get safely through the forest before we freeze to death.

Hooves pound on the road behind me. I curse as Lord Devereaux comes into view, his red tunic a sharp contrast against his black cloak and stallion.

He catches up to me with a shout. "Are you mad? What are you doing out here?"

I narrow my eyes. "Good afternoon to you, too, Lord Devereaux. Isn't a lovely day for a ride?"

He glares, his lips pressed into a flat line. "I'm trying to prevent you from dying in a blizzard, and you make a joke? We need to return to the palace before that storm buries us."

Is that concern I hear underneath that annoyance? I narrow my eyes at him. "Why do you care?

He shifts in the saddle. "You're a guest in my home, and therefore under my protection. I'm responsible for your safety."

Of course, it's all about him. Fates forbid Lord Devereaux actually care about someone other than himself. "You're planning to ruin my life because you think I looked through your papers. Something you decided without a single piece of evidence and that you refuse to discuss with me or consider any other possibilities. And now you want to pretend you're concerned about me?" I brush past him. "Consider yourself relieved of any obligation to me. I'm certainly not going to spend another moment worrying about you."

He mutters under his breath as he swings off the horse, moving to block my path. "You've wasted enough of my time today. It's dangerous to travel in winter, especially when you're unfamiliar with mountain storms. If you had any sense, you'd have stayed put until I said it was safe to leave."

"I can take care of myself. It was my decision to go, and it's my decision to continue to the village. Go home."

"I order you to turn around and return to the palace."

I tug Henri's reins, guiding him around Lord Devereaux. "I'm not one of your subjects to command. I'm leaving and you can't stop me."

He grabs my elbow. "I will if I have to."

I yank my arm away from him and brandish the knife. "Do you really think you can drag me back by force? I've knocked you down before, and that's when I was unarmed. Imagine what I can do with a weapon."

A vein pulses in his forehead. "You're being an idiot."

My voice drips with sarcasm. "Your sweet words have swayed me and I'm helpless to resist. I'll follow you wherever you lead."

"Miss Julietta," he grinds out. "Please come back to La Sailles. I don't want you to get caught in the storm."

"No, thank you." I keep my gaze straight ahead as I plow forward.

Lord Devereaux growls. "Stop being stubborn. You're going to get killed because you're too pig-headed to listen to reason."

That brings me up short. I whirl around and poke him in the chest. "Me! What about you, you oaf? All you do is yell at everyone! You refuse to listen to anybody, especially me." I glare at him with so much heat it's amazing he doesn't burst into flames. "Calling me a thief and a liar? I never touched your precious papers. It might surprise you, but most people think I'm very trustworthy and loyal. I've never had any complaints from my employers, not one! But then again, I've never worked for someone as obnoxious as you." My lungs heave, my fists clenched as I fight the urge to throw the knife at him.

He glances at the sky, then reaches for my arm again. "I don't have time for this."

I step back. "If you want me to even consider the possibility of coming back with you, then make the time. Otherwise, leave, and I'll find my way to the village."

He crosses his arms, his face setting to stone. "There's nothing to talk about. I know what you did. There's no excuse you could provide that I would accept."

"I didn't do anything to your papers! Yes, I talked to Lacee. But I—"

"So, you admit it."

I want to smack the smug look off his face. "You're impossible! Talking to someone isn't—"

The wind blasts me, sending me stumbling closer to the trees. A second blast knocks me off my feet, and I drop the knife in the snow. I struggle to stand, shielding my eyes from the relentless gale. Roaring and cracking shatters the air. Devereaux yells. An enormous darkness hurtles at me. There's no time to even scream. I'm hit from the side, the force sending me tumbling and rolling across the ground as the sky collapses and the earth shakes. Devereaux's shout cuts off.

The only sound is the howling wind.

All I can do is shake, curled up in a small ball as I try to sort out everything that just happened. Everything is odd shapes of darkness and white. Slowly, the world takes form again. My brain struggles to string coherent thoughts together.

A tree fell on me.

I'm buried in a cage of branches.

Bark and sticks scrape my skin with every motion. Gritting my teeth, I move carefully and methodically, testing my limbs until I confirm I'm not injured beyond scratches and bruises. Digging myself out of the tangled prison is slow and agonizing work. Most branches are too thick to snap, so I have to wriggle my way through the tangle. Every movement brings a fresh wave of pain. My head throbs and waves of nausea hit me. I inch my way out, wincing as cuts open on my face and arms where my clothing doesn't protect me.

After an eternity, I break free of my wooden prison and survey the damage.

My stomach drops.

A tree thicker than my height lays across the road, blocking the way. I can't see the ground under all the twisting snarls of branches. Henri and the prince's horse are standing down the road.

There's no sign of the prince.

10

"Lord Devereaux? Milord?" My heart thunders, ice creeping up my chest. "Lord Devereaux? Are you hurt? Where are you?"

I scramble through the branches, searching for any sign of him. "Devereaux?" My voice is shrill, the panic creeping in. "Devereaux? Answer me, you stubborn a—oh thank the Fates."

A corner of his red tunic shows through the tangle. I rip away branches and shove the snow aside until I've uncovered him. Devereaux's face is pale, his eyes closed. An angry red welt the size of an egg is growing on his forehead. I gently tap his cheek, calling out, but he doesn't react.

I swallow hard against the lump in my throat, then grab him under his arms to drag him away from the tree. Gritting my teeth, I keep my tone light. "Oomph, you're heavy. I hope you appreciate this when you wake up."

His limp body refuses to move. A sickening feeling grows in my stomach as I realize his leg is trapped under a branch. The limb is the size of my waist and still attached to the tree, making it impossible to lift off him. Cursing, I drop to my knees and dig at the ground under his trapped leg. Snowflakes fall into my eyes and down my back, soaking through my clothing as I frantically work. Too soon my hands scrape against rock. I tug his leg, but I wasn't able to dig down far enough to free him.

The panic threatens to overwhelm me. I shove it down, focusing on helping the prince. *I have to get him out from under that tree, but how? Digging him out won't work. Think, think, think.* My lungs can't get enough air and black spots dance in my vision. Closing my eyes, I force myself to take a deep breath. *There's only one way to possibly get him out. It won't work, but I have to try.*

My eyes sting as I tear through the wreckage, trying to find a branch large enough to act as a lever, but small enough that I can manage it. After too many minutes, I locate one and try to wedge it into place next to Devereaux's leg, using another sturdy branch as the pivot point. I curse under my breath when it takes several tries to get everything in position, my hands shaking so hard they're more hinderance than help. Once everything is in place, I look around for my horse.

"Henri. Come here. Easy, boy." I cluck at the stallion, encouraging him to stay put as I slowly get closer. Every nerve screams at me to run and grab the reins, but he's still skittish from the tree falling. He'll bolt if I startle him, and the prince's horse doesn't trust me. "I need your help. Can you help me get the prince free? There's a good boy."

Once I have hold of his bridle, I guide the horse back to where Devereaux is unconscious on the ground. I loop the reins around the prince's wrist, wincing in sympathy for what's about to come.

"One … two … three!"

Sending a prayer to the Fates to help me, I press down on the lever, forcing all my weight on to it. The branch pinning Devereaux doesn't budge. I clench my teeth and lift my feet up, bouncing against the wood. Slowly, slowly, the branch creeps up. The moment the weight lifts off his leg, I scream as loud as I can, spooking Henri into jumping forward, dragging Devereaux free. I collapse on the limb, my muscles turning to water.

I stumble over to Henri, soothing him as I untie the prince. "I'm so sorry, boy. Thank you, Henri. You're a good boy. Thank you."

The horse snorts, then gently blows on my hair. Gulping, I turn to focus on helping Devereaux.

A strangled sob escapes my lips. I drop to my knees next to the prince's motionless body. Devereaux looks even worse than before. His skin has gone ashy, his breathing shallow. I gently prod his leg, eliciting a groan from the unconscious man. I don't think the limb is broken, but I don't know enough of healing to be sure. My chest tightens, and it's hard to breathe. My mind races through my options. *I can't leave him out here alone while I get help. I don't know how long it'll take, not to mention he could freeze while I'm gone. He said a storm's coming. And there's the wolves.* I shudder. *So, we go together. The village or the palace?*

I bellow in his ear, "Devereaux, is La Sailles closer, or the village?"

No response.

All right, it's up to me to pick. Just because this is a literal life or death decision doesn't mean anything. Why, oh why, did he have to come after me? I could've found my way to the village while he was happily sulking in the palace and everything would be fine. But no, he had to chase after me because I'm his responsibility in his delusional mind.

My breath hitches as I ignore the little tug at my heart, not wishing to look too closely at the cause. A crash sounds nearby, making me jump. The snow falls faster, thicker. *We have to get out of here.* I tie Henri's reins to a branch, then cautiously approach the prince's black stallion while my mind whirls. *Focus on the problem and what I know.*

Devereaux doesn't seem completely without sense. Surely if the village was closer, he would've insisted on taking shelter there rather than trying to outrun the storm back to the palace? But he's so stubborn and arrogant! And controlling—I can't forget controlling. Would he risk his life just so he could ride out the storm in his own home? Village or palace? Palace or village? It comes down to whether I think Devereaux would put our safety ahead of his comfort ...

Devereaux is impossible for me to lift into the saddle, especially with my muscles already shaking from exhaustion and cold. Luckily, his horse is exceptionally well trained, and I convince him to kneel next to the prince. After a lot of swearing, sweating, and sobbing, I manage to sling Devereaux across the saddle. Using strips cut from his cloak, I secure him in place to ensure he won't slide off as his horse struggles to its feet.

I tether the black stallion to my saddle, then turn Henri toward La Sailles. "Let's go."

The heavy snowfall and increasingly powerful gusts of wind mean our time is running out—the storm is here. I pray to the Fates my optimism in Devereaux's judgment isn't misguided. Our lives literally depend on it.

But I've been wrong before ...

11

I thought my first journey to La Sailles was brutal, but it was a gentle spring walk compared to this nightmare of snow, wind, and ice. Blackness swallows the sky as more clouds gather overhead. The wind threatens to sweep us off our feet every moment, blasting from one direction, then another. My teeth chatter so hard I'm afraid they'll shatter. Ice cakes my cloak in layers, cracking with every movement. The only way to reassure myself that my legs are still attached is to look down and see them clamped around my horse. I stopped feeling anything hours ago and moved into complete numbness, my thoughts following as each minute slips away.

Poor Henri has his head hanging so low it's almost touching the ground, his hooves barely lifting with each step. I try to force myself to think of something—anything—I can do, but my thoughts are sluggish, refusing to form into anything sensible. Occasionally, I remember Lord Devereaux and the stallion behind us. If I can hang on to the thought long enough, I twist to check on them. They're dark blobs moving through the roaring white storm trying to smother us.

Our only advantage is the path Henri and I broke through the snow earlier. We wouldn't have a chance without it. Besides making traveling back faster and easier than going out, it also guarantees we don't get lost in the white blizzard shrieking around us, blinding us to any landmarks that might have guided us to the palace.

When Henri stops, I stare dumbly ahead, unable to register anything in our surroundings. A bright light cuts through the whiteness, followed by muffled voices. Something plucks at the reins gripped in my frozen fingers. I struggle briefly against the shapes pulling me off the horse, but my body has nothing left to give. The sounds morph into a dull buzzing as everything fades to black.

Extreme exhaustion, followed by a severe cold, keeps me bedridden for days. Most of that time is spent sleeping. Every time I wake up, I fly into a panic, and whoever's close by has to reassure me that Lord Devereaux and the horses are fine and recovering swiftly. I barely have the strength to lift my head off the pillow when Lacee clucks over me or hands me a hot cup of broth between naps. The staff takes turns checking in on me and dropping off treats. I have to admit, it's nice to have someone fussing and taking care of me for a change.

One morning I wake up enough to know I won't be going back to sleep soon. There's a fire burning in the grate, but the room has a lingering chill. I shiver and wrap the blankets tighter around me. Everything from my interrupted trip to the village comes flooding back: the accusations, the tree, the way the prince risked his life to come after me.

I rub a hand across my eyes with a sigh. There's time enough to dwell on the things that led me to leave the palace and brought me back. Right now, I want to put all my thoughts away for another day, and the best way to do that is to get lost in a good book. There's a small library on the floor below me that will be the perfect place to read in peace.

To my pleasant surprise, there's a huge gray robe lined with black fur and a pair of matching oversized slippers set next to my bed. The sleeves on the robe hang well past my fingertips, and the hem brushes the floor, wrapping me in a cozy bubble as I shuffle from the room on my errand.

My illness took more out of me than I thought. By the time I descend to the lower floor, my legs are shaking and I'm sweating with the effort of staying upright. I grit my teeth and push forward, using the wall for support, promising myself a nice long rest in the library. I finally reach my destination and shove the door open, then jump back in surprise as a wave of heat brushes my face. A large fire crackles in the fireplace and lamps are lit around the room. It takes a moment to glimpse Lord Devereaux hunched over a desk off to the side, his brow furrowed in concentration. I swing the door shut, not wanting to disturb him—or face him right now.

I quickly hobble down the hallway and duck around the corner as the library door clicks open. My trembling legs threaten to leave me in a puddle on the floor as I hold my breath, listening for his approach. A hundred heartbeats tick off before the door closes again. I heave a quick sigh of relief and creep away, resting frequently on the stairs. Back in my room, I collapse on a small settee, unwilling to move another inch. *Best to stay out of the prince's way until his temper dies down and his wounds heal. I'll ask Lacee to bring a book the next time she visits.*

Ten minutes later, there's a rap on my door.

I purse my lips. None of the staff has bothered knocking since I fell ill. I heave myself off the settee with a whimper and open the door to find the blank-faced butler waiting for me.

I smile, curious at the man's presence. "Good morning, Orvil. Please, come in."

"No, thank you, Miss Julietta. I've come on business." He clears his throat. "Lord Devereaux requests you join him for tea in the library at eleven. However, if you would like to decline, he'll be vacating the library at one, and you may have it for your personal use for the rest of the evening."

"Oh!" If given a million guesses, I'd never have predicted this. *Why would he invite me for tea? Is this some kind of trick?* Orvil stares at me, waiting for a response. "Um, yes. I'd be happy to join him for tea."

"Very good. I'll send Lacee to assist you." He turns on his heel and glides down the hallway as I stare at his back.

The prince must have spotted me near the library, after all. My stomach twists, and I have to fight the urge to shout after Orvil and take it back. *He must think me so childish for running away like that. What is he planning? Is he going to exile me from the kingdom? Shout at me for dragging him out into a storm and almost getting him killed?*

Tea would be an odd setting for a scolding. Perhaps ... Perhaps I should give him the benefit of the doubt? After all, he could have left me out there on my own. And he came after me himself instead of sending someone ...

Lacee bustles in with an armful of dresses, interrupting

my thoughts. "Julietta, you're going to look gorgeous! I think you should wear the red one. Although the blue one is so pretty. Or this yellow one. Which one do you think Lord Devereaux would prefer? It's so romantic! I knew he would fall in love with you."

I giggle nervously. "Lacee, it's just tea. He probably wants to make sure I'm not going to die on his watch." My pulse speeds up as a blush washes over my body. *It's nothing. Calm down. This doesn't mean anything.*

"Nonsense. He gets updates on you five times a day and he knows you're doing fine. This is something else." She drops the dresses on the bed and then puts her hands on her hips, surveying me with a critical eye. "We have a lot of work to do."

The next hour is a blur of Lacee whirling around the room. She brushes my hair until it shines, braiding it back and arranging it in elegant loops. The choice of dress is her biggest struggle, but she finally settles on a pink dress with cream insets. "It gives your face some color, which you desperately need," she tells me with a wrinkled nose. I talk her out of the tiny heeled slippers she tries to shove my feet into, opting instead for my boots so I don't lose any of my toes due to lack of circulation. A thick cream wrap lined with silver fur ensures I won't freeze on the journey between my room and the library.

Lacee wisely offers me her shoulder for support for the walk, so I don't arrive a quivering mess of jelly. She whispers good luck and throws me a grin before skipping away.

I stare at the library door, taking a deep breath. *There's still time to run away.* I knock quietly, then crack the door open and peek in.

Lord Devereaux paces in front of the fire, hands folded behind his back, muttering to himself. His skin has a healthy glow, his dark eyes bright. Except for the small yellow-green bump on his head, you'd never suspect he'd been downed by a tree just a few days prior. He looks … nervous? Some of the butterflies in my stomach settle and I step into the room. He abruptly halts, spinning to face me. The firelight casts a glow around him, highlighting the chiseled perfection of his features. *No wonder he's arrogant. The Fates shouldn't allow someone to have every advantage and still bless them with good looks that can take a girl's breath away.*

Lord Devereaux bows. "Miss Julietta. Thank you for joining me."

I hesitate, then curtsy. "Thank you for inviting me."

We stare awkwardly at each other for a moment. I bury my fingers in my skirt, unsure what to do next. Lord Devereaux seems equally bewildered, his eyes darting to mine, then the door, the fire, and back to me.

Well, he doesn't seem to want to yell at me. That's a good start. If this is some kind of elaborate trick, I can't see what purpose it serves. Could it be? Does he want to call a truce? A little thread of hope winds its way through me. *If so, I'll do my best to help.* "How are you feeling, my lord?"

He tucks his hands in his pockets, then pulls them back out and folds them behind his back. "Much better, thank you. And you?"

"Fine as well."

"Is there anything you need?"

"Um—no, no. Everyone has taken good care of me." My fingers crush the fabric as I search for something else to say. *Ugh, this is painful. Why are we so awkward? We should be able to have a simple conversation.*

There's a light tap on the door. The prince looks relieved as Nancey wheels in a tea service with covered plates. She sets everything up on the small table between the two plush chairs by the fire with practiced efficiency, then takes the cart out, throwing me a small smirk before the door closes.

Lord Devereaux gestures to the chairs. "Shall we?"

I settle on the edge of the seat, my muscles tense.

He perches on the chair across from me and picks up a plate. "Rosemarie makes the most delicious mushroom tarts. Would you like one?"

To my surprise, he assembles the delicacies with considerable courtesy, asking what pastries I prefer and if there's anything else I'd like from the kitchen. Lord Devereaux hands me a loaded plate and then pours tea for us both. We spend a few minutes busying ourselves munching on the savory treats, each one tastier than the last. The teacup looks tiny in Lord Devereaux's hands, but he handles it with practiced ease, every movement fluid and effortless.

I fiddle with an egg tart, crumbling the flakey pastry between my fingers, gathering my courage. "I wanted to thank you. You saved my life twice. Once by coming after me, and then by pushing me away from the tree. I'll never be able to repay you for that." I lower my eyes. "And I'm sorry about your arm. I hope it doesn't hurt too badly." At his puzzled look, I explain how I used Henri to pull him away from the tree. "I was afraid it would injure you, but I didn't know what else to do."

"Is that what happened?" He rubs his shoulder. "It was sore for a day or two, but no permanent damage. I can't believe you got that tree off me."

"I can't believe you survived that blow." I grimace in sympathy. "Does your head still hurt?"

"Only when I try to think. Thank the heavens I don't have to do that too often." He gives me a self-deprecating smile. "I've had worse knocks. I should be back to my normal, stubborn self in a few more days."

"Then I shall prepare to run for cover when that happens," I tease him with a smile.

He straightens up, his face sobering. "I wish to express my regrets for everything that has happened since you arrived. My behavior has been inexcusable and unworthy of a gentleman."

I lift an eyebrow. "Is that your way of saying you're sorry?"

He huffs out a breath. "Yes. I'm rather out of practice at it."

"I'm sure you'll do better next time." I reach over and touch his hand. "I'm sorry too. Can we start over and be friends?"

"Friends?" Lord Devereaux nods, his face relaxing. "Yes, I like that. Friends."

"Excellent. That means we can drop the formalities and act like normal people around each other." I snatch a macaron off the tray between us, grinning as he raises an eyebrow. "I never could resist a dessert."

He chuckles. "At last, I've found your weakness. Now I know how to get on your good side."

"'Tis true. Give me a sticky bun or a plate full of chocolate creams and I'm your eternal slave."

Lord Devereaux leans forward, tilting his head close to mine. "Mine is raspberry meringue. But don't tell anyone. I can't have other kingdoms using it against me."

I make a crossing motion over my heart. "My lips are sealed. I've never had raspberry meringue, but it sounds delicious."

His eyes widen in feigned shock. "Never had—this is a travesty! We need to fix this immediately." He jumps up from the chair.

Laughing, I tug him back down. "Another time. I'm too stuffed right now to eat another bite. You'll have to roll me out of the room."

"Nonsense. We'll just turn the library into your bedroom."

I melt back in the chair with a sigh. "Don't tempt me. If I could move in here, I would."

He leans on the arm of the chair. "That was you earlier, wasn't it? That came to the library?"

I shift uncomfortably and look away. "Yes."

"Why didn't you come in?"

"I—I didn't think I'd be welcome." I watch him out of the corner of my eye.

His brow furrows. "But you saved my life."

"After endangering it." I take a deep breath. "I thought you might blame me, since you were chasing me out into the storm. You wouldn't have been there if I hadn't left."

"True, but you left because of my actions." He drags a hand across his face. "I've thought about what you said in the forest. What I can remember of it, anyway. And you're right. I should've listened to your side of things before I started flinging accusations. I'm sorry."

"And I'm sorry I left instead of trying to talk to you again. We'll both do better the next time we argue." I nudge him with a grin. "See? I knew you'd be better at apologizing the second time. All it takes is a little practice."

His rich laughter sends warmth spreading through my chest. It's cozy chatting by the fire, but my eyes soon droop

and I'm stifling yawns every few seconds. Lord Devereaux
notices my fatigue and calls for one of the staff to assist me
to my room, over my protests.

He bows over my hand. "Thank you for joining me,
Miss Dantes."

I give his hand a gentle squeeze as I dip into a curtsy.
"Julietta, please. Anyone who knows my secret should call
me by my given name."

"As long as you call me Devereaux. I hope you'll join
me again tomorrow." He smiles, flashing dimples hidden to
me before now.

My heart stutters. *Just my exhaustion making me
overreact.* "It would be my pleasure."

Nancey is mercifully quiet as she helps me back to my
room, although I'm sure everything she witnessed in the
library will be described in detail to the rest of the staff. She
assists me out of the gown and I crawl into bed, sleep
chasing away consciousness before I have time to think
about my intriguing afternoon, leaving one lingering
thought.

Devereaux has a heart after all ...

The next morning, I dress quickly, ignoring the brief pang of guilt as I slip out of my room. *I'm not avoiding Lacee—not exactly. I just don't want to rehash every moment of my tea with the prince, because she'll read too much into it. This friendship with him is too new to analyze every word and look. Better to let it be and see what happens.*

When I open the library door, I'm unsurprised to see Lord Devereaux working at the small desk, his shirtsleeves rolled up. There's a thick blue robe hanging around his shoulders to supplement the heat from the fire. The rumpled clothing makes him look less the chiseled granite prince and a little more human. Even his hair seems a bit more disheveled today.

He looks up and smiles. "I see you decided not to run away this time."

I laugh. "I thought it worth the risk, but I don't want to interrupt you. I was looking for a book."

Lord Devereaux grimaces. "You probably won't have much luck in here. It's mostly histories, treaties, and maps, although there might be a couple of novels if you search long enough. Try Isabeau's room. She always seems to find a way to sneak her favorite romance stories past Mother."

"Histories are perfect. It's one of my passions." My eyes roam the rows of books, not bothering to hide my eagerness.

His brow furrows. "Really?"

I nod enthusiastically. "Do you have anything on the eastern kingdoms? Or something on Roma?"

He points to a shelf in the back and I happily wander over to browse, conscious of his gaze on me. Soon I have three thick books in my arms, with a few mentally marked to grab after I finish my current selections. After a moment of debate, I settle on a long couch near his desk. *It makes more sense to stay here than go back to my room. It's warmer in here. And it'll be easier to grab new books as I finish these. Going back to my room would be impractical. Really, reading here is the only logical thing to do.*

He puts down the quill, then stretches his arms out to the sides with a groan. "Have you had breakfast yet? I'm starving."

At the mention of food, my stomach growls, making him chuckle. He ducks out to arrange for trays to be delivered, then settles back at the desk and frowns at his papers.

"What are you working on?" I quickly add, "If it isn't too sensitive to talk about."

He hesitates, then shrugs. "Treaty proposals. There's several kingdoms I think we should approach to create mutually beneficial relationships. I wanted to draft some preliminary terms to present to my father when I return to Charistel."

I smirk. "*Mutually beneficial relationships.* What a bureaucratic phrase."

Lord Devereaux leans back and crosses his arms. "How would you say it?"

"Alliances or partnerships, depending on what you're proposing." I hold up my hands. "I'm not saying mine are any better. Despite my attempts to cling to my common roots, I've been around too many aristocrats to think differently."

"Ah, yes. Your previous contracts. I'm sure none of them were as difficult as I am."

"You're definitely the front runner in that category." I smile, thinking back on my past charges. "Although that little rascal from Sulomi comes in a close second. He kept trying to sneak snakes into my bed." At the prince's shocked expression, I giggle. "He was seven."

"That's right. You normally take care of children." He taps his chin, a thoughtful expression on his face. "Sulomi, you say? That's one kingdom I'm considering reaching out to. They have excellent copper and iron mines."

I open my mouth—then snap it shut. I could tell Lord Devereaux about my experiences in Sulomi to help with his negotiations, but the Guild has a strict code about disclosing information about our clientele. They'd be furious I even mentioned my contract there. But an agreement between Sulomi and Fallian Province could help both kingdoms. *Would it really harm anything to share a few details with him?*

I'm saved from deciding by the arrival of breakfast. Lord Devereaux and I eagerly dive into crepes stuffed with raspberry preserves and ricotta cheese, spiced apple slices, and cinnamon tea. There's a mischievous smile playing on Devereaux's lips whenever I glance at the remaining covered plate on his tray.

I take a sip of tea, eyeing him over the rim. "You seem too happy with yourself this morning. Should I be worried?"

He feigns an innocent look. "What could you possibly be concerned about?"

"Too many things to count. That's my job, after all." A twinge of guilt plucks at me. I've been ignoring my duties for too long, using my recent illness and fatigue as an excuse. I need to get back to work. *Tomorrow.* "Are you going to tell me what's under there?"

The prince grins as he whips off the cover to reveal a mound of chocolate cremes. He holds out the plate to me and inclines his head. "For you, milady."

I laugh in delight. "No raspberry meringues?"

"I thought I'd bribe you with your favorite first, just in case you don't love the meringues as much as I do."

"A wise man to see to the needs of his lady before himself." Heat rushes into my cheeks. I blurt out, "Not that I'm yours. I mean, I'm your friend, but not—oh, you know what I mean." I pop the treat into my mouth, groaning as the outer chocolate shell dissolves, flooding my mouth with the delicious creamy mousse inside.

Lord Devereaux watches me devour another three cremes, his eyebrows rising. "You weren't exaggerating when you said they're your weakness."

"Can you blame me? These are proof that the Fates want us to be happy." I lick my fingers, already plotting how I can bribe Rosemarie to make these for me every day.

He chews one thoughtfully, then shakes his head. "Delicious, but they're no raspberry meringues."

"You did not say that!" I shake my finger at him, aghast. "Blasphemy!"

He lifts his chin. "I said it and I refuse to budge. Fallian

Province always stands by its declarations.”

I cross my arms and scowl at him in mock annoyance. “You should be more open-minded. Are you this stubborn about everything?”

“Only desserts.” He winks. “But I’ll concede these may be my second favorite.”

“That’s because you didn’t try the sticky buns I made for the staff.” I debate throwing a chocolate at him, but eat it instead. *No point in wasting something this scrumptious.*

After the trays are cleared, Lord Devereaux and I settle back into our spots. The quiet scratching of his quill accompanies my dive into Roma culture and mythology. We take turns adding wood to the fire as the hours pass.

In the middle of a story about a Roma deity stirring up yet more mischief with mankind, I look up to find Devereaux standing behind me.

He holds up the blue robe he was wearing earlier. “It’s getting chilly in here.” He settles it across my shoulders, the fabric still warm from his body.

I snuggle back into the welcome heat, running my hand down the soft sleeve. “Thank you. But don’t you need it?”

“No, I’m closer to the fire than you are.” Lord Devereaux rocks back on his heels, clearing his throat. “You were smiling. Is the book funny?”

“Very.” I launch into a recount of the story that soon has him chuckling, flashing the dimples I glimpsed before.

“Why have I never heard that tale? All my tutors told me were facts about road building and aqueducts and territory.”

“Too many teachers avoid the best parts of history. Too many books, too. History is the past come alive. It lets us glimpse into the lives of our ancestors. What they were passionate about and the mistakes they made. There’s so much we can learn, and not just about roads and aqueducts. Although those are really important when you realize how large their empire was, and they—" I snap my mouth shut. "Sorry, I tend to ramble when I talk about my favorite topics."

"I can see that." Lord Devereaux clears his throat, then glances at the book. "I'd like to read it after you finish."

My pulse unaccountably speeds up. "Of—of course. It'd be nice to have someone to discuss it with." *Fates, I always seem to blush around this man! It must be the extra heat from the robe.* I covertly fan myself when he glances at the desk.

Sensing he's about to get back to work, I blurt out, "Do you like mythology?" I bite my lip. *What am I doing? He's my protectee. I should let him get back to his papers instead of distracting him.*

Lord Devereaux says, "I'm not sure."

"Aren't princes supposed to have an opinion on everything?" I tease.

He smirks. "I'm trying to learn to be more open-minded."

"Haha, well-played!" I fidget with the page edge, finding it oddly hard to meet his eyes. "That's something I need to learn, too. If you haven't noticed, I make snap judgments about people."

"But you're willing to reconsider, otherwise you probably would have tied me up and thrown me in the dungeon by now." He gives me a wry smile.

I ignore the warmth blossoming in my chest. *Dare I ask? I shouldn't.* "Why didn't you stay in Charistel?"

The animation drops from his face. "Why do you ask?"

My stomach twists, but I keep the smile on my face. "It

seems like a perfectly reasonable question. From what I've heard, Charistel is wonderful. Plays and musicals, beautiful parks, lively parties. I'd mention the food, but I doubt anything could surpass Rosemarie's creations."

"La Sailles' library is better for research. I should get back to it." Lord Devereaux returns to his desk, pointedly keeping his gaze away from mine.

I smother a sigh. *Why can't I resist pushing him? Mayhap it's better this way. Things were getting a bit too ... comfortable.* I rub the small ache in my chest, then shake my head.

Enough stalling. This has been a nice rest, but I need to get back to my job. There's a palace to map and an assassin to catch. I glance at the prince who's furiously scribbling on a piece a parchment, a deep crease between his eyebrows. *He won't notice if I slip out.*

My hand is on the doorknob when Lord Devereaux calls out.

"Are you leaving?"

I take a steadying breath, then smile over my shoulder. "You reminded me it's time I go back to my job. After all, your sister isn't paying me to sit around and read."

He frowns, tapping the quill against the desk. "That nonsense. It's ridiculous. I don't need anyone to protect me. Let me buy out your contract and then we'll put this whole silly thing behind us."

"I appreciate the offer. But as I said before, I can't accept it, even if the Guild would allow it. It's a matter of honor."

"Then I hope you're not planning to go outside. I'm not going to ride out in another storm to rescue you again," Lord Devereaux grumbles.

I barely manage not to roll my eyes. "Not today. I haven't finished looking around the chateau yet."

His frown deepens as he leans back in the chair, crossing his arms. "You're going to get lost if you don't know your way around. There are a lot of dead ends and odd passages."

If I didn't know better, I'd think he doesn't want me to leave. Laughter bubbles up inside me. "Someone will find me, eventually." I pause, watching the struggle behind his stoic mask, before adding, "Shall we have supper in here?"

His shoulders relax. "I'll let the staff know." The prince turns his attention back to the documents stacked on the desk.

I slip out the door, my steps as light as my heart.

Lord Devereaux eyes me as he takes a sip of tea. "Did you discover anything exciting today?"

I adjust the blanket that appeared in the library this afternoon, tucking it tighter around my legs. "Three assassins, two secret passages, and four deadly pit traps. Don't worry, I disabled them." At his exasperated look, I laugh. "A lot of dust and one leaky window, which I reported to Helene. I still have five floors to go and I'm not even a quarter done with this one. Why couldn't you have a nice tiny cabin in the mountains instead of this monstrosity?"

"My great-great-great ancestors didn't believe in modesty. The bigger the palace, the better to show how important they are."

"That seems to be sentiment among most many-great royal ancestors. You'd think one or two would prefer a little cottage in the woods."

"Can't fit an entourage in a cottage, unless you're going to store the footmen in the pantry."

I snort, tea going up my nose. As I sputter, Lord Devereaux gallantly looks away, a smile playing on the edges of his lips.

I take a long drink, letting the warm liquid soothe my throat. "You don't exactly travel with a large group. You could almost fit your staff in a cottage."

He waves away my comment. "There's already more people here than I'd like. But Helene insisted this was the minimum she needed."

"She overlooked some key people in her planning. Like guards. Somehow I doubt Orvil is secretly a master of knife throwing, or Helene can wrestle a two-hundred-pound man to the ground with one arm tied behind her back."

"Then it's a good thing you're here. There's probably an assassin hiding behind the couch right now."

"I'm not that lucky. If there was, you'd have to start taking me seriously." I sigh and sink back in the chair, my muscles relaxing in the warmth from the fire.

He chuckles. "I always take you seriously. It's my sister's judgment I question. I love her dearly, but Isa loves to create drama. You're in for a very boring time here."

"I would love nothing better. But I hope you have something fun planned for the winter besides preparing treaties."

"Nonsense! What could be more entertaining than reading crop reports and analyzing dry good exports for days on end?" Lord Devereaux's shoulders slump, the humor draining from his expression. "No. I'm going to need every minute to finish my proposals before I return to Charistel."

I tilt my head to the side and raise my eyebrow. "You know you're not responsible for solving all the problems in the world in one go, don't you?"

He runs a hand across his eyes. "Sometimes it feels like I am." He shakes his head. "But nobody's forcing me to do it, so I can't complain." His smile can't hide the exhaustion shadowing his face.

Don't say it, don't say it, don't say it … "I could help you. Give you some suggestions on how to approach each kingdom based on my experiences, if you want." I hold my breath, my heartbeat quickening.

He hesitates, but seems to think it over instead of laughing at me.

I hurry to add, "I don't have to see anything you're planning. We could just talk in generalities so you don't spill any royal secrets." *Why am I doing this? It's stupid. I could get into so much trouble with the Guild. But I know I can help both countries. If I can help, I should … shouldn't I?*

Devereaux drums his fingers on the chair arm. After an eternity, he inclines his head. "I can't see any harm in that. As long as you promise not to talk with anyone else about what we discuss, or kingdoms I'm considering."

I sit up straight, making a crossing motion across my thumping heart. "I swear. We could even talk about all the kingdoms. That way I won't know which ones you're planning to approach."

He nods slowly. "And I might get some new ideas I hadn't considered. Good. Where do you want to start?"

My mind goes completely blank. "Oh, um. Well … why don't you pick the first one and we'll go from there?"

We spend the next few hours talking. I throw out every detail I think could be helpful about the kingdoms I've worked in or researched for my contracts—*Sulomi gets annoyed by chitchat; what we consider polite, they view as patronizing, so be blunt. They've had famines, so trading grain and other foodstuffs for metals and gems would be the best approach*—and kingdoms that may be reluctant to set up a treaty—*Balut is a seaside kingdom that doesn't approach anything directly. Offer something as a show of goodwill without expecting anything in return. They love spices and delicate glasswork.* There are some where I'm not much help—*I haven't worked with Rus and they haven't contracted with the Guild. But I bet there's some books in here that can help us.* It's fun to put my knowledge to a different use, and Devereaux proves eager to share what he knows as well.

The fire is burning low when we start discussing one of the neighboring kingdoms.

I frown as I think it over. "Irelin values friendship and honor more than physical goods. I wouldn't bring up trade until you've established a relationship. Or let them bring it up first." I smirk. "I've heard the princess is agreeable. Perhaps you should consider a marriage alliance?"

"Agreeable." He shakes his head, his lip curling. "That's what everyone looks for in a potential spouse. Why would you suggest such a horrid thing as a marriage alliance?"

I giggle, ignoring the way my chest lightens at his obvious disgust. "Just doing my duty as your royal matchmaker."

He grumbles, "I can't believe the staff bought that hogwash. As though I would allow a matchmaker anywhere near me."

"Give them some credit. They think your sister is responsible for it, not you."

"It does sound like something she'd do." His eyes widen in alarm. "Heavens, I hope she doesn't hear about it. I don't want her getting any ideas."

"I'm sure she already has plans for you." I laugh at his loud groan. "If a marriage contract isn't on the table, then you'll have to figure out another approach. Their culture has deep ties to their mythology. They make a lot of references to their gods and legends as part of their normal conversation, and get their values from the stories." I jump to my feet and hurry to the bookshelf along the far wall. "I saw a book on Irelin's mythology that could help you."

Devereaux joins me in the search. There's no organization for how the books are placed, so it takes a few minutes to locate the slim volume jammed in on an overhead shelf.

"There." I stand on my toes, inching it out with my fingertips. The line of books shifts forward, reluctant to release the volume.

"Here, let me." Devereaux edges in front of me. "Where is it?"

"I can do it." I stretch past him, yanking the volume free and bringing the rest of the books crashing down on us. With a curse, Devereaux tucks me against his chest, shielding me from the onslaught.

This close, his scent of leather and something uniquely Devereaux wraps around me, flooding my senses. A strange heat spreads across my skin and I close my eyes against the dizziness, gripping his shirt, trying to keep my balance.

His chuckle rumbles through me. "I always seem to have things falling on me when you're around."

I take a faltering step back, hugging the book to my chest. A blush fills my cheeks as I avoid his eyes. "You're just lucky, I guess." My voice is breathless. *What's wrong with me? It must be some lingering effect of my illness.* I cling to the annoyance, shaking my head to clear the fog. *I'm just tired and being silly.* "Here." I shove the book at him, then stoop down to grab the fallen volumes.

We silently re-shelve the books, then return to our seats by the fire. I stare down into my lukewarm tea. *I shouldn't be helping Devereaux like this. He was going to ruin my life because he suspected I looked at his treaties and now I'm practically drafting them for him. I've already done more than I should. Anything else and the Guild will definitely blacklist me. I wanted to help the kingdoms, and now I have. It's enough. No more.*

"Julietta?" Devereaux is watching me, his brow furrowed. "Is everything all right?"

I jump, sloshing the tea over the edge of the cup. "Yes. Of course. My apologies, my mind is woolgathering. I should go to bed before I fall asleep."

Before I can stand, Devereaux reaches out and touches my hand, freezing me in place. "Thank you for your help today."

My stomach flutters as a warmth grows in my chest. "No need to thank me. There's nothing I'm telling you that you couldn't find out on your own with a little research and friendly spying." *At least, that's what I keep telling myself.*

"But I know I can trust your information." He chuckles. "My favorite part is your stories about the pranks you and the children pull on each other. I can see why you like them so much and I can't wait to hear more. See you tomorrow for breakfast?"

It's entirely too warm in the room. "Tomorrow."

"Keep your eyes closed."

Devereaux guides me down the hallway, his hands warm in mine. I resist the urge to peek at our destination as we walk, anticipation thrumming through my veins.

"You won't give me a hint?" I've been mentally following our path through the castle, but we're in a section I haven't scouted yet. I was planning to investigate outdoors today, but when the prince asked me to accompany him, my curiosity wouldn't let me say no. I never would've guessed his plans included him leading me blindly to some unknown destination.

"It's a surprise. We're almost there." He pauses. There's the quiet click of a door being opened, then we take a few shuffling steps inside. "Stay here and don't look yet."

There's a flurry of curtains being pulled back, and light bathes my face. I strain to pick up any clues to our location, but there are no hints.

He whispers in my ear, his tickling breath sending shivers down my body.

"Open your eyes."

A beautiful room decorated in light blue and white greets me. Small chairs and music stands are scattered around the floor. My eyes are drawn to a small dais set in an alcove, where a gorgeous pianoforte sits in a place of honor. Even from a distance, the craftsmanship and quality are clear. The gold filigree shines from a recent polish while the paintings around its side have exquisite details and bright colors. Truly a work of art that's a pleasure just to look at.

I clap my hands together, my heart bursting with happiness. "A pianoforte! You have a pianoforte!"

He beams. "It's yours to play, as much as you like. Lacee suggested it." Devereaux ducks his head, an unexpected shyness in his manners. "I wanted to say thank you for all the help you've given me over the past week."

He talked to Lacee about a present for me? A blush climbs into my cheeks. *I'm overreacting. As he said, it's just a thank you.* I beam at him, overcoming the momentary urge to throw my arms around him. "I love it. It's the most perfect thing you could ever give me."

Devereaux ushers me over to the small bench. "Sit, sit. Try it." His brow crinkles as he looks over the instrument. "It's been a while since anyone's played it, but I think there's someone in the village who can tune it."

I rest my hands on the ivory keys, savoring the moment. The first few notes sail through the air, filling the room with the pianoforte's deep tones. The notes swim around me, bringing a peaceful feeling I haven't had in a long time. My fingers fly across the keys, long-forgotten songs coming back to me. The ever-present tightness in my chest whenever I'm away from home loosens, then fades away. *I can't remember the last time I was this happy.*

My smile grows, and a lightness fills me as I lose myself in playing snatches of my favorite songs, letting each one transition seamlessly into the next as they come to mind. I have a hard time not laughing as the room echoes with music. I've forgotten Devereaux is standing next to me, forgotten I'm far from home, forgotten everything except the music.

Finally, I let my fingers come to a rest as the last chord fades away. I look up at Devereaux, tears stinging my eyes. "I'd forgotten how much I loved to play."

He beams at me. "You were amazing. Please, continue. There should be music in the bench, if you want to see if there's any new songs. Or really old ones, which is more likely." There's a warm glow in his eyes I haven't seen before.

I ignore the way my heart flutters and hop off the bench. "I'm a little rusty." I busy myself looking through the pile of sheet music, avoiding his eyes. "Thank you so much for this. Really. But you can go if you need to. I know you're busy."

Devereaux straightens and steps back. "I don't mean to make you self-conscious."

"It's not that. I played in front of Papa all the time at home, and I entertain my kids sometimes." I fidget with a sheet of music, curling the edge of the parchment. "You're welcome to stay, of course, but I know I'm not anywhere near the level of the musicians you normally hear. Just another amateur who loves playing music with more enthusiasm than skill."

"Nonsense, you're exceptional." Devereaux's face shines with sincerity.

A warmth grows in my chest. "You're flattering me, but I'll pretend it's true." I bite my lip and look away, searching for a way to change the subject, determined to keep a sense of normalcy in our conversation. I nod to four clay pots with little doors in their bellies scattered around the pianoforte. "What are those?"

"Ah, part of the surprise! They're portable warmers." He opens the door on one of them, revealing the coals glowing inside. "Orvil found these in the attic for me. I think they're from Sulomi. I know how cold this room can get and I didn't want your fingers getting stiff."

His thoughtfulness set my heart fluttering again. I smile impishly at him. "That's very kind. But now you'll have to drag me away from here, otherwise I'll be playing day and night. I've never seen such a beautiful pianoforte."

"As I said, it's yours to play as often as you like." He leans toward me, then abruptly pulls back. "For as long as you're here." His smile doesn't quite reach his eyes.

The tightness returns to my chest. "Yes, of course." *Don't be a ninny. After this contract is over, I'll go home and all my worries will be over.* I press my lips together, forcing a note of cheerfulness into my voice. "But I intend to take full advantage of your generosity while I'm here."

"Then I'll have a desk moved into here so I can enjoy a concert while I work. Anything to make it more tolerable."

"But you love drafting treaties, and revising treaties, and worrying about treaties. It's your favorite thing in the world," I tease him.

He tilts his nose up. "It's true. It's my first love. There's nothing I'd rather be doing than agonizing over whether I should propose to trade wheat for iron, or wheat for copper. Riveting stuff."

I chuckle. "Fascinating. I can see why you're so obsessed. Perhaps you should find a hobby that's actually fun."

He pretends to be offended. "Treaties are fun."

"If you enjoy torturing yourself by wasting hours writing something down and then crossing it out a minute later."

"You're judging how I spend my time when you read history?" Devereaux shakes his head, smirking.

"History is useful! And full of adventures! It has all the answers. If more people read histories, there would be a lot fewer problems in the world."

"Well, if I'm responsible for solving all the problems in the world, I better do my best to make sure everyone gets along and has what they need. Hence, the treaties." He makes a face. "But I agree, they're boring. And tedious. I have to go over every detail five times just to make sure I'm not making any mistakes. And then I go over it again. One misstep, and I could cause more problems than I solve."

I trail my fingers over the pianoforte keys. "Doesn't your father have councilors or advisors who should do the research instead of you?"

He folds his hands behind his back, his mouth twisting. "Yes. But then I wouldn't know the details or what they're leaving out. Having them draft the proposal gives them the power to slant the arguments and the decisions. It means they're running the kingdom, and we're merely figureheads."

I raise my eyebrow. "That's cynical, even for a prince. Don't you trust them?"

His brow furrows. "I don't trust anyone. Experience has taught me people will let you down and betray you, usually when you need them the most. I've been proven right too many times to be that innocent and naive again."

"You don't trust anybody? Not even Helene or

Rosemarie or Orvil?" I challenge him.

"Not when it comes to what's best for the kingdom." He shifts on his feet. "I've learned to rely on myself, and I think I'm better off for it."

It must be very lonely living that way. But it also explains how he treated me when I first got here. "I'm used to having a partner when I go on a job. If I didn't trust them, it would make everything ten times more difficult, and we wouldn't be as successful as we are. Working as a team means we're considerably more effective than we would be alone."

"That's fine for you, but I have to think about the kingdom."

"And I have to protect lives. Usually children's."

He shudders. "I can't imagine anyone targeting them."

I grimace. "It takes a special kind of viciousness to endanger a child for political gain. And that's why I take my work so seriously. "

"Any why you're so good at your job. One thing I know about my sister is she insists on hiring the best. If there was a threat, I'm sure you'd be the perfect one to handle it." Devereaux pretends to scowl at me. "But I'm completely safe here, so there's nothing for you to do."

"I'll be the judge of that. After all, I am the best." I smirk at his groan. "And since we're talking about my job, why did you come to La Sailles? We wouldn't have to worry about freezing to death in Charistel."

He sighs. "This again? Can't you let it go?"

I smile sweetly as my fingers play softly over the keys. "It's a mystery and I hate mysteries."

"Fine. I'll tell you if you tell me how you became a bodyguard."

"I told you, I'm not a bodyguard. I'm—"

"Yes, yes, you stop the knife before it's drawn. I was listening." His eyes crinkle at the corners.

I harrumph, smothering my smile. "Make sure you do more of that. The listening, I mean."

"I'll practice diligently every day. Starting with how you got into this line of work."

"My mother." At his surprised look, I grin. "It's a family business. She was in the Guild and met my father during one of her contracts. They fell in love the moment they set eyes on each other and were married as soon as her job was over. After, my father traveled with her, conducting business deals in whatever kingdom they were in at the moment. When I was born, she worked for a few more years before declaring she was ready to retire, and they settled in Cassia. But she taught me everything she knew about the Guild, and entertained me with stories and songs from all the kingdoms she'd visited. It made me want to join when I was old enough." I nod to him. "Now it's your turn. Why come to La Sailles?"

He crosses his arms and rocks back on his heels. "It's as simple as needing a place to work in peace and quiet. Moving here for the winter guaranteed me that. Nobody will drop by unannounced, or drag me into meetings. And I don't have to deal with Isa fussing over me with whatever silly idea she's gotten into her head at the moment."

"Like assassins targeting you?" I raise an eyebrow.

"Exactly. We're a small, boring kingdom. We don't start wars, we don't want to expand our borders, and we make sure our people are as happy as we can reasonably keep them. There's no reason for anybody to hire an assassin to target me, or anybody in my family. Some noble probably thought my coat was out of fashion and Isa flew into a tizzy over it."

Something isn't adding up ... "But you're worried about something. You accused me of spying on you and going through your papers."

"Yes, well." He clears his throat. "In that case, your presence was suspicious in itself. Here was this stranger that showed up unannounced and attacked me—"

"You mean defended myself from *your* attack."

"—and I didn't know why they were here or would be insane enough to travel in the middle of a blizzard. I was still trying to figure out who you were. Can you blame me for doubting you?"

"Yes, but being paranoid seems to be your normal reaction to everything and everyone." I play a soft melody, mulling over his words. *I can't tell if he's lying or holding something back. Either way, I still have a contract to fulfill.* "I can't disagree with anything you've said. But it doesn't mean someone hasn't decided you pose a threat. So." I fix him with a stern look. "I'll continue to do my job and see to your safety as long as you're here."

He shakes his head. "It's a waste of time, but I won't stop you. What are you planning today? More pianoforte, or wandering around the palace to find the nonexistent threat?"

"Since the snow stopped, I'm going to look around the grounds while I can." I hold up my hands before he can protest. "I know, I know. Another storm could blow in at any minute. I'll stay close to the palace."

"I thought you'd be stubborn about it." He smirks. "I had Orvil bring down snowshoes from the attic."

"Snowshoes?"

"You'll see. Come on, we should go before the snow

starts again."

I sit up straighter, my lips parting. "You're coming with me?"

"I can't have you getting lost. And mayhap this time you'll listen to me when I say we need to go back, before another tree falls on me."

"Technically, that tree fell on both of us. You just weren't quick enough to get out of the way."

He shakes his head, laughing. "Next time, I'll save myself instead of shoving you out of the way. But to be safe, I'll steer us away from any large trees today." He offers me his arm. "Shall we?"

I slide my arm through his. "Lead the way."

The snowshoes definitely make things easier, but it's still a struggle to walk outside in the deep snow. Somehow, I don't mind slipping and sliding around as Devereaux entertains me with stories about the trouble he and his sister caused growing up. His presence makes the day more enjoyable and time goes by quickly. It's an immense help to have him with me as he confirms where the other outbuildings are and their uses, and how far the grounds go. He proves the wisdom of his accompanying me when he prevents me from stumbling into a pond buried under the snow. At least he claims there's a pond there—until spring, I'll have no way of knowing if he's right or just teasing me.

I've always enjoyed working with a partner, but this is different. There's an extra spark of energy I get with Devereaux. I've gotten a chance to see more of the humor lurking behind that stoic mask. There's so much pressure on the prince to be perfect; it warms my heart to know he doesn't feel the need to keep up that pretense in front of me. That it's all right if I see him as a human being with flaws— even if he refuses to admit to having any until I point them out.

When the sky darkens, we return to the palace, stomping the snow and ice off the snowshoes.

Devereaux brushes some errant snowflakes out of his hair. "Was that enough, or are you going to go outside again to satisfy some masochistic need to freeze to death?"

"You thought that was cold? It felt like a lovely spring day to me." I bounce from foot to foot as I think it over, nodding to myself. "The outbuildings will need a more thorough look through, but there's no rush now that I've seen them. I'll finish looking around the palace first."

"Thank the heavens. I don't think my toes could take another trip tomorrow."

"I can go by myself now that I know the way."

"Nonsense. You'll get lost or fall into the pond. It's my responsibility to ensure your safety."

I fight back a grin and shake my head at him. "As I must keep reminding you, I'm responsible for your safety, not the other way around. But I won't say no to a guide if you're volunteering again."

"It's the only way I can make sure you don't get into trouble." He blows into his hands. "Let's see if Rosemarie will get a teapot brewing for us before my fingers fall off."

I wrinkle my nose and hold my dripping skirt out. "We'd better change first. I don't know about you, but I don't want to spend the rest of the day in this damp dress."

As we make our way through the halls, the prince insists

on taking the lead. Devereaux slinks along the wall, peeking around each corner before dragging me forward. After the third time he stops me, I laugh and tug on his arm.

"What are you doing?"

He whispers, "Looking for Helene. She's been nagging me to go over the household accounts with her. I don't know why the woman insists on reviewing every expense down to the sixpence. I don't know what's the normal price for salt is, nor do I care."

"So that's why you offered to escort me outside. You're hiding from her." I giggle at his growing aggravation as he pulls me down the hallway. "Have you told her you trust her to keep the accounts?"

"I've tried, but she refuses to do a thing without my approval."

"So, you do trust someone." I smirk.

He stops to glower at me. "It's the household accounts. And I expect people to do their jobs. After all, I don't make Rosemarie run every menu choice by me, or follow the maids around to ensure they're dusting the mantles."

"But you don't have faith in the councilors. Is there anybody you'd trust to advise you?"

He opens his mouth—then snaps it shut. "Come on, we need to hurry."

I shake my head as we continue sneaking through the palace. *Stubborn, arrogant man doesn't want to admit anything.*

Devereaux looks around the next corner, then leaps back. "She's coming. Hide!"

He drags me over to the closest door and yanks it open to reveal a tiny closet. His eyes are wild as he frantically looks to the left, then the right. "No time. Get in."

"There's no way we're both fitting in there," I squawk. "*You* can't fit in there."

"We have no choice." He wiggles his way into the small space, his arms pinned to his side. "Now you."

"I have a better idea." I swing the door shut as Helene comes around the corner. Giving the housekeeper a bright smile, I lean against the door, acting surprised to see her. "Oh, hello. Can you believe the storm finally stopped?"

She slows her steps and narrows her eyes at me. "Yes, and I can also see you've left quite a mess behind you." She glances pointedly at the trail of melted snow glistening on the granite floor.

The best revenge is to kill them with kindness. "I was going to clean that up just as soon as I'm changed and dry."

She sniffs, clearly not impressed with my excuse. "Where's Lord Devereaux? I understood he was out on the grounds with you earlier. There's some important business I need to speak with him about."

A groan sounds in the closet behind me. I raise my voice. "If I see him, I'll tell him you're looking for him."

"Be sure that you do." She steps closer to me. "I don't approve of you spending so much time with him. Whatever your business is, the prince came here for peace and quiet. You shouldn't be distracting him."

The closet door pops open an inch, pushing me forward a step. I throw my back against it, forcing it closed. It bounces twice more, jolting me before I can brace my feet to stop it from moving. Grumbles sound on the other side of the wood.

I smile angelically at Helene, acting like nothing happened. "Thank you for your concern. Lord Devereaux is more than capable of deciding how to spend his time, but I look forward to visiting more with you and the staff."

"Is that critical to your matchmaker duties?" She lifts an eyebrow, her voice dripping with sarcasm.

"Absolutely. I find how a person treats others says a lot about their character. But I'm sure you want to continue your search for Lord Devereaux, so I won't delay you any longer."

I keep the pleasant expression fixed on my face as Helene surveys me a moment longer, then continues down the hallway. After her footsteps have faded around the corner, I step away from the door with a chuckle.

Devereaux bursts out of the closet. "Why did you stop me?"

I widen my eyes innocently. "I thought you were hiding from her."

"How dare Helene say those things about us." He runs his hands through his hair, setting the damp strands astray. "She was rude. And impertinent. She needs to apologize to you."

I lift my shoulder. "She's just looking out for you, like the loyal housekeeper she is. She thinks I've set my cap for you and intend to snare you into marriage. It's harmless. And actually kind of sweet."

"She what? You? What?" He glances at me, then down the hallway, then back at me, his alarm growing.

I laugh at his adorable befuddlement. *For being so distrustful of everyone, he sure has some blind spots.* "Surely, you've been around women in the court who hoped to catch your eye? Or a visiting princess who proposed an alliance be sealed with a kiss?"

"Certainly, but I don't understand why Helene thinks you're like them."

"I'm sure she views any woman within a mile of you that way. But have no fear, my handsome prince. I would never get involved with a client. Personally, I find this hilarious. Usually nobody is worried about me, since most of my male protectees are still in short pants. I have to admit it's flattering she thinks I could catch your eye. Especially looking like this." I gesture to my drab, water-stained brown dress and my mussed hair.

Devereaux frowns as he looks me over. "What do you mean? You always look nice."

I snicker. *Men.* "I'm glad you think so. You'd better hurry before she comes looking for you."

He hurries down the hallway, then half-turns back. "Will I see you in the library?"

My heart skips a beat. "I'll join you there for supper. I was going to help Rosemarie prepare for the meal after I get into some dry clothes."

His brow furrows. "Doesn't she have assistants?"

"Yes, but another set of hands is usually welcome, and I enjoy it. Supper tastes better when you've made it."

His eyes take on a faraway look, and he gives a distracted nod. "I'll leave you to it then."

I watch him stride down the hallway, curious about what he's thinking, then shake my head. *Time to get out of these damp clothes before I catch another cold.*

Lacee intercepts me in the hallway. "Julietta, can you believe it? I'm so excited!" She bounces on her toes.

Her giddiness rubs off on me and I grab her hands. "What? What's going on?"

"I've found him. The love of my life." She heaves a lustful sigh.

I rack my brain, trying to think who on the staff could

have caught her eye. "Is it Perrin? Or Jon?"

She burst into laughter. "Of course not! Edmon's from the village. He came to deliver a message to Rosemarie from the innkeeper." Her blue eyes shine. "Have you ever heard a more perfect name? Edmon. Oh, he's so handsome, and funny, and sweet, and I've never met anyone like him. It's destiny we found each other."

I grin at her enthusiasm. "That's wonderful. Here, walk with me and tell me all about him."

She links her arm through mine, dancing down the hallway. "As soon as our eyes met, we knew. He works for the village inn during the winter and helps his family out in the fields in spring and summer. Edmon said he remembered meeting me last year, although I don't know how I could have forgotten him. He has the greenest eyes I've ever seen, like new leaves. And the best smile! He's so funny. His freckles are adorable. I love each and every one of them. Rosemarie thought he was very handsome, too. I wish you could've met him, but he'll be back soon."

She prattles on as I lead her to my room. I change out of my wet clothes and into a warm woolen dress from Lady Isabeau's collection. Lacee helps me do up the back, barely stopping to breathe as she fills me in on every detail about Edmon.

As the descriptions about his eyes, freckles, and smile get repeated, my curiosity grows. "How long did you talk to him?"

"Only an hour, but he promises he'll visit again as soon as he can."

An hour and she's in love? I mentally shrug. *Sometimes you just know. Besides, Lacee's young, despite her protests. She still has that ability to fall in love over a conversation. I*

*have to admit, I'm a little envious. I've never been as in love
as she is with her new beau, even when I was her age.*

Lacee leaves me at the kitchen, promising to find me the
next day and tell me more about Edmon. I present myself to
Rosemarie. "I'm here to help with supper if you could use an
extra set of hands."

The red-cheeked woman wipes her hands on her apron.
"Always, and thanks for your help. You can start by peeling
and chopping those into large chunks for the stew." She nods
to a pile of vegetables.

I grab an apron off the peg on the wall and get started on
the carrots. Rosemarie sings quietly as she works. After a
few moments, I join in with the parts I know, earning a smile
from the cook.

Her voice cuts off abruptly. I look up to find Devereaux
standing in the doorway, my breath catching. He's back to
polished perfection, not a hair out of place. Despite the
immaculate clothing, he appears a little boyish as he looks
around the kitchen, something I'd never have thought before.
I twist my braid up, the heat from the fire suddenly making
me uncomfortably warm.

Rosemarie says, "Is there something I can assist you
with, milord?" She shoots a worried look in my direction.

He smooths down his jacket, then smooths it again. "If
you could use another assistant, I'd like to volunteer."

"That's not necessary, Lord Devereaux. I'm sure you
have more important things to be doing with your time." Her
cheeks grow redder as she fidgets with her apron strings.

"Oh. All right." He hesitates in the doorway. "I'll go
then."

I call out, "You can help me cut these up."

Devereaux's shoulders relax. "Certainly."

Rosemarie watches with a combination of fascination and horror as I direct the prince to get an apron, then demonstrate how to peel and chop the vegetables. Devereaux wrinkles his brow, as always paying close attention and putting more thought into the task than a normal person would. The kitchen is silent except for quiet chopping and footsteps as we move around our tasks.

Devereaux places more perfectly sliced carrots on the growing pile. "What are you humming?"

"Am I?" I laugh self-consciously. "Apologies. I tend to do that without realizing it."

"It sounded familiar. Mayhap something my mother used to sing to me?"

"In my kingdom, we call it 'Star Dream Bedtime.' My mother used to sing it to me, too." I hum a few more bars.

He nods along to the tune. "It feels so familiar, but I can't remember where or when I heard it."

"A lot of my childhood memories are like that." I raise my voice. "Rosemarie, what's your favorite song to sing to children?"

She answers without hesitation. "Little Sheep. They always fall asleep as soon as I start singing it."

Devereaux's face lights up. "I know that one."

He sings the first few lines in a beautiful baritone that sends shivers over my skin. When he falters on the second verse, Rosemarie joins him, filling in the gaps. Soon we're trading songs as we prepare supper. Devereaux and I work together with a casual ease, as though we've known each other for years. Helene peers in the room at one point, then shakes her head and leaves. Time flies by and before we know it, Rosemarie is shooing us out of the kitchen, claiming we'll be more hinderance than help at this point.

Devereaux and I share a smile and surrender. By silent agreement, we move to the library. Instead of settling at the desk, the prince picks up the book of Irelin mythology and takes a seat on the couch next to me.

This close, I'm overwhelmed by his scent of leather and parchment, a hint of the apple slice he snatched in the kitchen on his breath. My heart stutters and I have to fight the urge to lean closer to him. *What am I doing?* Heat floods my cheeks. *I have to get control of myself.* I've already had enough disasters on this job; the last thing I need is to embarrass myself by mooning over my protectee like one of the silly court ladies I shake my head at.

I haven't had many close friends, or spent this much time with a man before, so it's not surprising I'm mistaking feelings of friendship with something else. It's perfectly natural. Happens all the time. No reason to think anything more about it. And the couch is more comfortable for reading, so of course he's sitting here. It's only logical. Practical. There's plenty of room for both of us. Nothing confusing or suggestive about it. It's all completely normal and ordinary.

I clear my throat and nod to the book. "No treaties tonight?"

"I decided to take a break from my favorite activity." He chuckles. "I'm actually ahead of schedule, and Irelin is the last one I need to draft. I wanted to do more research before I decide what approach to use with them."

"That's wonderful! I'm sure your father will be grateful to see all the work you've done. It could really make a difference for your kingdom." I look down at the book in my lap, fiddling with the cover. "Since you're almost finished, you can go back to Charistel as soon as the pass opens."

Devereaux shifts on the cushion. "No need to get ahead of ourselves. It won't open until spring, at the earliest."

I should leave it alone. No point in talking about possibilities that may not happen. "But if it does, you'll leave?" I hold my breath.

"I'll decide what to do when the time comes. Until then, I'm going to focus on practical matters." He waves the book in his hand. "Unlike these deities. They're ridiculous! If they had an ounce of sense between them, most of these disasters would've been avoided."

I scrunch my nose. "Where's the fun in that?"

"This isn't fun, it's chaos." His growing smile betrays his words. "Always sneaking into each other's beds, or stealing powers, or interfering with the mortals in their realm. As far as I can tell, they're a curse on the land."

We keep up a spirited conversation about mythology through supper. Then the topic shifts to the different kingdoms and our favorite memories. Surprisingly, I've been to more kingdoms than Devereaux. Fallian Province uses ambassadors rather than sending members of the royal family, which has both benefits and drawbacks.

Devereaux shakes his head. "That's something I plan to talk to father about when I return to Charistel. Isa and I can do more to build stronger ties between the kingdoms if we visit them."

"But that places you both in greater danger."

He chuckles. "Always thinking about the risk."

"It comes with the job." I frown. "I see your point, though. It would be better if you had ambassadors you really trust, who could lay the groundwork, then you could have a shorter visit to give them a personal touch. That way, you'd get the best of both options. But I know how you feel about trust."

He sticks his tongue out at me.

I gasp. "Did you—? No. Did you stick your tongue out at me?" I burst out laughing. "I can't believe you did that!"

He sniffs. "I felt it was the most appropriate response to your comment." That devastating grin with the dimples breaks out across his face, making my heart beat faster.

The door clicks open. I glance over my shoulder, expecting to see Nancey or one of the other staff. Instead, the shadow in the hallway disappears, accompanied by pounding footsteps.

My body is moving before my mind has time to catch up.

Assassin.

14

I burst into the hallway barely in time to catch a flash of movement disappearing around the corner. Devereaux calls after me, but I can't stop. The staff wouldn't run. It could be one of their children playing games again, but my instincts say otherwise. Besides, I would rather be wrong again than ignore something dangerous.

My focus narrows to catching the shadow ahead of me. The long afternoon trek in the cold and the late night are working against me. My lungs burn and my legs are clumsy. I curse my slowness and growing fatigue. The best I can do is glimpse a brown shirt here and there. It's enough to let me know they're too big to be a child, but not enough to get a description or even determine the gender of the person.

The distance between us grows wider and wider until I come to an intersection, and I have no idea which way the person went, no footsteps or other noises from any of the passageways to follow. I study the floor as I try to catch my breath, but there's nothing to guide me.

Devereaux sprints up beside me, panting. "What in the

blazes are you doing? Why did you run off like that?”

“There was a person at the door.” I keep scanning the floor, listening for any footsteps over my thundering heartbeat.

“It was probably one of the staff.”

“Then why did they run? You know the palace better than I do. Where’s a good place to hide from here?”

He shrugs. “You’ve seen enough to know this place is a maze of hallways and rooms. That one leads to the backrooms, including the butteries, pantries, and storerooms. This one has a bunch of solars and sitting rooms and reception rooms. That one …” He scratches a hand along his chin. “I think that one leads to some old guest suites and a bunch of empty rooms, but I’m not sure what they’re for.”

I blow the loose strands of hair off my face and shake my head. “They could be anywhere by now. I can’t believe I lost them!” Grinding my teeth, I pick a hallway at random and stalk down it. “I’ve been letting my guard down. Relaxing. Acting like I’m on holiday instead of a job. And now they know I’m on to them. Gah!”

Devereaux matches his stride to mine. “What are you doing?”

“I need to search the passages.”

“Who do you think you’ll find? Another six-year-old spying on you?” He grins.

Ugh, he’ll never let me live that down. “Oh, I don’t know. Perhaps the assassin your sister hired me to protect you from?” I growl. “And now they’ll be doubly on their guard. Lady Isabeau should fire me on the spot.”

Devereaux says hopefully, “I don’t suppose I can fire you?”

“Not a chance. You’re stuck with me until she hears

about this colossal mess." *Fates save me from pretentious royals with their stupid castles built like mazes. I missed my chance! How am I going to protect Devereaux now?*

Devereaux grimaces, massaging his right thigh. "How far did you want to search tonight?"

I jerk to a stop. "My apologies. I don't mean to drag you all over the palace with me. I'll escort you to your rooms."

He rocks back on his heels, his hands clasped behind his back. "You're going to escort me?"

I put my hands on my hips. "Do you need me to knock you down again?"

"And how are you at wrestling a two-hundred-pound man with one arm tied behind your back?" He grins.

"Not the best," I admit. "In my line of work, you usually only need a few offensive and defensive moves. But I'm confident I could keep an assassin off you long enough for you to escape."

The smile drops from his face. "What about you?"

"I'm not the target. Besides, I can take care of myself. Now, let's get you into bed." My cheeks heat. "I mean, get you back to your rooms."

"Are you going to stand guard outside my door all night?"

"Someone should. If you had a lick of sense, you'd have brought at least a couple of guards with you." I hold up my hands before he can respond and take a deep breath. "Sorry. I'm just frustrated. And mad at myself."

"And me too?" He rubs a hand over his face, exhaustion creating new lines around his eyes. "I can see why you'd be upset I didn't bring any guards, but I couldn't risk it."

My ears perk up. "So, you did come up here with a purpose. Something beyond needing peace and quiet to work?"

"Yes, hm." He clears his throat. "I began to suspect … after some investigation … and several instances …"

I clench my fists to keep from strangling him.

"There's a spy."

A spy, not an assassin. So, Lady Isabeau had a right to worry, but was wrong about what was going on. Wait— Devereaux has known this whole time about a spy? "You lied to me! You said nobody was targeting you."

He glowers at me and folds his arms. "I was trying to get rid of you. Telling you the truth would hardly have helped my case."

"But you knew there was trouble and still tried to send me away!"

"Yes. As I already admitted." His overly patient tone fans the flames of my temper.

I narrow my eyes. "You didn't say you were sorry about it."

"That's because I'm not. I made the best decision at the time, and now I've changed my position based on new information."

"Do you know how arrogant you sound?"

"Making hard choices is part of my job. I won't apologize for doing what I think is right."

"You mean what's easiest for you."

"Sometimes those coincide, yes. But I always do what I think is best."

The conceit! He refuses to see past his nose. But does that explain …? "When I came here, you thought I was the spy."

He shrugs nonchalantly. "Of course. It seemed too much of a coincidence that you arrived when you did. Who but the spy would brave a snowstorm with a ridiculous story about being hired by my sister, knowing I couldn't verify it until spring?"

"And now?"

"Eighty to eighty-five percent chance you're not the spy." He flashes his dimples.

My chest tightens. "That day in the forest, you actually came after me because you wanted to make sure I didn't report back to my employer."

He folds his hands behind his back, his eyes dropping away from mine. "No. I knew by then you weren't a spy."

"But you accused me of going through your papers!"

"Yes. Well. I thought I was wrong about you at that moment, and I was mad at myself for being fooled. When I had a few moments to think it over, I realized I had unjustly accused you."

My mouth drops open. "But when you caught up to me, you didn't say anything. You didn't apologize."

"I was too angry with you for being foolish and running off into an oncoming storm."

"And you hate admitting when you're wrong."

Devereaux glares at me. "Perhaps."

I smirk. "I'm going to set aside your stubbornness for now since you might actually be useful. Tell me everything you know while we check the other passages."

I turn to retrace our steps to the intersection, Devereaux grumbling beside me. As we walk down another hallway, the prince fills me in.

"For the last six months, I've noticed someone has been going through my papers and correspondence. I wasn't sure at first, since whoever it is has been very careful. But I did a few tests to confirm. A white hair inside a sealed letter. A few grains of salt sprinkled on the ledge of a desk drawer. That kind of thing. That's when I knew. Someone had gained access to my rooms."

I shake my head. "That's unbelievable."

"Now you understand why I'm not putting much faith in guards these days. If they can't protect me in Charistel, what good would they be here? They might even be the ones doing the spying."

"You still should have stayed in Charistel instead of running off to the mountains alone. The spy aside, you're practically begging for someone to assassinate you by coming up here without any guards. You're too important to risk your life so cavalierly. Like chasing me out into that storm. You were almost killed." I meant to sound annoyed, but my voice has gone soft.

He shrugs away my comment. "What choice did I have?"

"You could've left me on my own, or sent someone else out after me."

"I'm sure Helene would've loved being ordered to fetch you back." He grins, then sobers. "You're my responsibility. I won't put anyone else in danger if I don't have to."

"But why? Why do you feel responsible for me when I don't need or want it?"

He shrugs, his eyes avoiding mine. "That's the way things are."

"Hmph." *I'll never understand him.* "Was anyone else being spied on?"

"I did some discreet inquiries with my family. Isabeau tries to keep out of state affairs as much as possible, although she loves entertaining diplomats. Mother and Father always carefully check their papers and such, but they took a few more precautions and didn't notice any interference."

"You're always the lucky one," I tease. "So why target you? Why not anybody else?"

"I have no burning idea." He runs his hand through his hair, his brown eyes flashing. "My parents have all the power. I'm learning and I advise them, but there's nothing that should single me out."

"And that's everything? There haven't been any attempts on your life?"

"Isn't being spied on enough?"

"Lady Isabeau was convinced you're in danger. I don't think she would have contracted with the Guild over some routine espionage."

"I told you, my sister considers someone stepping on her foot during the waltz an assassination attempt." He smooths a hand down his jacket, his gaze going everywhere but my direction.

"Somehow, I'm starting to doubt that." I glare at him. "What's really been happening?"

"There've been a few … accidents." He quickly adds, "Nothing definitive. And nothing the guards felt warranted investigating."

"The same guards who may or may not be aiding the spy? What happened?"

He shrugs uncomfortably. "Nothing, really."

Stubborn, stubborn, stubborn. "And that 'nothing' would be …?"

"A poisonous mushroom was accidentally mixed in with the normal ones in the kitchen. A mistake, obviously, that the cook caught when sorting through them. And some oil spilled on the stairs. Like I said, nothing but a few minor accidents.”

Every muscle stiffens. My fists clench and I want to stab something, starting with Devereaux. *I can't believe he hid this from me!* “Those don't sound like nothing.”

“Neither of them were targeted directly at me. Besides— wait, look, over there.” Devereaux crouches down next to a silver coin.

I stop him before he can pick it up and kneel next to him. “Careful, it could be poisoned.” Using a corner of my dress, I lift it up.

It's about the size of the larger ten-pieces Fallian Province uses for currency. Both sides are covered with small symbols made up of stark lines, but nothing I recognize as either letters or numbers in any kingdom.

Hmm, not currency. “Some sort of pendant? Perhaps a luck piece?”

“Some of those markings look familiar, but I can't place it.” He studies it intently.

“We can research it in the library. One of those books must have something on it.”

Devereaux's face is inches from mine. Our eyes meet and I'm frozen in place, my heartbeat thundering in my ears. I gulp and shoot up, losing my balance for a moment.

“Whoa, steady.” He puts a hand on my arm. “Careful there.”

My skin warms under his grip, sending shivers down my arm. The air rushes out of my lungs. I step away, clutching the spot where he touched me. “You said this is the hallway that leads to the extra guest suites and empty rooms?”

“As far as I know.” He shrugs. “Helene or Orvil would have a better idea whether there's anything noteworthy in this direction. I haven't done much exploring since my childhood days, so it's possible I'm misremembering, or that the rooms have changed purpose over the years."

"I'll ask the staff about it. It'll be less suspicious coming from me since I'm still learning the layout and have been asking questions since I got here." I carefully wrap the silver piece in a handkerchief and tuck it in my pocket. "One thing I still don't understand is why you came here."

"Isn't it obvious? If I'm the one being singled out, I needed to draw the spy away from everyone else. What better way to do that by coming all the way out here in the middle of nowhere? I'm hoping they'll follow me and stay away from my family."

"Hence the limited number of staff you brought with you. You wanted to ensure you knew everyone who would be around you. Because … you suspect one of them?"

Devereaux stumbles to a stop. "What? No! The opposite. I brought people I think are loyal to me, although I could be wrong. They're the perfect target for blackmail and bribes. And if you saw someone tonight, it must be one of the staff."

"Not necessarily. This morning, someone came from the village to deliver a message, which means anyone could've snuck in today." I bite my lip, pondering everything we know. "That day you accused me of going through your papers—are you sure they were disturbed? Would anybody have touched them if they were straightening up, or had another reason to be around them?"

"I'm not sure," he says reluctantly. "My mind was elsewhere. I thought they were rearranged, but I wasn't paying as close attention as I normally do."

"If they were rifled through, then it's better odds it was a staff member. Although, the village isn't that far. Someone could have come to the palace in the morning and gotten back before the storm hit." My heart wants to believe the staff would never turn against him, but my head knows better. *How many times I have rooted out a traitor among the staff on other contracts? No, we have to be cautious.* "But you're right. It's impossible to know who to trust in these situations. We can't rule out someone who works for you. Mayhap they panicked when I spotted them and ran."

"Either way, it's a relief. If they're here, then they won't be harassing my family. And now I can seek them out."

The hallway branches off in four different directions. *I feel like a rat in a maze.* "There's no point in continuing, since the spy has crawled back into their hole by now. I'll search again tomorrow and see if I can guess where they went." I steer Devereaux back to the library. "But if you think I'm letting you go after a spy on your own, you're crazy. And I know you're too stubborn to let me handle it. We're going to work together on this. Starting with figuring out what the spy dropped and where it came from."

He nods, his steps gaining an extra spring. "If we know its origin, we can see if anyone here or the village has ties to that kingdom."

"It's going to be tough. We don't have much to go on aside from the symbols on it. It might take a while to figure out."

"But at least it's a clue." His eyes have a dangerous glint. "It's time I did a little hunting of my own."

"Julietta!" Devereaux's voice booms from outside the library a split second before the door flings open.

I stifle my giggles. "Good morning, Lord Devereaux. Did you call me?"

He storms across the room, the vein in his forehead pulsating. "Someone set up a net over my bedroom door. It dropped on my head when I opened it."

I widen my eyes in mock surprise. "That's terrible."

"Orvil had to cut me out." He presses his lips together. "You wouldn't happen to know anything about it, would you?"

"Me? Why would I?"

"Perhaps you thought it was some sort of revenge?"

"Why would I possibly want to get revenge on you? For lying and hiding threats on your life from me?" I tap my chin thoughtfully. "No, not that. Accusing me of being a spy and then refusing to apologize? Hmm, that can't be it either." I pretend to think it over. "If someone's setting up traps, it might be—and this is only a guess—to catch an assassin if they're attempting to break into your room."

He narrows his eyes. "There's a big difference between routine spying on other kingdoms and ordering an assassination."

I narrow mine right back. "You don't know how desperate they might be. Better to be safe than sorry. Besides, it has the added benefit of teaching you to be aware of your surroundings in case the spy gets orders to make an attempt on your life. That net could've been an assassin's knife." I grin. "And it's funny."

"I didn't find it amusing." His tone is as dry as the Sulomi desert.

"I'm sure Orvil did. Now, did you find that book on Rus languages? I thought one of those symbols on the coin the spy dropped looked familiar."

"Don't change the subject. I won't be attacked in my own home. There's enough going on with trying to catch this infiltrator without having to worry about dye in my soap or trained chickens assaulting me in the hallways."

"Of course, of course. Now, about that book?" I smile innocently.

He yanks open the bottom desk drawer and reaches inside while glaring at me. "And another thing, I—ahhh!" Devereaux glowers at the mousetrap dangling from his finger. "Let me guess. Another trap for the spy?"

"Mayhap Helene was worried about rodents nibbling on your papers?" I smirk when he scoffs. "That one was just for fun. But I do want to set up some traps in your desk to help identify whoever is behind this. How about ink smears that'll stain their skin? And oil on the stairs is too dangerous, but we could spread a thin oil layer around your desk. Then I could follow the footsteps to the spy's lair, or at least where they're coming from."

He grimaces as he disentangles his hand from the contraption. "Still no luck on finding out how they're getting into the palace?"

I growl, slumping down in my chair. "No, Fates curse them. Not a hint. They're probably being extra careful after our close encounter the other night. Orvil and Helene have kept all the doors locked since you spoke with them. And it's not like anybody is going to leave a window cracked in the middle of winter."

"If it's one of the staff, then locking the doors isn't going to do much good."

"I'm still hoping it's an outsider. I can't imagine anyone here betraying you."

"Even Helene?" He grins.

I roll my eyes. "Please. I'd sooner believe you have a dragon hidden in the stable than that woman turn traitor. She's the most overprotective caretaker I've ever seen. She's constantly watching me and making remarks to ensure I'm not overstepping polite boundaries with you. I pity whatever woman catches your fancy, because Helene is going to make their life miserable."

"She's not that bad. She just doesn't express her approval easily."

"Or at all. But I won't fault her for that. It's good you have someone like her watching over you, since you insist on abandoning all precautions."

He raises his hands. "We've already been over this a hundred times."

"True, but such foolish actions require at least a hundred and fifty-two reminders of how harebrained they are."

Devereaux shakes his head. "Patience is going to win

this war. We have until spring to catch them.”

“It would be nice if we caught them sooner and I could stop worrying. Constant vigilance is exhausting.” I set my book on a side table and stand with a stretch. “I’m going to finish scouting the castle. Do you want to join me?”

“As much fun as poking my nose into dusty rooms is, I’m going to finish my treaty proposals. Once they’re done, I can hide them safely away and turn my full attention to this spy business.”

I nod, pushing aside my disappointment. *It was silly to think he’d come with me.* “Happy drafting and lock the door behind me.”

Devereaux calls out before I leave, “No more booby-traps.”

I give him my sweetest smile over my shoulder. “Of course not.”

Balancing on my toes, I teeter on the footstool, careful not to overturn the bucket of water in my hands. The open door bumps against my perch, threatening to send me tumbling. Cursing under my breath, I nudge the door with my hip. Once the opening is a scant few inches, I lift the bucket and perch it on the top rail, balancing it so it just touches the doorframe. Slowly, I pull my support away, hands hovering on either side of the bucket, ready to grab it at the slightest movement.

The bucket slips. I grab it, water sloshing over the edge. I bite my lip and narrow my eyes as I scrutinize the setup. *Does it need a wider opening? Or should I put more weight against the doorframe for better balance?*

"Good afternoon, Miss Julietta."

I start, nearly dumping the water on my head. Heat floods my cheeks as my pulse kicks into a gallop. "Good afternoon, Orvil." I lower my arms and clutch the pail to my chest, heedless of the wetness seeping into my dress. "Did you need something?"

His face doesn't betray a hint of curiosity. "My lord wished to inquire if it would be acceptable to have supper in the sunroom this evening instead of the library."

"That's, um, fine. Do you know why he's suggesting the change?"

"He didn't say, milady. Would you like me to enquire?"

"No, no. It doesn't matter." I grin guiltily at the butler. "You're probably wondering what I'm doing here. I was planning a small surprise for Deve—Lord Devereaux."

"I would never pry into your personal affairs, milady." Orvil pauses in the doorway and clears his throat. "His lordship usually comes through the other door."

My eyebrows fly up. "Thanks."

Orvil bows, then turns away, but not fast enough to hide the grin on his face.

I peer around the corner, watching for Devereaux's approach. A door opens down the hallway. My heart speeds up and I hold my breath.

"Julietta!" Lacee runs up to me and grabs my hands. "Edmon came again today. That's the third time this week."

That's quite a few visits. Love, or a convenient excuse to be at the palace? I grin at her. "It sounds like he's thoroughly smitten. When am I going to meet your mysterious Edmon?"

"Soon, I hope. He never can stay long." She juts out her lip in a pout. "He's always running back to the village in case a storm blows in, although it never does."

I risk another look around the corner. "I can't blame him. After my first few weeks here, I thought there would be a storm every night. But it's been quiet these past two weeks. Is it saving up for a world-ending blizzard at the end of the month?"

She laughs. "I think we're safe. Rosemarie grew up in the mountains and she said some dry years are normal. I'm going to keep my fingers crossed that the weather stays nice so Edmon can keep visiting me."

I bite my lip. "If the snow is lighter this year, does that mean the pass is open?" *If that's true, Devereaux definitely isn't safe here. Could I convince him to go home? If not, the guards would have to come here. Surely he wouldn't object to taking some normal precautions if the pass isn't providing the protection he thought it would. What am I saying? Of course he would. Stubborn prince.*

Lacee shrugs. "I'm not sure, but I can ask Edmon. The villagers would know better when the pass opens and closes."

"Please do. I—"

A loud crash echoes down the hall. Devereaux bellows, "Julietta!"

I yell back—"Could have been a knife!"—then grin at Lacee. "Gotta go. Find me tonight and tell me everything about Edmon's visit." I run for the stairway just as a soaking Devereaux comes sloshing around the corner, his dark eyes flashing.

16

It's exhausting to search this much—even for snacks. Conducting a thorough investigation of anything takes time and patience. My explorations of late have kept me away from the library and, by association, Devereaux. I tell myself it's because I need to finish mapping the palace. That's easier than admitting how much I enjoy our breakfast and suppers, and my reluctance to leave his side when they're over. A reluctance that grows every day. Being friends with my protectee is proving to be more complicated than I imagined. Focusing on something as straightforward as my job is a welcome break.

I've been working my way through the more frequented areas like the stockrooms, pantries, and washrooms, but it's risky to search when someone could come wandering in at any moment. Now the kitchen is calling me for an entirely different reason: my stomach is growling.

I hum as I make my way through the palace, debating whether I can convince Rosemarie to let me make sticky buns, or should opt for something quicker so I can get back to searching. *I shouldn't waste time. I don't need anything special when supper is only a few hours away ... Who am I kidding? Sticky buns it is.* The hint of guilt is easily overcome by picturing the steaming rolls coming out of the oven.

The hair on the back of my neck flies up. *Something's wrong.* I keep my steps steady, humming as I look around me.

There. A shadow where it shouldn't be in the doorway near the kitchen. I get closer, details emerging. Someone crouched, trying to remain unnoticed. *The spy.* My heartbeat kicks into a gallop. I casually stretch my arm, using the motion to move my dagger from my sleeve to my hand. *You're not getting away this time. You're mine.*

The shadow twitches. With a shout, I burst into action, hurtling toward the spy. They take off down the hallway at a run. I follow, my vision narrowing to the person ahead of me. Slowly, I close the gap. Today I'm not exhausted or half frozen. Today I'm going to catch them.

Closer. They keep running. Closer.

I tackle the runaway, knocking them to the ground. He yelps, going down in a tangle of arms and legs. I trap him under me and yank his hair back, my dagger pressed against his throat.

Lowering my face close to his, I growl, "Who do you work for?"

The man staring back at me is barely into adulthood, the freckles sprinkled across his nose a stark contrast to his pale skin. His green eyes dart back and forth frantically as his mouth works, trying to form words. "I—I—I—"

I press the dagger closer, a thin line of blood appearing at the edge. "You better start talking or you're going to be sorry."

"I—I'm here—Lacee—I thought—she was—" He winces, eyes blinking rapidly. "The village, and I—I—wanted—I—please don't hurt me!"

Did he say Lacee? I look him over. *Brown hair. Green eyes. Freckles. Uh-oh ...* I mentally groan. "Edmon?"

He cringes. "Yes."

Fire rushes into my cheeks. "Oh. Sorry." I jump away, hastily hiding the dagger up my sleeve. Clearing my throat, I pull him to his feet. "I'm Julietta, Lacee's friend. Why were you hiding?"

Edmon's close to my height, but his limbs are too long for his body, hinting at a coming growth spurt. He wraps his arms around his middle, backing away. "I was, um, looking, um, for Lacee. She wasn't, um, in the kitchen and I, um, I thought you might be Madame Deneuve."

"Aren't you supposed to stay in the kitchen when you come here?" *Do all the villagers wander around the palace on a whim?*

He winces, shaking. "Yes, milady. But Rosemarie couldn't leave, and she said Lacee was just down the hall. I didn't think it would hurt nothing after I came all this way."

Lying, or just nervous because I just assaulted him and held a knife to his throat? Impossible to tell. I force my shoulders to relax and give him a friendly smile. "Let me find her for you."

He backs away. "No, no. I need to get home anyway, before it's too late. I'm sorry to disturb you. It won't happen again."

"Edmon, it's all right. I know Lacee enjoys seeing you and would be disappointed if you left before she could say hello. And I'd like to chat with you after hearing all her stories about you."

He keeps inching down the wall away from me, his face growing impossibly paler. "Sure, um, sure, but I can't now. No. Another time. It was, um, nice to meet you." Edmon gives me a last panicked look, then flees through the kitchen.

I sigh and slump to the ground in a puddle of skirts. *Great. I've scared another boy half to death. Wonderful job. If he's not the spy, he'll probably be afraid to visit Lacee here ever again. I'll have to figure out a way to convince him it's safe to come back.*

"Search going that bad?" Devereaux strolls up behind me.

"No, I just thought this would be a great place to rest for a moment." I groan and lay on my back, staring up at the ceiling. "I had an unfortunate encounter with Lacee's beau, Edmon."

The prince glances around the empty hallway. "Is he invisible?"

"He just left. He came looking for her when she wasn't in the kitchen."

"And then you decided to take a nap in the hallway?"

"When I saw him, I thought he was the spy and I might have … perhaps …" I cover my face. "Knocked him down and threatened him with a knife."

Devereaux bursts out laughing.

I sit up and glare at him. "It's not funny!"

"On the contrary, it's hilarious."

I sigh. "I hope Lacee thinks so. She'll never forgive me if I scared him away."

"Have no fear. He'll be back as soon as he gets over the humiliation of being taken down by a tiny woman." Devereaux helps me to my feet.

Ignoring the sudden spark when his hand grips mine, I roll my eyes. "There's nothing embarrassing about a trained person taking down an untrained one."

"You know that, and I know that. But I suspect Edmon is too young to realize it."

"You aren't embarrassed I knocked you down?" I lift an eyebrow, a smile playing on my lips.

He sniffs. "Not at all. I'm confident I could take you on now that I'm aware of your style. After all, I know how to defend myself. Shall we have another bout?" Devereaux steps closer with a wicked grin, sending an exciting and dangerous thrill through me.

I step back and smooth my skirt, trying to calm my racing pulse. "Mayhap another time. Right now, I'd rather make a snack to tide us over until supper." *And ask Rosemarie about the other villagers stopping by the palace that I don't know about.*

His eyes light up. "Raspberry meringue?"

Laughing, I swat his arm. "Not unless you're going to make them. I was thinking about sticky buns. I might even let you have some if you help."

He puffs out his chest. "I was planning on doing some work on the treaties today so I can cross it out tomorrow and start all over. But I guess I can set it aside. It's important that a gentleman always comes to the aid of a lady in need."

I nod knowingly. "It's the chivalrous thing to do."

"And afterwards we can put our plan into action. I have everything ready in the library."

My grin turns wicked. "That spy won't know what hit them."

17

Devereaux spreads the parchments across the library desk. "I mocked these up as bait so the spy will still find something when they come searching. There should be enough information in them to fool anyone into thinking these are the real documents."

I study the fake treaties, excitement thrumming through my veins. "Perfect. We'll lock them in the desk drawers. If they saw the real ones in there before, the spy will come back to check for changes. I have a few fun surprises in mind for them."

He frowns. "You think they've broken into the drawer? I haven't noticed any disturbances, or evidence the lock's been picked. And I have the only key."

"It's only a matter of time if they haven't already. They were probably going to search the desk and the rest of the library the other night when we scared them off. They might avoid it for now, but they'll be back soon."

"What about the desk in my study? That's where I was working before you arrived and turned my life upside down."

"You mean, brought fun and excitement into your otherwise dull and dreary world." I purse my lips and think it over for a moment, then shake my head. "It's a good idea, but I'd like to keep our traps in one place for now. This one makes the most sense since everyone knows we've been working in here lately. The spy might get suspicious if we rig both desks, and I want them to get comfortable. If they think we've given up looking for them, they'll get sloppy. That's when we'll catch them."

"The staff knows we're working in here, but not the villagers. And you heard Rosemarie; it sounds like half the population comes by once a week to visit or deliver something. Clever of you to ask her about that without making her suspicious." He grimaces. "I don't know why they can't burning stay home instead of coming here."

I nudge his side with a grin. "You can't blame them. You're their prince, they're curious! They want to know if you're going to tax their tea, or make them wear polka dots on Tuesdays, or force them to only eat raspberry meringue for dessert. But I agree. It makes identifying the spy more difficult."

"And if it's a villager, they'll search the study. They won't know we're working in here."

I shake my head. "Any halfway decent spy will find that out from the staff. Nobody would see the harm in mentioning we spend most of our time in this library."

He blows out a noisy breath. "I still don't like it."

"You just don't like people talking about you." I switch tactics. "Why don't you spend some time in the village? Let them get to know you. That'll help satisfy their curiosity and ease their fears."

"Fear?" He blinks. "Why would they be afraid of me?"

"Oh, I don't know. Your ultimate power of life and death over them. The ability to make their lives easier or miserable. What's to worry about?" I nudge him again. "Think about it. If you never talk to them, all they can do is listen to rumors."

He crosses his arms, perching on the edge of the desk with a frown. "They'll listen to rumors, anyway."

"True, but this could give them something more to think about. You won't be loved by everyone, but at least they could decide to hate you for who you really are."

He pretends to be grouchy, but I can see the smile fighting to break through. "I'm surprised you'd let me out of the palace. You're always so worried about assassins."

"That's because I won't let you near the village until you have a full complement of guards." I lean closer, narrowing my eyes. "And if you try, I'm going to tie you up and stuff you back into that closet."

He laughs, raising his hands. "Noted. Now, let's catch this spy."

We work together seamlessly over the next few hours to carefully booby-trap the desk: ink mixed with oil to prevent it from drying out placed on strategic surfaces to stain fingers; snap traps to bruise the skin, but mounted so they look like pieces of broken locks; oil smeared on the stone floor beneath the desk to attach to someone's unsuspecting shoe. Last, shards of wood to prick fingertips that would be mistaken for splinters at a glance.

When we're finished, Devereaux rocks back on his heels with a satisfied nod. "If nothing else, we'll make the spy miserable when they try to break in here."

I wipe my hands with a rag, removing the last traces of

oil from my fingers. "We should start taking our meals in the sunroom instead of the library again. It'll give them more opportunities to break into the desk without looking like we're trying to lure them here." *And put us back under the footmen's scrutiny.* I push aside the unhappy twinge at losing our private meals together and focus on my job. "Will anyone on the staff accidentally get caught in these? I don't want to unjustly brand someone as a spy if they're going about their duties and have a reason to touch a drawer."

"Everyone is under strict instructions to stay away from it since I've started working in here instead of my study. If they're around it, then they're already disobeying my orders. We won't have a problem." Devereaux's dark eyes sparkle with mischief. "Don't you want to know where I hid my real treaties?"

I smirk. "No need. I already know."

"There's no possib—"

"The second-to-last row of bookcases, top shelf. Hidden in the books on Scara history."

An adorable, befuddled look falls over his face. "How did you …?"

I wiggle my fingers at him. "Magic." Then I laugh. "You can't stop glancing at them. At least four times since we came in here."

"Hrmph." Devereaux folds his arms and glares at the books. "I'll have to find a better spot for them."

"Don't bother. The top of your wardrobe is too obvious. Whoever's spying on you will find them in minutes."

His jaw drops open.

I burst into giggles. "Don't worry, your predictability is one of the most charming things about you."

"Nobody has ever called me predictable before."

"Then I daresay they don't know you well. I'm certain you could never surprise me now that I've spent more time with you."

Devereaux raises an eyebrow, his smile taking on a roguish edge. "Is that so? Challenge accepted."

My breath catches, a spark warming my belly that I do my best to ignore. "Prepare for disappointment."

18

My fingers fly across the pianoforte's keys, pounding out my frustrations through the powerful notes. Our investigation keeps running into dead ends. The upper floors of the palace were simple to check, since layers of dust verified nobody has been up there in some time. Another search of the outbuildings on the palace grounds proved equally useless, although I wasn't holding out much hope for them. Whoever the spy is, they're sticking to the ground floor of the palace. The staff—and I can't assume one of them isn't the spy— make it impossible to track their movements. As Ysabel would say, it's like trying to find a needle in a needle pile.

And now that travel between the village and La Sailles is easier, I'm spending every waking moment at Devereaux's side. With deliveries and people visiting the staff, there's too many people I don't know in the palace and I'm the only one who can protect him. I knew not having a partner on this contract would be hard, but I had no idea what I was in for.

Normally my Guild partner and I can juggle guarding our protectee with research and interviews, trading duties as needed. But here everything falls on my shoulders. I really am just a bodyguard these days because watching Devereaux leaves no time for snooping around the village or the villagers. Even when the prince locks himself in a room like now so I can take a breath, I still worry about him and I can't stay away for too long. Not that being around Devereaux is ever a chore. He's funny and sweet and unbelievably kind now that I've gotten to know him as a friend. But tripping over someone twenty-four hours a day can wear on anyone, especially when we're both used to having some privacy. A few breaks from each other makes our time together that much more enjoyable. Now if I could just get him to see how serious this is instead of merely indulging me.

Devereaux is convinced we're only dealing with a spy, but I know how quickly things can escalate from spying to assassinations. Not to mention other threats he may not know about or is hiding from me. It's hard to sleep even though I walk Devereaux to his suite each night and make sure he locks the door before I find my own bed. I usually end up waking up in the middle of the night to prowl the hallways, driven by nightmares of assassins breaking into his room while I sleep, cursing myself for accepting this Fates-forsaken contract.

Thankfully, I have Orvil. While most of the staff still believes my matchmaker story, Orvil suspects my real purpose at the palace and heartily approves. Knowing he shares my concerns about Devereaux's safety, I ask the butler to discreetly watch over the prince whenever we're separated. Orvil may not be a Guild member, but he has a lifetime of experience in common sense and dealing with palace backstabbing. I would be lost without him.

Even with Orvil's help, I'm exhausted. If we can't catch

the spy, or find a way to bring in more help, I'm going to make a mistake. And that could mean Devereaux's life. *I can't let that happen. I won't let that happen.*

Devereaux is too important to trust anyone else to help me. Even relying on Orvil is risky since I don't know who is targeting the prince. But I'll never find out who is behind the threat if I can't conduct some reconnaissance away from him, and I can't leave him long enough to do anything useful.

I finish the song, then bang my head against the keys and groan. "This is hopeless."

"Pardon me, milady."

I squeak, twisting around, my hand at my throat.

A man near my father's age stands in the doorway, twisting his battered hat in his hands. He's lanky, with the weathered skin that comes from a lifetime working outdoors. His clothing is neat and serviceable, but worn thin around the hems. Bright blue eyes shine from beneath his wrinkles.

"I'm sorry to interrupt you, Lady Saint-Veil. Madame Deneuve hired me to tune the pianoforte." He chuckles. "Although, I don't know why. It sounds perfectly fine with what you were playing now."

I try to calm my racing heart. "No need to apologize. You just surprised me. And I'm not Lady Saint-Veil. Please, call me Julietta."

"Kane. Pleased to make your acquaintance." He ambles over and lifts the lid of the pianoforte, studying the inner workings. "Are you a musician?"

"No, I work for Lord Saint-Veil. He lets me use it from time to time."

Kane's eyebrows go up as he glances from me to the expensive instrument.

My neck goes hot. "Yes. Well, I'll get out of your way."

As I rise, he waves me back into my seat. "Begging your pardon, miss, but if you'll assist me, this'll go a lot quicker and then you can get back to your playing." He pulls a tuning key out of his pocket and ducks his head closer to the strings.

"Oh, of course." I settle back on the bench, spreading out my skirts. I clasp my hands tightly in my lap, crossing my ankles and then uncrossing them. "Do you, um, live in the village?"

His voice is muffled. "Mmm-hmm. But I grew up in Charistel, which is how I learned this trade. Can you hit the middle C?"

I press the requested key, my mind racing. *Charistel! And he lives in the village. But would he admit that so freely if he's the spy?* "I haven't been to Charistel, but I've heard it's lovely. What brought you back here?"

"My wife's from the village and didn't care for the city. Neither did I, truth be told. I don't like a place where you don't know your neighbors. Can you press it again?" He listens intently, then makes an imperceptible adjustment with the key. "There, that should do it. One more time."

I dutifully follow his instructions. "I know exactly what you mean. Although I don't know if I'd like being cut off from everyone else in winter year after year. It's odd being so isolated. No offense."

"Not at all. I felt the same way before I moved here, but it's been peaceful and everyone makes more of an effort to get along since tempers run short in the cold." Kane runs his hands over the strings, then uses his tuner to twist another part. "'Course, the merchants and travelers keep things interesting in the summer."

He launches into a story about a merchant who drank an entire cask of his wine during supper, then accused the fae of stealing it while he slept. He chuckles. "Those Irelin folks are always good for a few laughs. I hope the merchants that arrived last night are half as entertaining."

My fingers slam down on the keys, making Kane wince. My mouth goes dry as my heart leaps into a gallop.

I swallow hard, trying to appear outwardly calm. "Sorry, I slipped. You said merchants came to the village. Does that mean the pass is open?"

"Yup. You wouldn't know it from the way the valley's still buried in snow, but the pass is easy traveling right now. Has been for a couple of weeks." He casts a wary eye at me. "Try the next one, miss. But a little gentler, if you please."

Fumbling, I place my hands on the keys as my stomach twists. *The pass is open. We're out of time.*

Kane and I slowly work through the pianoforte's notes while my mind whirls, running through all the implications of the news. I've been subconsciously counting on some measure of isolation with the pass blocked, but now that's vanished. Anyone can come to the chateau at any time. Protecting the prince here, alone, is impossible.

Every way I look at it, there's only one conclusion: Devereaux has to leave La Sailles.

19

Convincing Devereaux to return to Charistel is going to take every ounce of persuasion, charm, and bullying I can muster. And when he refuses—because, of course, he will—then I need to convince him to at least bring in more people to protect him. If not palace guards, then help from the Guild. There's a few people I could recommend, and Marcel can suggest more. *He's a prince, for Fates' sake! It's ridiculous not to have guards here. And I won't be around forever. He needs to find people he'll trust after I'm gone.*

A lump forms in my throat. My contract is technically over now that the pass is open, but I was planning to stay until he returns to Charistel. It's been too easy to forget that after we leave, I'll never have another debate with him about Irelin mythology or whether Roma expansion happened too quickly to sustain the empire. Devereaux's the only person I've ever met who enjoys breaking down things into their finer points as much as I do. I rub the growing ache in my chest, knowing one day soon I'll say goodbye to all the friends I've made here, including the prince.

But not today. I shake my head, pulling my thoughts back to practical matters. I'm betting Devereaux won't agree to leave if I order him to go home. Strange how he doesn't listen to me when it goes against what he wants. *Fates take him, why does he have to be so frustrating? He's worse than a toddler at nap time. I need to get him in a good mood before I bring it up ... I'll ask Rosemarie for a plate of raspberry meringues. If he can use my weakness against me, I can use his.*

The first step in my plan decided, I set off through the palace with a determined stride. But soon, loud voices coming from the kitchen slow my steps, making me wary of what I'll find.

My eyes pop at the crowd stuffed into the room. *Rosemarie said more people were coming to the palace, but this is ridiculous.* There's barely any standing room with women chatting and arranging jars along the counters, men hanging smoked meats and herbs from the ceiling, and children chasing each other and playing on the floor. Rosemarie's nowhere to be seen, and I don't recognize a single person. The violet dress with white lace I selected this morning feels horribly out of place among everyone's practical brown and gray homespun.

A woman glances at me, then does a double take. She tugs on her friend's sleeve, whispering in her ear without taking her eyes off me. Silence sweeps across the crowd as everyone stares at me.

Great. Just like my first night here. Ignoring the fluttering in my stomach, I smile at the group. "Sorry to interrupt. Do you know where Rosemarie is?"

One woman steps forward. "She'll be back in a moment. You must be the matchmaker we've heard so much about."

She tilts her head to the side, her calculating eyes running boldly over me. "You're a bit older than I thought you'd be. Pretty enough, though. Ladylike."

I blink, fighting the blush threatening to bloom at her blunt assessment. "Yes. Well. I'll check back later, then." I back out of the room, ears burning as whispers and giggles break out. *Yep. Exactly like my first night.*

I keep my gaze straight ahead, avoiding eye contact with everybody as I hurry toward the library. It's impossible to settle my racing thoughts and growing uneasiness. *Too many people. I need to stay close to Devereaux until they leave. But if this is happening every day ... I can't watch him every minute ...* My heart sinks as my chest tightens. *A few guards won't be enough. He has to go home.* I swallow hard. *Really, it's a good thing. Life can go back to normal. I'll finish this contract and spend time with Papa before figuring out what I want to do next. Something outside the Guild. It's the best thing for all of us.*

I pause outside the library door, soothing the frenzy of worries assaulting me. Nightmares about what could happen to Devereaux loop through my mind. Stabbed in the back, strangled, poisoned, tortured—the possibilities are endless. *What I wouldn't give to have a partner right now ...*

No more stalling. No matter what it takes, I have to convince him to go back to Charistel. I check the door is locked, then give a quick knock, waiting for Devereaux to let me in. *At least he's following some of my suggestions. But it's not enough. Not anymore.*

Devereaux opens the door, a distracted look on his face. He motions me inside, hurrying away as I lock the door behind us. By the time I turn around, he's sitting on the floor next to one of the back shelves, surrounded by stacks of books. He glances up to give me a quick smile as I walk over, then returns to studying the pages of the thin pamphlet in his hand. "One symbol on that coin the spy dropped keeps bothering me. I know I've seen it."

I settle outside his ring of books. "Which one?"

"The wavy one with the thing over it."

I roll my eyes with a laugh. "Helpful."

He holds out his hand without looking up from the page. "I'll show you."

"It's hidden behind the sideboard in the sunroom. We've stared at it long enough by now to memorize all the symbols. Where's the one you're thinking of?"

"At the edge, under the one that looks like a blocky mouse."

My brow wrinkles as I run through the image's stark lines in my mind's eye. "Hmm. Wait, that's not a mouse. That's definitely a swan."

His head snaps up. "You must be blind. There's a tail coming out the back."

"That's the swan's head, and the tear-shaped part is the body. I can't believe you think it's a mouse."

He glares at me in mock outrage. "As the future ruler of this kingdom, if I say it's a mouse, then it's a mouse."

"Good thing I'm not one of your subjects, because it's a swan." I stick my tongue out at him.

We grin at each other.

The humor drains out of me, knowing what I have to do next. *Unfortunately, the prince is a stubborn and annoying man who's convinced he's always right. I have to make him see reason. He has to leave.*

I close my eyes and take a deep breath. *It's now or never.* "Devereaux, you need to go back to Charistel."

He picks a book off the top of a stack, avoiding my eyes. "The road is barely passable. The next storm will hit any day now and close it again until spring." He flips through the pages with a studied concentration. "I was thinking about the traps on the desk. We should add ink on the drawer handles in case the spy is bad at picking locks."

I refuse to be distracted. "You don't know another storm is coming. Everyone I've talked to thinks the pass is going to stay open the rest of the year. Merchant trains and travelers are coming through now with no issues. And there are already too many strangers coming and going from the village. There's no point in staying here any longer."

He leans back and crosses his arms. "I told you, the Charistel guards can't be trusted."

"But you're defenseless here." All the imagined horrors flash before my eyes, sending ice through my veins. "You're making yourself an easy target."

"A spy is a long way from an assassin. There hasn't been poison in my toothpowder or a scorpion in my boots. The worst thing that's happened is someone nosing through my documents. It's annoying, but hardly dangerous."

Great, new nightmares to add to the list. "That doesn't mean it'll end there." I swallow around the growing lump in my throat. "If someone's taken enough interest to hire a spy, another kingdom could have a reason to send assassins. I might be able to stop one or two alone, but not three or four. And I have to sleep sometime." I wrap my arms around my waist, my voice going soft. "Please. Go home. I couldn't stand it if something happened to you."

He looks down, thinking it over. I hold my breath, praying to the Fates he comes to the right conclusion.

Devereaux looks up, eyes full of resolve. He shakes his

head. "I'm staying."

I clench my fists, my stomach twisting. "You're not being reasonable. Your plan had a teeny, tiny smidgeon of logic when the pass was closed. But everything's changed, and you're refusing to adapt."

He lifts an eyebrow. "And why does that surprise you? You've been saying how stubborn I am since you got here."

"I was hoping by now I'd have pounded some sense into you." I sigh. "Will you at least bring some guards here? There must be a few you can trust. Or the Guild can supply them. I can't keep you safe by myself. Not anymore."

"My welfare isn't your responsibility."

I poke his chest. "Yes, it is. It's literally the reason I'm here."

He waves his hand. "That's because of Isa's misguided concerns. My reasons for coming here are still valid. If I want to catch the spy, my best chance is to stay here and lure them to me."

Grrrr. "Why does your asinine plan have a better chance of working here instead of Charistel?"

"We just need to be patient. It'll work."

"That's not an answer." I throw my hands out. "It's been weeks since we booby-trapped the desk, and nothing! Not one hint of someone snooping around, or looking for the treaties, or going through your study or rooms. Mayhap if you go back to Charistel, they'll try again and you can catch them there. Did you think about that?"

He shrugs, unconcerned.

I glare at him. "You're a very frustrating, annoying man."

"I'll take that as a compliment." He tilts his head to the side. "I won't leave, but you should."

There's a sharp pain in my chest, but I keep my face unchanged. "And then who would help you hunt out the spy? Besides, I have a contract." *Which is technically over, but he doesn't need to know that.*

Devereaux narrows his eyes. "Mayhap now that the pass is open, I'll write Isabeau and request she fire you."

I give him a bored look. "You used to be better at trying to intimidate me. You should practice more. Use a mirror to work on your glare. Eventually, you'll be able to scare small children."

"Something to strive for." He surveys the stacks of books surrounding him. "Shall we switch to Sulomi symbols?"

"I think I'll spend some time with the pianoforte. Clear my head. I get my best ideas when I'm playing." I stand, shaking out the skirt on the violet dress, avoiding his eyes. "Would you like to join me? I can provide the background music while you work. I'm sure you're dying to memorize a grain inventory from ten years ago, or critique an essay claiming cows that eat clover produce more milk."

Devereaux's face lights up, making my heart skip a beat. "I have something I need to take care of first, but I'll join you in a few minutes."

"I don't mind waiting."

He makes a face. "Nobody is going to attack me if you leave me alone for five minutes." At my raised eyebrow, he adds, "I'll lock the door and you can send Orvil over to pretend to polish the library doorknobs until I'm done. I'll be fine."

"All right, but don't take too long or I'll come find you." I pause in the doorway. "And I agree. Putting your treaties with the copies of the old Balut treaties is clever. Treaties hiding in treaties. Funny."

His draw drops open.

I wink "I told you. Predictable."

20

Devereaux's refusal to go home wasn't unexpected, but that doesn't make it any less annoying. *Stubborn, arrogant, infuriating prince. Always convinced he's right, even when logic says otherwise. What if something happens to him? It'll be all my fault. I can't do all this on my own. But he refuses to trust anyone. I'm not even sure he trusts me. If he did, wouldn't he listen to my suggestions instead of sticking to his harebrained plan?*

I shake my head as I stride through the palace, shoving aside my exasperation for another day. *I'll convince him. I have to. But I'll give him time to think about our discussion—all right, argument—before trying again. Devereaux can be slow to change, but he's not unreasonable. All right, he's totally unreasonable, but I can make him see he's wrong eventually. And this means I can stay at La Sailles for a bit longer ...* I shove aside the pang of guilt. *I did my best, and I won't give up until he changes his mind.*

Orvil promises to watch over Devereaux during

whatever errand the prince wants to run without me, letting me set aside one worry for the moment. Nancey drops off a pitcher of cider on a corner table as I leaf through the sheet music. I give her an absent-minded thank you, my attention on selecting something that will lighten my mood.

I pick an older song that reminds me of springtime, when the world is full of endless possibilities and new beginnings. The music transforms the room into a place where flowers bloom and warmth wraps around me, sunshine slipping into every corner. I always fancied it a song to fall in love to because of the way it gently takes your hand and leads you down the path, everything soft and dreamlike. If I ever fall in love, I want it to be like this song.

Devereaux enters near the end of the composition, a worn leather case clutched in his hands as he moves to the side of the pianoforte. He puts the case by his feet, then picks it up again and places it on the lid of the pianoforte. He puts his hands in his pocket, then takes them out again. Rests his right hand on the case. Runs a finger across his upper lip. Rocks back on his heels, clasping his hands behind his back.

He's nervous about something. It's rather adorable, actually. I don't think I've ever seen Devereaux fidget this much in the entire time I've been here.

He claps as the last notes ring through the room. "Beautiful."

"Thank you." I nod to the leather case. "What's that?"

"Yes, er." Devereaux glances at the floor, then looks back at me. He clears his throat, shifting his weight from one foot to the other. "It's my violin."

I raise my eyebrows as my eyes widen. "I didn't know you played."

"Would you say this proves I'm unpredictable?" He

grins.

Chuckling, I tilt my head, acknowledging my defeat. "Completely. But why didn't you say something earlier?"

"It's not something I tell many people. Being a musician doesn't go well with the ruthless reputation I've cultivated."

A warmth grows in my chest. *But he's sharing it with me.* I wrinkle my nose. "Ruthless?"

"People find me quite cold-blooded." He lifts his nose, his lips twitching.

"Obviously, they don't know you very well if they actually believe that. You put on a good mask, but underneath you have a heart of gold."

He leans closer and lowers his voice. "Don't tell anyone."

"Never." I make a crossing gesture over my heart. "Now, did you bring your violin here just to tell me about it, or do you have something else in mind?" I hold my breath, giving him an encouraging look.

"I—I thought we could play. Together." He rushes to add, "You don't have to if you prefer to play alone. I just thought since you played for me, it was only fair I return the favor. So. That. Yes," he finishes lamely. Devereaux blushes, his brown eyes avoiding mine.

I beam. "I'd love to."

Devereaux's shoulders relax and he takes out a beautiful violin, polished to bring out the red and honey tones in the wood. He sets the instrument under his chin, bow at the ready. "Dance of the Four Seasons?"

I nod, my fingers settling on the ivory keys. The first chords of the haunting melody never fail to make me shiver, even when I'm the one playing. But when Devereaux's violin joins me, the music takes on a life of its own, sending delightful chills over my skin from head to toe. Caught up in his enchantment, I let my hands drop into my lap, mesmerized.

His eyes are closed, his face the picture of relaxed concentration. His body sways to the rhythm of the song, every movement fluid and graceful. Devereaux weaves a spell with his playing, capturing the music and making it dance to his whim.

A flicker by the doorway distracts me. Helene stands there with her hands clasped to her mouth, her face soft, eyes shining with unshed tears. When she notices me watching her, she straightens, her mouth hardening back into its stern lines. The housekeeper gives me a curt nod, then slips out of the room.

Devereaux plays on, oblivious to the silent exchange that just took place. He holds the last note, then ends it with a flourish, running the bow quickly across the strings in a sweeping gesture.

"Devereaux …" I put a hand to my heart, shaking my head slowly.

His arms drop, his brow crinkling. "Was it that bad?"

"Bad—what? No! It was beautiful. Possibly the most perfect, magical thing I've ever heard." I touch his hand. "Devereaux, you're incredibly talented."

"Really?"

The edge of shyness in his smile sends butterflies to my stomach. "Yes. Truly. I've never heard your equal, not in any of the kingdoms I've been to. You're exceptional."

"Thank you." He clears his throat, his neck and ears reddening. "Sometimes it's hard to tell what's shallow flattery and what's a genuine compliment. It's nice I never have that worry around you."

I grin, intentionally lightening the mood. "Because I'll tell you when you're being an arrogant beast?"

He flashes his dimples. "Exactly. Just like I'll tell you when you're being a stubborn know-it-all."

"I am the best, after all." I chuckle. "What a pair we make. Only trusting the people who insult us."

"Indeed. It's pretty obvious why I'm this way with people always trying to get favors and special attention. What's your excuse?"

"The same as you. My time around royals has soured me on compliments. I've seen too many people fawn over aristocrats and tell them whatever they think they want to hear."

Devereaux tilts his head, studying me. "No, there's more to it than that."

I shift on the bench, uneasy at how clearly he can read me sometimes. Nobody else can do that except Papa. "I distrust compliments because they're rarely given without an ulterior motive. There's a man in my village who's convinced everything he does is justified, even when it's cruel, because nobody will naysay him. All they do is fawn at his feet and tell him how wonderful he is because he's rich and handsome and a bully. They either want to gain his favor, or they're afraid of him. Or both." I force my fists to unclench and blow out a long breath. "Sorry. I'm concerned about the example he's setting for everyone else. I'm afraid of what'll happen if he keeps going unchecked."

Devereaux watches me closely. "This man. He hurt you."

I shake my head. "He's been an annoyance, but nothing more."

"Good. If it had been otherwise, I'd have to kill him."

Devereaux lifts the violin and settles the end under his chin. "Shall we play another?"

"You did what?" My stomach plummets as I drop into the chair.

"I told the staff we'd be gone all day tomorrow." Devereaux spreads his arms wide and beams. "It's brilliant. Now the spy will definitely search the palace and we'll discover who it is. And I think we should actually leave the castle. That way, they'll see us go and know we won't interrupt them when they search the library."

"That could work," I admit grudgingly. "We could keep watch from the stable's hayloft. We won't be able to see everyone who comes to the palace, but most villagers will pass that way."

He holds up a finger. "Or, we go far away."

I bolt up. "That's a terrible idea!"

He gives me a steady look until I fold my arms and gesture for him to continue.

Devereaux settles into the other chair. "If we stay nearby, they could spot us and get spooked. Besides, the stables are too far to spot something small, like stained fingertips. Watching won't help us." He lifts a shoulder. "You said it's been too long since we've seen any sign of the spy. I figure this is our best chance to see if they're still around."

"And if they're not, you'll go back to Charistel?" I hold my breath, not sure what answer I want.

He waves his hand. "This'll work."

I tap my foot as I think it over. "Fine. We'll be able to see if the staff has tampered with the desk the next day, but what will you do if it's a villager? They could just stay away from La Sailles until any evidence from our traps has disappeared."

"I'll tell Orvil and Helene someone broke an ink jar in the hallway near my study today and I'll ask them to be on the lookout for any villagers with injuries or ink stains on their fingertips. I'm even going to spill some ink in the hallway to confirm my story." He gives me a smug grin.

I raise an eyebrow. "Won't that make them extra watchful, and they'll stop people from going into the library, or scare the spy into staying away completely?"

His shoulders slump, then his expression brightens. "They can't watch everyone, and the spy is used to sneaking around undetected. This'll be too good an opportunity for them to pass up. I'm sure they'll find a way to slip past them."

"If the spy is good enough to get past them, they can also leave without being spotted."

"Then you'll discreetly find out from the staff who used to come around the palace, but stopped suddenly. That's your specialty."

I sigh in defeat. "It's terrible logic, but I can't think of a better idea." I lightly smack his arm. "Next time you'd better talk to me before making an announcement to everyone. If we're supposedly working together, we both need to agree on our plans." *I might as well make the best of this. And a day alone with Devereaux won't be the worst thing in the world.* I dismiss the way my heart flutters. *Nerves, that's all.* "You'll get to spend a day in the village after all. I'll talk to Jon about getting some horses saddled tomorrow."

He shakes his head with a mischievous grin. "This is my plan, so I'm in charge. I'll arrange everything."

I groan and cover my eyes. "This is going to be a disaster."

22

Dawn hasn't yet crested the horizon when a soft knock on my door jerks me out of sleep. *Staying here is making me soft. Not too long ago, I would've woken up just because someone walked near my room.* I stumble to the door, pulling on my robe and wiping the sleep from my eyes. The sight of the prince waiting outside my room brings a blush to my cheeks. His clothes are disheveled and his cheeks are too flushed for it to be caused by the chilly air alone.

Devereaux grins excitedly at me. "I have a surprise for you."

"Another one?" My heart skips a beat as I cross my arms and lean against the doorjamb, pretending to be annoyed. "I'm beginning to think you love giving people surprises as much as you adore drafting treaties."

"It's impossible to choose between them, since both bring me so much joy."

He grabs my hand, but I tug him to a stop before he can drag me down the hallway, giving him a stern look.

"Do you think I'm available at your whim? What if I'm

in the middle of something?"

His eyebrows scrunch together. "Are you?"

I grin. "No, but that's not the point. It's usually polite to ask permission before you abduct someone."

He clears his throat dramatically. "Miss Julietta Dantes. It would give me immeasurable pleasure if you allowed me to escort you on an excursion that will both delight and amaze you." Devereaux drops into a deep court bow, keeping his eyes locked on mine, his dark gaze drawing me in.

Oh, my. It's suddenly too hot. I sweep into a curtsy, purposefully dropping my gaze to the floor, nervous of what he might see in my face. "Thank you, kind sir. I most gratefully accept." Face composed, I straighten. "Can I get dressed first?"

"Oh, right. Yes." Devereaux looks at me, then quickly glances away, his ears turning red. He holds out a thick coat and oversized boots, both lined with fur. "You'll need these."

"We'll be outside that long? Really?" I pretend to be annoyed while secretly thrilled. *Those weren't in his sister's closet. He's gone to a lot of trouble planning this.* I point my finger at him—"Stay here"—then shut the door.

It only takes a few minutes to dress. I take the precaution of pulling on a second pair of thick wool stockings, falling over as I try to stuff my padded feet inside the boots. With all the extra clothes, I feel like an overstuffed crepe and I'm in danger of passing out from overheating, but I suspect I'll be grateful for the layers later. I hesitate, my hand hovering over my knives, before finally tucking them into the sleeves of my dress with a reluctant sigh.

When I open the door, Devereaux has donned a thick

coat similar to mine. His hand is warm as he tugs me through the palace to the front entrance, where he wraps a scarf around my neck, then plops a thick wool hat on my head. Leather gloves lined with more fur complete the outfit. "Perfect. Now, close your eyes."

I narrow my eyes in mock suspicion, then close them with a smile, excitement thrumming through me. He takes my hands and leads me out the door, where we're immediately greeted with a blast of cold trying to force its way through all the clothing layers.

"I've seen the stables before," I tease him.

"We're not going there." His smugness comes through clearly as he guides me carefully down the stairs and across the ground.

Not going to the stables? I wrack my brain, trying to think if there's anything of interest this way, but nothing comes to mind.

The tension builds until I can't stand it. "Can I open my eyes yet?"

"Don't you trust me?" He jokes.

"Of course, I do."

His hands tighten on mine and he stops. "You do?"

I smile blindly at him, my heart warming at the vulnerability in his voice. "I'm letting you lead me around in the cold with my eyes closed after I've been ambushing you for months. If this isn't trust, then I don't know what is." I hold up a finger. "However, if you end up dunking me in a freezing pond or something equally horrible, I'll have to reconsider."

He squeezes my hand. "I promise your faith will be rewarded." After a few more steps, he stops and stands next to me. "My lady, your chariot awaits."

A large red sleigh sits in front of us, blankets and furs piled high on the black leather seat. The railings on the sleigh are wound with fresh evergreen branches, with delicate silver bells tied to the greenery by gold ribbons. A pair of matched black draft horses stand ready to pull the sleigh, blowing white breaths into the air.

I jump and clap my hands, making the horses turn their heads toward us. "This is wonderful! I can't believe you did all this."

His eyes glow as he ducks his head. "No trouble at all. Except for the sap. That stuff is impossible to scrub off."

My heart skips a beat. *He decorated it himself instead of asking the staff. Does he—no. No. I'm being silly. He's not used to having friends is all. No need to make things awkward.*

Devereaux helps me up into the sleigh, tucking the blankets in around me. I can't help but blush as he fusses over me, then stashes one of the clay pots from the music room by my feet. A delicious warmth wafts up, enveloping me in a bubble of warm air.

"It's a bit of a ride and I didn't want you freezing," he says as he settles in next to me.

"This isn't the surprise?"

"It's part of it."

I clutch at his sleeve, brimming with excitement. "Where are we going?"

"You'll have to wait and see. And we're off!" He snaps the reins, the horses breaking into a gentle trot.

The snow has settled enough that the horses have an easy time pulling the sleigh. Devereaux controls them with an experienced hand, guiding them through the grounds and past the gate, turning away from the pass. He takes a small trail I hadn't noticed that quickly turns steep. The horses slow to a fast walk as we climb higher into the mountains.

Devereaux grins at my obvious impatience as I squirm in the seat. "Relax and enjoy the ride. And before you ask, I told the staff we're going to check the pass and then stop by the village for supper. Everyone knows we're gone and won't be home until late, but won't actually know where we are. And it'll be easy to tell if anyone is following us the farther up we get. So, there's nothing for you to worry about. I've taken care of everything."

Devereaux keeps me entertained, telling me stories about his childhood and asking about mine. It's impossible not the be aware of where our bodies press against each other, but I do my best to keep my mind on our conversation. He fiendishly refuses to answer any questions about our plans for the day, but soon has me laughing as his excitement grows.

Regardless of our destination, the scenery is beautiful enough to justify our trip, with stunning vistas and awe-inspiring panoramic views laid out around us. Winter has its own fantastical beauty that I haven't appreciated until now. The previous storm brought a crisp stillness to the air, the skies a vibrant blue I never see in Cassia. The mountains are impossibly tall, even at this elevation, with hues of purples and greens gentling the black rock. I can spot glimpses of thick forests and pristine lakes beneath the snow in the valley below. At one point we pass under four delicate waterfalls frozen for the season, the tumbling water locked in place until it's released with the spring thaw. Even the rocks appear magic-touched, with cracks full of shining ice glinting in the sunlight.

"Almost there." He grins.

I lean over the side of the sleigh, trying to peer ahead on the curvy trail. "And where is there?"

"You'll see."

We turn around the bend, dropping into darkness. The horses neigh unhappily, but don't stop.

I yelp, heart racing, and grab his arm. "What happened? Where are we?"

Devereaux reaches over and covers my hand with his. "It's fine, you're fine. I'm so sorry. I forgot we wouldn't see the tunnel entrance before we're in it."

"Tunnel?" Since we haven't plunged to our deaths yet, my heart slows to its normal rhythm. Vague, rocky shapes form in the darkness. I grumble, "Why didn't it scare the horses?"

He chuckles. "They know the trail from previous trips up here. We'll be out of it in just a moment." Devereaux's warm voice wraps around me, reminding me I'm not alone in the darkness.

I'm still clinging to his arm, his hand a solid weight on mine. *He hasn't moved. Why hasn't he let go?* I shake my head. *Because I haven't. He's just being nice since he knows I had a fright.* I slide back on the seat, releasing my hold on his jacket.

The prince continues, "The tunnel was partly natural and partly manmade. My father would take me and Isabeau here at least once every summer before he became king."

"Not your mother?"

I can hear the smile in his voice. "She pretended it was too rugged for her, but really it was so we could have some time alone with him. It's the only place we had our father completely to ourselves. Mother is better at making room for us, but Father has always had too many demands on his attention." He hurries to add, "Don't misunderstand. We know he loves us, and he's always there when we need him—"

"It's just hard when you're competing with an entire kingdom," I finish for him. "I understand. A lot of the kids I've worked with have the same situation."

"Exactly. Now, brace yourself. We're about to come out of the dark."

As if on cue, the sleigh leans into a sharp turn and a blinding light floods the tunnel. I blink at the brightness— then gasp.

We're inside a shining blue crystal. The walls arch around us in smooth waves, reflecting and refracting the light that seems to come from within. Every shade of light blue shines in the walls: sapphire, cornflower, azure, robin's egg, and a thousand other colors I can't name. The entire space seems to pulse with a living force. Even the air feels different, somehow thicker, without a trace of moisture.

"What is it?" My heart races, my voice breathless.

Devereaux slows the horses to a stop. "It's a glacier."

"This is all … ice?"

He nods. "Isn't it amazing?"

"I've never seen anything like it." It's thrilling and somewhat unsettling to be surrounded by glowing blue ice, like being in an air bubble at the bottom of the ocean. I'm standing, with no memory of getting up from my seat. Our hands are clasped together, his grip warm in mine.

After a few minutes, Devereaux sits down with a reluctant sigh and picks up the reins. "We'd better keep going, otherwise we won't have time for the best part."

My eyes go wide. "Better than this? Impossible. This is unbelievable."

"I'll take that bet. Prepare to be astounded."

The glacier covers the next mile of our travel. I sit back and enjoy the enchanting ride, the silver bells and the soft tapping of the horses' hooves lulling me into a serene, dreamlike state. The light brightens until the glacier ends, revealing a lush pocket valley filled with greenery. The air is heavy with moisture, a steaming pool in the middle of the scenery.

Devereaux stops the horses at the edge of the grass, then makes a sweeping gesture encompassing the valley. "Welcome to Dei-Les-Tains." He points to the water. "Those are natural hot springs that the Roma believed had healing properties. They used to come here from all over the empire to soak in them. They left a few artifacts here, including—" he pauses for dramatic effect, his eyes twinkling. "The remains of a bathhouse and a temple to the goddess Altena."

Fates! "Honest to goodness Roma ruins?" I bounce up and down, grabbing his hand with both of mine. "Where? Where?"

He laughs. "I'll show you."

Devereaux helps me out of the sleigh, his hands lingering a moment on my hips. I bite my lip, looking around the valley, pretending my stomach didn't flip at his touch.

The prince gives a quick shake of his head before tugging me toward some standing stones and a thick wall of greenery. "Let's start over here. You're going to love this."

He's right. The bases of the structures are mostly intact, making it easy to imagine the graceful buildings standing near the hot springs. The bathhouse was huge, with at least seven chambers connected by shallow steps to guide visitors. But it's the temple that takes my breath away. Bits of the colorful mosaic floor are still visible where nature hasn't claimed it. Fluted columns lay in their final resting places on the ground. There's even a few remains of statues scattered around the area, their graceful lines letting me picture the missing parts. Devereaux indulges me, spending hours climbing around the ruins, pointing out carvings and script he and his sister discovered over the years.

I run my hands over the faint lines chiseled into the stone closest to the pools. "Can you imagine seeing this place in its full glory, with people visiting the temple and making offerings? It'd be amazing if we could travel back in time and visit it then."

Devereaux makes a face. "I think I'll stick with our modern amenities."

"But they were so advanced! The aqueducts they built hundreds of years ago are still standing. They perfected roads—we're still using their techniques—and they turned the world from isolated little villages to an empire. They were just as advanced as we are, mayhap more so."

He chuckles. "If I hear about a time travel doorway, you'll be the first one I tell. And then you can report back to me on whether it lived up to your expectations."

"Deal. They wore beautiful clothes and had amazing architecture, as hinted at here. Oh, and the food! So many exotic spices and fruits from far-away lands."

"Speaking of which …"

Devereaux grabs a basket tucked in the corner of the sleigh. Inside is a variety of meats, cheeses, and bread, along with a flagon of apple cider, somehow still warm even after a day out in the cold. He pours us each a mug and we relax on a blanket, our legs dangling over the edge of the cliff. More mountains sit across from us, a dark emerald lake in the valley below our feet.

I lean back with a contented sigh. "I admit it. This is even better than the glacier. It's amazing."

He lifts his cup in my direction. "I thought you'd appreciate it. When I found out about your crazy obsession—" he pretends to clear his throat. "I mean, your deep and passionate love of history, I knew you had to see it in person."

"It's so much better than reading about it. To actually touch the same carvings as they did, I—they—I—there aren't any words!" I laugh. "I've been moony all day. It must be getting on your nerves. I can't imagine anyone else you brought up here made such a fuss over some old rocks."

There's an intensity in his eyes as he stares at me. "I've never brought anyone here."

"Oh." I lower my gaze to my mug as the blush rushes into my cheeks. "Then thank you for letting me be the first. I love it." There's an energy charging the air, cracking between us. "I can't believe you arranged all this on your own."

He leans back on his hands, smirking. "I have a few skills besides drafting treaties."

"Apparently." I bump my shoulder against his. "Really, though. I'm impressed. And touched." I fidget with my mug, my stomach fluttering. "Nobody's ever done anything like this for me."

"I'm glad I could share it with you before you go home. I wasn't sure the weather would cooperate long enough to make the trip."

It takes a moment for the meaning to sink in, the flutters transforming into knots. *Home. How long have I been thinking about La Sailles as home? That's the danger of staying somewhere too long* ... I look back at the ruins. "I wish I could see it in spring. It must be beautiful."

"Hm." Devereaux stares out across the valley, his face back to the stone mask that's been absent these past months together.

What did I say? I sip my cooling cider and shrug. *Perhaps thoughts of the future have us both in an odd mood. I'd never would have guessed it when I met him, but I'm going to miss Devereaux when I leave. He's not at all what I thought he would be. Not everyone would go to such extremes to give their friend an enchanting day out.* I grin. *Especially when that friend was such a disruption to their peace and quiet. I'm sure he wanted to strangle me a few times before we got to know each other. But now ...* I shake my head. *Friends. Friends is good. Uncomplicated.*

The twitch of movement off to the right catches my eye. A white mountain hare with black tips on his ears nibbles the grass, his little nose bobbing happily. Devereaux appears lost in thought, unaware of our visitor. I touch his hand and lift a finger to my lips, then nod in the bunny's direction.

Devereaux starts, then grins. He silently points to the hare's mate, crouched a few feet further away. Her ears twitch back as she watches us warily.

Devereaux's breath tickles my ear, sending shivers over my skin. "Remind you of anyone?"

I ignore the way my heart speeds up, forcing my breathing to remain steady. "The way he's oblivious to any predators potentially lurking nearby, so she has to protect him?" I pretend to think it over. "Nope, doesn't sound familiar."

His quiet laugh sends the two rabbits vanishing into the greenery as silently as if they'd never been there. We grin at each other. That strange spark ignites the air around us. Heat spreads across my skin. His scent is everywhere, mixing with the sweet cider. Devereaux's pupils dilate and my heart slams against my ribs. I'm suddenly too close—and not close enough. His eyes burn into mine, and I fight the urge to press against him. My lips part as I stare helplessly at him, wanting … something. Everything. It's thrilling—and terrifying.

Devereaux breaks the moment by jerking to his feet. "We'd better start home or we're going to be driving the sleigh in the dark."

I flinch at the sudden loss. "Yes." I jump up, grateful we avoided … whatever that was. *Best not to think about it.* "Let's hurry. I'd rather not fall off a cliff."

We awkwardly pack up the blanket and the remains of our picnic. Soon, the sleigh bells are jingling as we make our way back through the glacier. By silent agreement, we ignore the odd moment and chat like old friends on the ride back down the mountain.

We reach the valley floor as the sun sets. Devereaux slows the sleigh as we reach the main road.

"Did you want to go to the village for supper?"

I dart a quick look at him before staring down at my hands, unaccountably nervous. "I'm fine. Unless you'd like to?" *Since when am I indecisive?* "I mean, our picnic was plenty of food. But if you're hungry, going to the village could be nice." *Great recovery, fluff brain. Ugh.*

"Let's return to the palace." There's a tightness around his eyes.

It's quiet for the short ride back to the stables. La Sailles is dark. Even the kitchen doesn't have its customary glow in the windows, and nobody comes out to greet us as we stop in front of the stables.

Devereaux looks around with a furrowed brow. "Hmm. I told everyone they could have the evening off if they wanted. I guess they all took me up on it."

"That was nice of you." I steal the reins from him, trying to recapture some of our earlier good humor. "And if you know where the sleigh goes, I think we can handle stabling two horses. Well, I can. I have some doubts about you."

He puffs out his chest, his eyes twinkling. "I'm in line to rule an entire kingdom. I can manage this."

I snicker. "We'll see."

We deposit the sleigh in the stable since "Jon made me swear on my crown I wouldn't try to put it away because I'll damage it." Over his protests, I help Devereaux unhitch the horses and get them settled in the stalls with some warm mash. I'm intensely aware of him as he moves around the building. Our normally easy comradery has a strange undercurrent tonight as we complete the chores.

The stars are coming out by the time we leave the stable. Halfway to the kitchen door, I pull him to a stop. I twist the hem of my coat in my hands, unaccountably nervous as I let out a shaky breath. "I just wanted to say again that today was magical. Truly one of the best days of my life. Thank you."

His eyes soften a fraction, but remain shuttered. "It was my pleasure. It's nice to visit the ruins with someone who likes them for their history."

I smirk. "Your sister isn't a history fanatic like me?"

"More like a mischief maker. She was convinced there was buried treasure somewhere in the valley. We spent two summers trying to find a hidden chamber in the temple ruins before she decided romance novels were more interesting." He glances at the kitchen door, rubbing his hands together. "Let's get inside before we freeze. I hope the kitchen fire is still burning.”

As Devereaux hurries toward the palace, I call out, “Just one more thing.”

A snowball explodes against his coat. Devereaux spins back, glaring.

I grin. “That could’ve been a knife, little bunny.”

He growls, his lips twitching. “That’s it. You’re getting dunked in the pond.” He leaps toward me.

I shriek and take off running. The oversized boots and thick skirt hamper my movements, but I manage to dart out of his grasp twice before he catches me.

He grabs me, trapping me against his chest. “Ah-ha!”

The look of triumph morphs into alarm as he yelps. Devereaux overbalances, sending us both tumbling into the snow. We go down in a tangle of legs and coats. He keeps his arms around me, twisting so I land on top of him.

“Julietta, are you all right?” He grabs my waist, steadying me, his eyes wide. “Did I hurt you?”

I laugh and tap him on the nose. “Only my pride. I can’t believe you caught me! I blame these ridiculously gigantic boots. They’re impossible to run in.”

His eyes crinkle. “Or perhaps you can’t admit I’m faster.”

“There’s only one way to settle this. A footrace in the hallway.”

“And risk losing? Never.”

“You’re impossible.”

“Admit it, you love it.”

The gleam in his brown eyes darkens to something thrilling. His gaze searches mine as his grip on my waist tightens. Tension simmers between us, threatening to ignite. Heat burns through me, tempting me with something beautiful and a little scary in its intensity. My pulse speeds up as I squirm against the strange warmth burning in my belly, his muscles twitching with my movements.

"Devereaux?" My voice trembles.

I suck in a breath as he slides his fingers into my hair. He whispers my name and leans toward me, slowly, slowly, giving me time to pull away. An urgency I've never felt before pushes me forward, brushing my lips gently against his.

A storm of need and hunger explodes between us.

Every thought except the scorching urgency to kiss Devereaux is driven from my head. I pull him closer, needing more of this, more of him. His growl shoots straight through me, his body warm and solid against mine. He deepens the kiss, somehow mixing overwhelming need and heat with softness. His lips send ripples of pleasure through to the center of me. Every nerve is on fire, every touch leaving me burning for more. Suddenly, the world feels right in a way it never had before. Something I never knew I needed unexpectedly here and now and perfect.

Too soon, we break apart with a gasp, my heart thundering in my chest. Devereaux buries his face in my hair, his breath hot against my skin. I stare at him in a daze, my mind a haze of yearning and amazement, with something much more dangerous hiding at the edges.

Devereaux's hand cups my cheek. "I've wanted to do that for a long time."

I gaze at him from under my lashes, finding it hard to meet his eyes. "I've wanted you to do that, too. I just didn't want to admit it to myself."

"Because I'm too charming?" he teases, a hint of worry flashing in his eyes.

"Of course. But also because you're my protectee and a prince." I run the back of my fingers down his cheek, loving the way he leans into my touch. "But that doesn't mean I'm not happy here, in this moment. Or that I don't want to kiss you again very, very badly."

"It would be ungentlemanly of me to deny a lady any request within my power," he murmurs, closing the small gap between us.

Every doubt, every question, every thought disappears as his lips touch mine. After I've lost track of time in a whirl of lips and heat and passion, he pulls away with a sharp intake of breath. I whimper, desperate for more, already mourning the loss of his lips. He presses his forehead to mine and we both let out a shaky breath.

He looks at me, moonlight shining in his eyes. "As much as I'm enjoying our time under the stars, I don't want you to freeze out here." Devereaux pulls me to my feet. He brushes a strand of my hair back, his hands lingering on my skin.

I wrap my arms around him, amazed at how natural it feels. "You're doing a pretty good job of keeping me warm right now."

The corners of his eyes crinkle as he flashes those devastating dimples. "A compliment. Careful, or I'll turn back into that arrogant man you met the first night."

"You're still a beast, but now I know it's a mask to hide the kind gentleman underneath."

"A beast, am I?" His eyes spark with mischief. "Then I guess I can do *this*!"

He tickles my sides, his fingers finding every vulnerable spot. I shriek with laughter, twisting and writhing to get away from his attack. Breaking free, I run toward the kitchen door, Devereaux close on my heels.

23

I pace the floor in my room, morning light streaming in the windows and my mind buzzing with too many thoughts to contain. *We're incredibly lucky nobody saw us! How could I kiss him? What was I thinking? I wasn't. But I can't regret it. It feels like there's potential for us to grow into ... something. Something amazing and a tiny bit terrifying. Something that only comes along once in a lifetime.*

But I came to La Sailles for a job. My contract might be over now that the pass is open, but I've botched it from the moment I got here. No. To be fair, my efforts were passable until I let him sweep me off my feet with books and chocolate. Then I started acting like this was some silly game instead of life and death consequences. And that's not even considering how inappropriate I've been with Devereaux.

Devereaux ... A warm haze drifts over me and a silly grin spreads across my face, remembering last night. *All that passion hidden under that stony exterior. The way he kissed me ...*

I shake my head. *Ack, stop it. Focus. I've been allowing myself to be distracted at every turn. No, I've been chasing distractions.*

I've let my feelings determine how I do my job instead of being a professional. Staying by Devereaux's side because I wanted to, not because of some threat. And I can't pretend I've been objective about the people here. I've tried to make friends with the staff instead of keeping my distance. I never thought for a moment Lacee was the spy, or Rosemarie, or Orvil. Nobody, really.

I'm a disgrace. I haven't been looking for an assassin, or even a spy. No, I've been making moon eyes at the prince. Yes—a prince. And my protectee. It's reprehensible. Inexcusable. I have to return Lady Isabeau's money and beg her forgiveness. I've put my entire future at risk. If the Guild knew how I've been behaving, the best case they'd deny list me for life. Worst case—better not to think about it.

But it's so hard to care about everything I've done wrong when I remember how Devereaux smiles at me, and all the little ways he makes sure I'm comfortable and happy, and how much he cares about everyone and everything, though he doesn't want anyone to know it. Devereaux's so much more than that haughty noble I met on my first night. If he could learn to trust people, to open up to them, everyone would see him as clearly as I do. They have no idea how deep his kindness and love run.

And he chose me, just as I chose him—even if I hid it from myself until now. Looking back, it's laughable I didn't see this coming. *I should've paid more attention to those stories of Guild members accidentally falling in love with their protectees. How naive I was, to assume it could never happen to me.*

There's no denying our feelings. Stealing heated glances across the breakfast table this morning while desperately trying to keep up appearances for the staff only added to the thrill. It was impossible to keep my mind on the conversation. Knowing what it feels like to kiss him, to be in his arms, it nearly drove me mad to keep my distance. Every moment was delicious torture. I can't imagine I'll feel different tomorrow, unless I somehow become even more obsessed with him. Could it someday become—dare I say it—love?

Mayhap it's time I toss caution into the wind and let my heart lead.

It goes against my nature to take a leap of faith, but this time I'm willing to put my happiness in the hands of the Fates and see what they have planned for Devereaux and me.

But trusting the Fates doesn't mean I'm going to ignore common sense. *We have to talk about this. There needs to be an understanding so we don't inadvertently ruin our lives as we're figuring things out. Having a ... something ... with Devereaux isn't without consequences for either of us.*

Pounding steps outside my room drag me out of the whirlwind of thoughts.

Lacee bursts through the doors. "Julietta, I missed you. And I have so much to tell you!" She bounds over to me and wraps me in a fierce hug.

I can't help but smile. "It's only been a day."

"But so much has happened." She sighs and sits on the bed, wrapping her arms around the bedpost. "I spent the whole day with Edmon in the village. It was magical."

I perch next to her, giving her a quizzical look. "Day? I thought you only had the evening off."

She giggles. "Don't tell. Caitlin offered to cover for me

so I could sneak off early." She flops back on the comforter with a happy sigh. "He bought me caramels, and told me how beautiful I am. He's absolutely perfect."

Laying on my side, I prop my head on my hand and grin. "Tell me everything."

Lacee's visit lets me forget my situation for a bit. Too soon, she leaves, needing to get back to her duties. I spend another hour fussing and pacing around my rooms, practicing what I need to say before pulling together enough courage to venture out and find Devereaux.

Instinct steers me away from our library and to his study. I slip inside and lean against the door, observing him. Devereaux is bent over his large ebony desk, studying a parchment with the fierce intensity he gives to everything in life. He looks as unsettled and agitated as I feel, with his hair mussed from running his hand through it and his jacket unbuttoned despite the chill.

My stomach turns somersaults while my heart threatens to leap out of my chest. There's so much I need to say to him, but all I want to do is fall into his arms and kiss him.

Devereaux looks up from his desk, his scowl melting into a warm smile just for me. "You found me."

"I told you, predictable."

"I'm not the only one." He holds up his hand. "I know what you're going to say."

I gulp. "You do?" My heartbeat thunders in my ears. *Does he regret kissing me? Does he want to take it all back?*

"It didn't work like we planned. But just because the spy

didn't set off the traps, it doesn't mean they aren't still snooping around."

Guilt and shame pour through me. I hadn't given a thought to the reason for our outing yesterday. All I've been able to think about is Devereaux. *How can I be so stupid? I've been daydreaming about kissing him while he's been occupied with the spy. Obviously, those heated glances at breakfast were one-sided. Fates, he must think I'm such a fool!*

He hurries around the desk and takes my arm, peering into my face. "Julietta? Are you all right? You've gone white."

"Yes, I—I just got lightheaded for a moment."

Devereaux guides me to his chair. "Can I get you anything? Do you want a cup of tea?" He hovers over me, his face full of concern.

"I'm fine. Really." I take a deep breath, shoving all my self-recriminations and embarrassment aside for later when I'm alone. *I need to act normal. Don't make him uncomfortable because I put too much importance on last night. It was just a kiss. He's probably kissed hundreds of girls.* I swallow hard to clear the sour taste in my mouth. "You can't possibly think the spy is still around. In your own words, that was an opportunity too good to pass up. It's time to admit defeat and go back to Charistel like you said you would."

"I never agreed to that. Besides, I can think of a few advantages La Sailles has over Charistel at the moment." He perches on the edge of the desk and takes my hand, his thumb tracing delicious circles on my palm that set my nerves singing, giving me a smoldering look. "Don't you agree?"

I drop my gaze to my lap. "I thought you … might …" *Get it over with.* I blurt out, "Want to pretend last night never happened?" I dart a quick look at him, holding my breath.

"No—do you?" He goes still, the corners of his eyes tightening. He suddenly pales. "If I've pressured you, or misunderstood your feelings—"

"No! Devereaux, no." I leap forward, wrapping my arms around him, my cheek resting against his chest. It breaks my heart he could think that for even a second. Giddiness bubbles up in my chest. I bite my lip to keep from smiling. "But it's been so long since you kissed me, I'm not sure I remember what it's like. Perhaps if you remind me?" I give him a mischievous smile.

A roguish gleam lights up his eyes. "I might assist with that."

Devereaux's lips capture mine in a searing kiss. Heat curls inside my chest, his warmth soaking through me. Every kiss is a thrill, new and exciting and perfect. There's no more reason, only burning need and desire and right now. I hope this feeling never goes away. His hands brush my waist, my sides, until I gasp at the intimacy of it. My knees go weak and I cling to his shirt, his arms the only thing keeping me upright.

When I'm sure I'll burst into flames, a shudder ripples through him and he pulls gently away. I put my hands on his chest, feeling his heart racing.

I try to catch my breath. "Ah, yes. I remember now. I think we can both agree we should continue that pursuit."

His dimples flash. "You make it sound like a contract."

I bring my lips a hairsbreadth away from his, teasing him. "I told you, a lifetime around nobles has warped my vocabulary."

His eyes darken, drawing me in. "Is it odd I find it enchanting?"

"No wonder you love working on treaties together. You like hearing me say things like leverage and concessions and stakeholders."

"It's definitely one of the unexpected perks."

Devereaux brushes a soft kiss against my lips, leaving them tingling. I pull him down and deepen the contact as he slides his fingers into my hair. My heart stutters, then kicks into a full gallop. His lips move to my neck, tasting my skin, until I'm ready to explode.

"It's a good thing I didn't mention preambles or cargo manifests," I pant.

A blissful smile bursts out on his face. He cradles my face in his hands. "How did I ever find you?" His breath catches as I trail my fingers down his bare arm.

"Just lucky, I guess."

He captures my hand. "As much as I'm enjoying myself, I know you well enough to guess you came here with some purpose." Devereaux perches back on the edge of the desk. "Something that involves what's happening between us."

My pulse speeds up for an entirely different reason as I nod.

He squeezes my hand. "You could get in trouble with the Guild. They must have strict rules about fraternizing with the subjects of your contracts."

He's thought about this too. My shoulders relax. "Draconian. And there's a whole list of people who would frown on you getting involved with the help." I chuckle, shushing him before he can protest. "I don't work for you, as I've made perfectly clear since I came here. But other people may not make that distinction, and the perception could be hard on you politically. Not to mention it would put the staff in an awkward position. Helene's head might explode."

"So what do we do?"

If only I knew. "I think we should keep things quiet for now. Let's enjoy this—whatever it is—without everyone watching and worrying about the fate of the kingdom."

His face reveals nothing. "And what is this thing between us?"

"I don't know, but I would like to find out. What are you thinking?" I bite my lip, my chest tightening.

"Julietta." His voice is soft as he cups my cheek. "I know I care about you, and I think you care about me."

I give a shaky laugh. "What gave you that impression?"

He kisses the inside of my wrist, sending delightful shivers over my skin. "You're right. This is new. I'd like us to figure out what it means without involving the rest of the country. Keeping it between us for the time being is the right thing to do." His eyes take on a mischievous gleam. "And it's fun."

My mind flashes back to breakfast, my cheeks heating. "It has some rewards. It's definitely better than chasing people through the sewers."

He chuckles. "I'm glad to see your standards are so high." His hand tightens on mine. "I worry at the thought of you hunting assassins somewhere."

"Actually, I was considering a career change before all … this." I smile at him. "Something where I can get to know people and have a bigger impact on them than leaving a fleeting memory. I don't know what that will be yet, since my skills are rather unique."

"If you came to Charistel, you wouldn't have to work.

I'd—" He raises his hand. "Forget I said that. I know you'd never be happy if you weren't supporting yourself."

"That includes working for you. Or someone you ask to hire me, which amounts to the same thing." I shake my head. "I don't want a token job to keep me busy. I need something real. Something that makes a difference."

"Noted. I'll give it some thought and see if I can come up with any ideas." He runs his hand down my hair, twirling a strand between his fingers. "Did you see your surprise?"

A grin springs to my lips. "Another one? This is getting out of hand. You're spoiling me."

"You're the only one I'm allowed to surprise. Spontaneity and unpredictability in the future king make people nervous. They want a steady, staid, and boring person on the throne. Predictable." He tucks the lock of hair behind my ear, his fingers lingering on my skin. "And you deserve to feel special, so let me enjoy spoiling you."

"All right, but only because you insist." I pretend to peek over his shoulder, then slide my hands into his jacket and look up at him. "Is it in here?"

"No, but you're welcome to keep looking." He chuckles at my pout. "It's somewhere in the palace."

"This place is huge! It could take me days of searching." I link my arms around his neck. "Give me a hint. How will I know when I find it?"

"You'll know." He tugs me out to the middle of the study. "Dance with me."

"Now?" I laugh. "Someone could see us."

"It's worth the risk. If I don't have you in my arms again soon, terrible things might happen." He wraps me in a warm, protective circle, resting his head on mine.

"We can't have that." I sigh. "I'm going to have to add

you to my lists of weaknesses."

"You're already on mine." He leans back and ducks his head to meet my gaze. "If you're finished with what you wanted to say …" He waits for my nod, then his gaze flits to my lips. "First, I need to kiss you again."

Always too soon, he breaks away with a regretful sigh, then kisses the tip of my nose.

"Now, I believe I asked you to dance."

I shiver as his hand settles on the small of my back, my senses still heightened. "What are we dancing, a waltz or the minuet?"

"I thought I'd show you a few local court dances. You never know when they'll be useful in your line of work."

I giggle, snuggling closer to his chest. "Ball attendance isn't usually required when I'm trying to root out assassins."

"I was talking about being a matchmaker." He winks. "Besides, assassins probably like to dance too."

Devereaux whirls me around the room, guiding me through the steps and combinations of the local dances. It doesn't take long for the choreographed moves to dissolve into gentle swaying across the floor, gazing at each other, lost to the rest of the world.

24

Devereaux was right: I knew his surprise when I saw it.

I add the newest rose to the others already in the vase, admiring the exquisite bouquet. Each rose is a deep red edged with a vibrant gold, a combination I've never seen before. Every day one has appeared somewhere where only I would find it. The older roses have loosened, opening up into a cascade of petals, while the newer flowers are still tight buds. Most of the staff must suspect something by now, but they haven't hinted at anything beyond Helene pressing her lips together a little harder than normal. Devereaux and I are careful to keep things polite in front of everyone, but they would have to be completely oblivious not to feel the sparks flying between us whenever we're in the same room. *And the times we find to be alone ...* A blush sweeps over my skin.

I check my reflection in the mirror, shaking my head at the extra sparkle in my eyes and the pink in my cheeks. *I can't go to breakfast looking all dewy-eyed.* I fan my face, to no avail. *It's time to surrender. If I can't hide it, I should at least make the most of it.* I brush my thick brown hair until it shines, then tie it back with a sky-blue ribbon that matches my dress.

Devereaux stands when I enter the sunroom and bows with exaggerated politeness. "Miss Julietta. I'm so glad you could join me." He holds my chair for me as I settle in it, his hand lingering on my shoulder before he returns to his seat. "I hope you had a pleasant night."

I smother my giggles at his feigned formality. "I did, thank you. And I hope you had an equally agreeable evening."

"Quite. The weather has been so temperate, I'm predicting we'll have an early spring. I'll miss the snow. It's led to so many *interesting* events this year." He winks as he folds his napkin into his lap.

Two can play this game. "Perhaps you could host a ball to lessen the pain of losing winter. Fallian Province has so many lovely dances. Or so I've heard. I don't have much opportunity to dance in my line of work."

"What a shame. I imagine you're a lovely dancer." He gives me a heated look that has me reaching for a cool drink.

Loud voices come from down the hallway. Devereaux and I exchange confused looks as the voices get closer.

Orvil pauses in the doorway. "Miss Julietta, you have a visitor."

Who could be looking for me? A knot forms in my stomach. *Did the Guild send someone to check up on me?* "Who is it? Did they give their name?"

A familiar voice pipes up behind him. "Is she in here?"

My jaw drops open. "Papa?"

A familiar face peers around Orvil, adjusting his thick spectacles. "Julietta, there you are." He staggers into the room, his arms overflowing with wrapped packages. "I've missed you, dear girl."

With a joyful cry, I leap at him and wrapping him in a hug, knocking most of the parcels to the floor. Tears spring to my eyes. "I can't believe you're here. What are you doing here? You must be exhausted. I'm so glad to see you."

I step back, really seeing him for the first time. He's dressed in trousers with a matching jacket I've never seen before, each tailored to fit him perfectly. His hair and beard have been recently trimmed. A dusty hat with a long feather is crushed under his arm. But it takes a moment to recognize the biggest change: the perpetual air of worry has disappeared from his face. "Papa, you look wonderful."

He fixes his spectacles with one hand, beaming at me. "It finally happened, my girl. Our ship has literally come in. When I arrived in Lyvon, I found *The Belle* had docked the day before. It'd been blown off course and needed repairs, but the captain brought her home safe and sound with our cargo."

"That's—that's amazing, Papa! I can't believe it." I notice Devereaux lingering awkwardly by the table. "Oh, where are my manners? Lord Devereaux, allow me to introduce you to my father, Nathanael Dantes. Papa, this is Lord Devereaux Saint-Veil of Fallian Province."

Devereaux bows. "Sir, it's a pleasure to meet you."

"I'm glad to make your acquaintance." My father returns the bow, dropping several more packages. "You look different as well, Julietta. Is that a new dress?"

I smooth the skirt of the blue satin dress, suddenly uncomfortable in the outfit. "Lord Devereaux was kind enough to let me borrow a few things from his sister's wardrobe, since my clothing isn't warm enough. I wasn't prepared for how cold it can get here."

"I can help you with that." Papa hands me the few packages he's hung on to. "While I was waiting for the pass to open, I got everything ready for you. Madame LeFleur had your measurements on file and Monsieur Gerrard sent over a pile of books. And, of course, I couldn't forget the most important thing. Your new pianoforte is waiting for you at home. Your contract ended when the pass opened, correct? Go pack. We can be home in less than a week if we make good time."

I shoot Devereaux a helpless look.

He steps forward. "But you can't leave before the masquerade. It's being held in your daughter's honor to thank her for all her help these past months."

I widen my eyes at him and he lifts a shoulder in a half-shrug.

"That's wonderful." Papa rocks back on his heels, his face beaming with pride. "I know my girl is talented, but nobody's ever thrown a ball for her."

"She's been invaluable." Devereaux nods to both of us. "I'll let you two catch up while I talk to Helene about the arrangements." He motions to the two footmen to follow him out, signaling me we'll talk later.

I almost forget to curtsy as he leaves the sunroom, closing the door behind him. Everything has changed so fast! I set the packages down and hug my father again. "I'm so happy to see you. Are you hungry? Let me dish you up a plate while you tell me everything that's happened since I left."

Papa settles at the table, talking about his journey to Lyvon and the discovery of the missing ship. I try to keep my mind on his story, but too many thoughts keep demanding my attention.

My father showing up unannounced adds a new wrinkle to my plans. As he said, my contact ended when the pass opened. I'd already decided to have the Guild send someone else to protect Devereaux until he returns to Charistel, so there's really nothing to keep me at La Sailles except my growing affection for Devereaux and desire to spend as much time with him as I can. *And that's a great reason for me to stay, but how can I explain that to my father without things getting embarrassing?*

I'm going to put that conversation off for a long, long time.

While Papa gets settled into a guest room, I slip away to our library, bumping into Helene as she's leaving.

"Miss Julietta."

Did it get colder in here? "Madame Deneuve."

"The lord informed me we're honoring you with a ball." She makes the bland statement sound like an accusation.

"He said something about that this morning." *But I never thought he'd go through with it!* "It's very kind, but unnecessary."

"Indeed. I'm curious what help a matchmaker could offer to warrant such an extravagant show of gratitude. But of course, that's Lord Devereaux's business. If you'll excuse me, the staff and I will be very busy planning this *unnecessary* ball."

I barely keep from cringing as she continues on her way. *What a mess.* At my soft knock, Devereaux calls to come in.

Instead of perusing the bookshelves, he's standing over a dozen pieces of parchment spread across the floor.

"What's all this?" I gaze down at the clutter, trying to figure out what all the diagrams and lists are for.

"Plans for the masquerade." He frowns and kneels down, swapping two documents. "I've never organized one before. Usually, Isabeau takes care of them. It's a lot harder than I've given her credit for. There's so many details that need to be worked out."

"About that. It's a lovely gesture, but I don't need a ball. Really." I take his hand, thrilling at the tingle that runs through my skin, then frown at the scribbled parchments littering the floor. "You did all this since breakfast?"

"I've been planning it for the past two weeks. I told you those dance lessons would come in handy. We'll invite the villagers and have a proper party." He brings my hand up to his lips, pressing a gentle kiss on the back of it. "Remember what I said about letting me spoil you? I want to do this for you." He tugs me closer, wrapping his arms around me.

My knees go weak at the glint in his eyes. "But Devereaux, there'll be rumors. Everyone will suspect something, including your family. There's no way to keep this from getting back to them."

"There's always gossip. It'll be novel to have it based on facts this time, instead of the normal scandalous innuendo and speculation."

"But a ball … It's too much. You might as well have publicly declared your intentions toward me."

He presses his forehead against mine. "Would that be so terrible?"

I feel like I'm being torn in two. Part of me is ready to promise myself to him, but the other part has doubts. Not about Devereaux—never about him—but all the unresolved questions around what the future will hold. I know I said I was going to trust in the Fates, but I didn't know it would be so unnerving.

"It's not that simple. You have an entire kingdom to think of. Royalty doesn't marry for love."

His eyes soften as he runs his fingers through my hair, tugging it free of the ribbon. "But that doesn't mean I can't. I've never felt like this before, and I can't imagine ever feeling it with someone else again. You're special, Julietta. You're smart, and beautiful, and stubborn, and you tell me when I'm wrong. Repeatedly. And emphatically. The only thing I want is to make you smile. I'm falling in love with you."

My heart soars as tears spring to my eyes. "Devereaux, I feel the same way."

"You like it when I tell you that you're wrong?"

I giggle, feeling like I might explode with happiness. "Exactly. You're the most frustrating, annoying, vexing man I've ever known, and I can't imagine my life without you. Who else would ignore my suggestions and come up with harebrained plans? How could I resist you?" I tug him closer. "Now, kiss me, you arrogant beast."

He murmurs my name as he cradles my face, lowering his lips to mine. Devereaux is so much more than I could have ever dreamed of. One touch from him and my skin is on fire, passion and the need to keep him close, shoving practicality aside. Every moment with him pushes me a little closer to falling off the cliff I'm trying so hard to avoid.

He gently breaks away, trailing kisses up my jaw. "We should probably go to the kitchen. The staff must have a list of questions about the masquerade by now." Devereaux nuzzles the sensitive spot behind my ear.

I grip his shoulders as he sends delicious shivers down my back. "About that. I don't think it's a good idea."

He murmurs against my jaw, "An entire evening with you in my arms? I can't imagine anything better." He moves his lips to my neck.

I gasp, trying to keep my thoughts straight. "No, I'm serious. It would be the perfect time for someone dangerous to sneak in the palace. To spy, or worse. If everyone is in costume, they could hide in plain sight."

"So can we. Nobody will know who I am or who you are. We can finally be together without sneaking around." His lips brush against mine. "Not that I'm unhappy sharing this secret with you."

I protest between kisses. "But how will we know who anybody else is?"

He chuckles. "I've never known someone who wants to worry as much as you."

"It's my job. Or at least, it was."

Devereaux pulls back, his eyes wide. "What?"

I take a deep breath. "I'm going to return Lady Isabeau's money. I'd already decided before Papa showed up that I haven't been doing my job, not for a long time. I'm too infatuated with you to pay attention to anything else. And I'm spending every moment with you instead of rooting out threats or watching for danger. Even if I'm not with you, I'm thinking about you instead of what I should be doing." At Devereaux's broad grin, I shove his shoulder. "I'm telling you how I've utterly failed and you're smiling?"

"It's the best confession I've ever heard. And I'm thrilled to be the reason you're terrible at your job. I wouldn't have it any other way."

"Don't be too excited. I'm still going to arrange for someone from the Guild to come here and protect you." I press a finger to his lips to silence his protests. "There's a threat that needs to be addressed. I'm not going to leave you vulnerable. It's either someone from the Guild, or you go back to Charistel."

"You remember I was the one who discovered the spy in Charistel, don't you?"

"Where there is one threat, there are bound to be more. You have actual guards there to protect you, unlike here."

He sighs. "You're not leaving me much choice."

"None, really. I'm sending messages to Lady Isabeau and the Guild tomorrow."

"I still think you're being ridiculous, but if it makes you feel better, do whatever you need to do." He kisses me again until my head's spinning. "Now, we're going to have the masquerade. You're going to have a wonderful time. And I need to see what the staff requires."

I trail my fingers along his jaw, enjoying the way his heartbeat quickens under my touch. "Let me know if there's anything I can do besides fret. I'm going to check on Papa and make sure he's settling in."

At the knock on the door, Devereaux and I spring apart. I quickly smooth my mussed hair as he calls out.

Orvil opens the door, his face impassive. "Lord Devereaux, you have a visitor."

A woman's voice sings out, "Where's my big brother? He knows how I hate waiting."

Devereaux blinks. "Isabeau?"

25

A beautiful woman with Devereaux's honey-colored hair and deep brown eyes sweeps past the butler, her arms wide. "Dev, darling. I've missed you."

Devereaux grins as he swings her into a huge hug. "Isa, I can't believe you're here."

"I knew you'd be miserable and bored up here without me, so I had to come." She smirks. "Actually, I knew you were perfectly happy hiding away from the court, but I couldn't take being in Charistel anymore. Without you there, everyone keeps running to me with all their problems and concerns, as if I have any idea what to do about them."

"And you decided to hide here with me?"

She laughs, the musical sound filling the room. "Of course not. I came to bring you home so you can manage the boring meetings and complaints, and I can go back to entertaining. Mother and Father were ecstatic at the idea. They would've come if they could, but you know how things are."

"Everything will fall apart without them." Devereaux

hugs her again. "I didn't realize how much I missed you. Now everything's perfect." He pulls her over to where I'm lingering uncertainly by the fireplace. "Isa, let me introduce you to Miss Julietta Dantes." At her blank face, he adds, "The Guild member you hired to babysit me."

I curtsy. "A pleasure to meet you, milady."

"Oh, I'd forgotten all about that. Nice to meet you. I hope you've been taking good care of my brother." She beams up at him, patting his cheek. "I know how stubborn and grumpy Dev can get."

I twist my hands behind my back. "Yes, of course."

Devereaux says, "Julietta's been keeping me on my toes. She even set up traps to make me pay attention to my surroundings."

Lady Isabeau tilts her head to the side, her brown eyes wide. "Is ambushing your clients a normal part of protecting them? I thought it'd be things like standing guard at his door, or patrolling the hallways."

"The children I normally work with have fun finding the traps I set for them." My voice is faint.

Devereaux chuckles. "Fun wasn't the word I used when a bucket of water dumped on my head, but I certainly learned something. Orvil has a wicked sense of humor. He was laughing and ready with a towel before the bucket hit the floor."

Lady Isabeau gasps. "Orvil? No! That man hasn't cracked a smile since the day he was born."

"He's hidden it all these years. But Julietta has done a lot more than guard me. She's also been invaluable in crafting the treaty terms for Father's review."

Lady Isabeau looks at me with interest. "Really? I wouldn't think a bodyguard would know much about negotiations between kingdoms."

I blush. "Lord Devereaux's giving me too much credit. I just shared my experiences from working in other kingdoms."

"And your obsession with history also helped." He winks.

Lady Isabeau says, "I'm glad to see it well spent my money."

"About that." I take a deep breath. "Lady Isabeau, I—"

"Julietta, was it? I would love to speak with you more, but first I'd like to spend some time with my brother." Lady Isabeau links arms with Devereaux, leading him to the chairs by the fire. "I have so much to tell you. Mother and Father sent over a long list of things to bore you with, but first I simply must fill you in on all the gossip."

He shoots a resigned look over his shoulder. Recognizing my dismissal, I slip out of the room and press my back against the door. *My father and his sister. This is going to make things interesting.*

Should Devereaux and I tell them about our relationship? I love Papa, but he's not the best at keeping a secret, and from Devereaux's descriptions of his sister, I can't imagine she's any better. If we tell them, everyone will know. Is that all right? Does Devereaux want that? Keeping it from the staff while we figured out our feelings was one thing, but this is family. I don't want to put anyone in an awkward position. I chew on my lip for a moment. *We should decide this together. Until then, I won't say anything, just in case.*

I shake my head and push away from the door. *Enough worrying.* I'm going to have a busy afternoon, starting with returning Lady Isabeau's dresses to her wardrobe.

Devereaux's sister didn't bring a large entourage, but it makes the small staff here before her arrival seem laughable. Adding to the crowd are the villagers brought in to assist with the extra guests and the upcoming masquerade. After spending months with twenty-two people in the palace, it feels like it's bursting with someone lingering around every corner. Nobles come and go from the little library, and there are too many strange faces in the kitchen.

Since Lady Isabeau isn't Devereaux, she brought a large contingent of guards with her. They take charge of Devereaux's safety, leaving me with nothing to do. But I keep Devereaux's concerns about the Charistel guards in mind, and watch for my Guild replacements. They'll protect him and can't be bought off. But it could be a month before someone arrives, longer if the weather is bad.

Papa was understanding when I explain I want to pay Lady Isabeau back, and he luckily has enough money with him to cover the debt. But it's been impossible to get a moment of Lady Isabeau's time to return her money. I'm not sure she cares, but I feel honor bound to settle the matter between us.

To avoid any awkwardness, Papa and I take our meals in the sunroom while Devereaux, Lady Isabeau, and the nobles that accompanied her dine in the banquet room. Papa's arrival was both a blessing by the Fates and a burden. Having him with me really has been wonderful. I haven't seen him this happy in a very long time. Without financial worries, Papa is his old, lighthearted self again. He tells me stories about the people in our village and his ideas for our future. Our conversations get me thinking about what I want when we leave La Sailles. My path used to be so clear, but everything's become muddled.

But having him here means I have to keep up a happy appearance, acting as though nothing is troubling me, even though I'm struggling. Days pass with Devereaux and I only catching a rare glimpse of each other in the hallways. The one time I hear from him is a note asking me to dismantle all the traps after the first noble's fingers get caught in a snap trap while searching for parchment.

It's a loneliness of longing I've never experienced before. I can't help but crave the feel of Devereaux's arms around me again, needing to hear his voice as we debate an idea or laugh at a shared joke. It's frightening how quickly he became a vital part of my existence, and how much his absence hurts now. Each day that passes brings the chasm between our worlds a little more into focus, despite my best attempts to ignore it. But when I try to see a future together, I can't find our happy ending.

Papa always says I'm borrowing trouble when I don't need to. One of the hazards of my job, I guess. Another is facing harsh realities I'd rather ignore. If Devereaux joins his family in Charistel and I go back to Cassia, we'll likely never see each other again. Just the thought of it breaks my heart. Devereaux can't give up his throne, nor would I ask him to. No, I have to find a way to live in his world, since he can never fit into mine.

I could go to Charistel with him. Devereaux's the most amazing man I've ever met, and I can easily fall in love with him if I let myself. Knowing he cares about me, that he could feel that way about me, is a dream come true. But the past week has shown me the harsh reality of how our days would play out. If he's this busy now, I can only imagine how his days are filled when he's surrounded by councilors and nobles and a thousand other people who need his attention.

And I would be one of them. Waiting. Lonely. Overlooked. There would be nothing for me to do there. I can't haunt the court, trying to snatch a moment or two with Devereaux every few weeks. I would be an object of scorn and pity, without an ounce of pride for myself. No, I can't do that. I might be falling in love with him, but I love myself, too. And if I found meaningful work to occupy me, the odds of Devereaux and I finding ourselves free at the same time would shrink to nothing. My only hope is to find something that keeps me close to him, but if we can't figure that out now, when will we? What place is there in a prince's life for a commoner from another kingdom?

Every day that passes without seeing Devereaux makes the likelihood of finding an answer slip farther and farther away. Only the red and gold roses appearing on my pillow every night keep me from despair. Knowing Devereaux is thinking of me lets me cling to the bit of tattered hope I have left that we'll find an answer together.

Tonight, there's a note accompanying the rose: *Library 2am.*

My heart goes into a gallop, feeling alive for the first time since everyone showed up at our doorstep. It's torture waiting for the minutes to count down. I change my dress three times, then change it again. It's silly to think he'll care what I'm wearing, but my frazzled nerves won't let me rest. The blush in my cheeks won't cool as I pace my room, counting down to the appointed time. Finally, I can't stand waiting a moment longer and sneak down to the library, keeping my steps quiet on the stone floors.

The moment I walk through the door, Devereaux crushes me to his chest, his lips seeking mine. I wrap my arms around him, pressing as close to him as I can, barely registering the click of the door locking. Devereaux sweeps me up into his arms and carries me over to the couch, never breaking our kiss. I lose track of time as I remember the smell and feel of him, the memories paling compared to reality.

Devereaux runs the back of his fingers down my cheek. "Julietta, my heart. I've missed you."

I lean into his touch, gazing into his eyes. "I couldn't tell." Laughing, I capture his hand and kiss his fingertips. "It's been impossible being away from you. Thank you for the roses. They kept me sane."

"I only wish I could have given them to you in person. I love my sister, but her timing could've been better."

"Speaking of which, did she ever say why she hired me?"

He chuckles. "I honestly think she doesn't remember doing it. Isa's like that. Something catches her attention one moment, then she's obsessed with something else the next. But I'm grateful she did, because it brought you to me."

His hand strokes my hair as I settle my head on his chest, listening to his heartbeat. Devereaux tells me about his sister's antics, and I share the stories from Papa. A feeling of rightness settles over me, even as a small part of me whispers this is only temporary.

Devereaux twirls a strand of my hair around his finger. "Are you looking forward to the ball?"

"Would you be hurt if I said no?" I twist to look up at him. "I'd rather have you all to myself for an evening, with nobody around to perform for or demand our attentions. But if I can't have that, I'll take anything that lets me spend more time with you."

He sighs. "It's harder than I thought it would be, especially since I can't tell anyone about you. Have you changed your mind about that?" He waits for me to shake my head, then nods. "I haven't either. In some ways, it would make things easier, but in other ways, it would make everything a mess. And it wouldn't really make a difference in how often we could see each other, anyway." He scrubs a hand over his face. "I barely had any free time in Charistel, and now there's even more things that need my attention. You'd think I was running the kingdom and not my parents."

A fist squeezes my heart at hearing my fears confirmed. *It doesn't matter. I'm going to enjoy the time we have now.* "They probably want to give you the experience and make you feel involved since you'll be doing it all one day."

"I could do with a little less experience and a little more time to myself right now." He takes my hand and interlaces our fingers. "Enough business. What are you dressing as for the masquerade?"

I lift a shoulder. "Nothing really. I was going to wear my nicest dress and fashion a simple mask. I imagine most of the villagers won't have much of a costume, so I'll blend right in with them. What about you?"

"It's a—"

"Surprise," I finish for him, tweaking his nose. I tease, "But how will I know who you are if you're wearing a mask? I could accidentally dance with another man, thinking it's you."

"Not possible. I can instantly find you in a crowd, and I know you can do the same," he answers easily. "I'll know it's you the moment you enter the room."

I press a kiss to the corner of his jaw, then snuggle further into his arms. The fire has burned down to embers. Our hour of parting is far past due, but neither one of us wants to be the one to say it.

As dawn approaches, a melancholy feeling creeps over me. "Devereaux, what are we going to do?"

He doesn't pretend to misunderstand my question. "We'll continue as we've been, finding times like this to be together." His thumb traces my cheek tenderly and my eyes slide shut. "I don't know what my future holds, but I know I want you in it."

"When are you going back to Charistel?" I hope he doesn't hear the slight tremor in my voice.

There's a long pause. "Soon."

My heart gives a sad lurch as he lays his head on mine, his arms tightening around me.

"I can't put Isabeau off much longer. There's too much that needs my attention at home."

"I understand." I close my eyes and let his heartbeat soothe the growing ache in my chest. There's no blame here, but our two worlds are being pulled apart, and there's nothing we can do to stop it.

26

Soon.

The word haunts me, following me like a shadow as I move through the next few days. I've been frantically going through our options, reviewing every possibility I can think of, from somehow becoming a royal councilor to scheming to get assigned as his personal guard. But logic won't be pushed aside, no matter how much it breaks my heart. Nothing I can come up with will actually work.

The glimpses of Devereaux in the hallways are even rarer these days, the distracted smiles I see from a distance only reinforcing how preoccupied he is with his duties. I make excuses. He's still catching up from his time away from Charistel. Lady Isabeau missed her brother and wants to spend time with him. He's worried another late-night meeting might draw the wrong person's attention. The rationalizations pile up. Anything to prove my fears are unfounded.

Each day chips away at my hopes until I only have one left. *I have to talk to Devereaux. Mayhap he sees something I don't.*

I wait a week in vain for another one of Devereaux's notes to appear before I finally swallow my pride and ask Orvil to arrange a few minutes on his schedule. The painful lump in my throat burns with the effort of not crying at the flash of pity in the butler's eyes when he promises to find an opening the next day. Before I can slink back to my room, he gives my shoulder a sympathetic squeeze.

When my appointed time arrives, I stand outside the library like I've done on countless other occasions, knowing everything will change after this. Heat runs through my veins, replaced by ice. I grip my fingers together tighter as my stomach twists. The guards standing nearby thankfully don't bat an eye at my odd behavior, though they must be convinced I'm a fluff brain with how long I'm taking to announce myself.

Finally, I work up the courage to knock. It takes another minute and a deep breath to actually open the door.

Devereaux hurriedly finishes scribbling something on a parchment, standing while the quill flies across the paper. "Almost finished … and done."

Before he can drop the pen, I fling myself into his arms, holding on with all of my being, kissing him desperately.

He eventually pulls back, a smile playing over his lips. "That's quite a greeting."

"I've missed you." I nuzzle his neck, feeling his heart skip a beat. It's so tempting to lose myself in his touch again, but knowing our allotted time is already running out tugs me away regretfully.

Devereaux chuckles. "I've missed you too. It's been too long since we've had a moment alone." He presses his forehead against mine, staring as though he's drinking in every detail about me. "I'm glad you thought to arrange this meeting. I'll ask Orvil to include more after the masquerade. Isa's been pestering me to return to Charistel after the ball, but I'll stall her for a few weeks. Have you thought of another excuse for your father? I can always claim there's a storm on the way, so you can't travel yet."

Scheduled meetings after the masquerade? Bitter disappointment floods my mind. *Is this the life he imagines for himself? For us?* I shake my head. *That's the fear talking. I know he cares for me and misses me. I have to remember our feelings are not our circumstances.*

I step back and clasp my hands together to keep them from shaking. My heart slams against my ribs. "I need you to listen—really listen. Because I can only get through this once." *Mayhap not even once.* Despite my careful attempts not to place any blame on him, Devereaux's eyes fill with pain as I stumble through my feelings and fears from the past weeks, my voice cracking throughout. When I finish, I grab his hand. "Please, tell me you see a way. That I've missed something that will solve everything."

He gives a heavy sigh. "I don't have an answer now, but we'll find one. And I promise I'll make more time for you soon."

Soon. A spark of anger ignites in my chest as tears sting my eyes. "How? I know you too well to think you haven't already tried and failed these past few weeks. Why will next week or the week after be any different?" I close my eyes and take a deep breath, calming the frustration boiling inside me. "Devereaux, I've tried. I really have. But I can't go on like this. What am I going to do—sit in my room, waiting for weeks on the off chance we can slip away for a few stolen hours, if that? And what happens when we leave La Sailles?

You've said yourself, you're going to be even busier in Charistel. I don't want you to turn your life upside-down for me, but I expect to be a priority."

Devereaux grips my shoulders, his eyes intense. "Julietta, you're the most important thing in my life. Don't you know that? I love you."

My heart soars—then plummets into darkness. My chest tightens. I can't breathe, can't handle this. "This isn't about love."

His shoulders slump. "You don't feel that way about me." His tone is flat.

"No! It's just … I …" I press my hands against his chest, struggling to find the words.

He lays his hand against my cheek, his eyes pleading. "Then say it. Please."

Something inside me breaks. My heart is already too invested. If I say it, if I make it real, when we say goodbye, there'll be no recovering from the loss of him. But I can't see a way to be together, and Devereaux hasn't offered one. I can't destroy myself when there's no hope. "I—I can't."

His hand drops, and he turns away. The loss is like a slap, sending me reeling back. I wrap my arms around my chest, trying to keep the fractured pieces of my heart from pouring out.

Devereaux's words are so quiet, I almost miss them. "You've been holding a part of yourself back. I didn't want to admit it to myself, but I could tell. You're so open and friendly with everyone else, but with me, there's always a hesitation."

I lay my hand on his arm. "You're right. I'm scared. You're kind and funny, and you care so much about everyone and everything. You're amazing—anything and everything I could ever want. But I'm terrified there's no place for us after we leave La Sailles. If I lose you … If we can't … If I have to …" A sob chokes me, the agony I've been trying to push down finally breaking through my walls.

The library door opens.

Devereaux curses and steps in front of me, shielding me from view. He bellows, "Not now."

There's a startled squeak as the door slams shut.

I give him a sad smile. "Your next appointment is waiting for you."

"Burn them, I don't care." His face is determined, his body tense. "I love you, and I know you love me, even if you won't admit it. Why do you insist on seeing problems instead of hoping there's a way for us?"

"I have hoped! I've done nothing but think through every scenario and a lot of impossible ones. Believe me, I've clung to every scrap of hope I can, but it doesn't change reality. No matter what we feel about each other, I don't fit into your life. It shouldn't be this hard just to see each other. Tell me, how will tomorrow be any different?"

"I'll find time for you. You just have to have to be patient."

"Why? What's going to change?"

His face darkens and he spins away, staring into the fireplace. There's a hitch in his chest, then his shoulders droop.

Devereaux's realizing how impossible we are. The thought gives me no pleasure. I really wanted the Fates to come up with a miracle.

"I could leave now, if that would be easier for you." My heart shatters even as I say the words, loath to give up even a minute with him. But I would do it, if that's what he needs.

"I want you to trust in us, not run away." His voice is harsh.

I flinch, my stomach twisting. "Is that what you think I'm doing?"

"Yes. No." He runs his hand through his hair, the movement jerky. Finally, he turns and faces me. "What I don't understand how you could be so willing to go, when I can't stand the thought of parting from you."

My voice breaks as tears stream down my cheeks. "And you think I don't feel that too? Leaving you would be like ripping my heart from my chest."

"Julietta." His voice is soft as he gathers me in his arms. "My heart, I'm sorry. I'm not being fair. I should've realized how hard this was on you. How can I ask you to hope when I've neglected you so badly for so long? But since I'm a selfish beast, I'll ask you to be patient a little longer. Stay until the masquerade. We'll think of something by then."

I squeeze my eyes shut, holding on with all my might. "Until the masquerade."

27

Devereaux tries. He really does.

There are notes with the roses every night now, telling me how much he misses me and loves me.

He has Rosemarie make chocolate cremes for my and Papa's supper each evening.

Books on history and mythology, and even a Roma vase, appear in my room.

What he can't give me is time.

Each day Orvil appears with an apology, I really understand, but a little part of my heart dies. Still, I hope. Hope that he'll be able to make our next meeting. That he'll ask me for another midnight rendezvous in the library. That he's found the answer that's still evading me.

The morning of the masquerade comes too quickly. The staff has been busy since before dawn with the preparations, while the rest of the palace slept late in anticipation of the long evening.

I'm preparing to join Papa for breakfast when Lacee bursts into my room in her usual whirlwind of energy. Her arms are filled by a large black box tied with a bright yellow ribbon. "Look! Someone left this for you."

"Good morning," I laugh. "It's nice to see you, too."

She drops the box on a side table, then bounces over to give me a hug. "Sorry, sorry. I've been so busy running around with errands for the ball tonight, I haven't had a chance to catch my breath. It's going to be wonderful, better than any of the parties held in Charistel. Rosemarie's been cooking for days and everyone's been polishing and decorating the ballroom. It looks like a winter faery land."

"I'm sure it's going to be amazing. Is Edmon coming?"

She bounces from foot to foot, her smile widening. "He promised he would. Lord Devereaux even hired extra help from the village so the staff could take turns attending the ball throughout the evening. Tonight's going to be amazing."

"I hope you both have a wonderful time." A pang of jealousy hits me at Lacee's giddiness. Everything is so simple for her and Edmon. *If only maybe way for Devereaux and me.*

"We will. And you will too. It's going to be so romantic." She gives me another hug. "I have to run and help Rosemarie. I'll see you tonight." With a last squeal, Lacee disappears out the door.

My heart quickens as I take a long look at the wrapped box on the table. I drag my feet as I make my way across the room, both anticipating and dreading what I'll find inside. The present has to be from Devereaux. As dearly as I adore Papa, he's more straightforward about such things. The prince is the one who loves surprises. I bite my lip as I tug the ribbon loose and pull off the box top.

A card sits on top of a layer of gauzy silver material:

An Irelish myth tells of a maiden who ventured into

My heart is hammering in my chest as I set the card aside and peel back the covering with shaking hands. Under the first layer sits a delicate yellow mask covered in beautiful gold filigree. Next are yellow dancing slippers with long gold ribbons designed to be wrapped around the leg. Finally, a stunning yellow ballgown. Delicate embroidery on the neckline adds embellishment to the simple bust, while the skirt flares out into a wide bell with delicate gatherings in the fabric. It's a dress fit for a princess.

I sit on the floor, staring at the items in silent despair. Despite trying to safeguard the last piece of my heart, I've fallen in love with Lord Devereaux Saint-Veil, the prince of Fallian Province.

The ache in my chest grows to a throbbing pain. I drop my head to my knees and wrap my arms around my legs, trying to hold myself together, though all I want to do is shatter into a thousand pieces.

I can't take anymore. This has to end.

After a good cry, I drag myself to the sunroom for breakfast, where Papa fills the silence with enthusiastic descriptions about the friends he's looking forward to visiting on our way home. Once we part ways, I write a letter to Lady Isabeau explaining that I'm returning my payment and attach it to the wrapped box of coins. When I ask Nancey to deliver it to the princess's suite after the ball starts, the maid gives me a curious look, but blessedly keeps her questions to herself.

Now I somehow need to get through tonight without breaking. One last night with my prince ...

I'm mesmerized by the image in the mirror.

I've always avoided yellow, convinced it makes me look sallow, but the gown makes my skin glow and brings out the subtle gold flecks in my brown eyes. The soft dancing slippers fit perfectly, the gold ribbons wrapping around my calves before being tied off in a bow. My hair is left in soft brown waves cascading down my shoulders, crowned with a wreath of red and gold roses. The beautiful yellow mask completes my outfit, making me look mysterious and alluring. I've never felt more beautiful.

One last look, then I take a deep breath and turn toward the door. It's time to stop admiring myself and join the party.

The masquerade has been in full swing for an hour, but the villagers and attending staff are still trickling in. My costume shines among the simpler dresses and outfits in the hallways. I'm not immune to the admiring stares sent my way, but I'm thankful the elaborate mask hides my identity. A lifetime spent in the shadows makes it hard to be the center of so much attention.

It's a relief when I can finally duck into the ballroom and blend in with the crowd. As I look around the vibrant room, my feet stumble to a stop.

The ballroom was a dark, cavernous space when I scouted it at the beginning of winter. Now it's transformed into the winter faery land Lacee promised. Silver chandeliers with dozens of candles float near the ceiling. Mirrors in gold and silver frames bounce the light around the room, making it a dazzling sight. Silver and pale blue drapes line the windows and long doors leading to the outdoor balcony.

White and silver linens cover every table along the far wall, their surfaces groaning under the platters of food. Another table holds sparkling crystal glasses filled with a bubbly pink wine. What appears to be a small orchestra is tucked on a dais in the corner, their beautiful music floating across the room.

And the clothes. Despite almost no notice, the nobles have pulled together a dazzling array of costumes. Some outfits seem entirely impractical for the cold weather, like the thin linens of the Roma gods and goddesses, while others are elaborate and covered in so many feathers I wonder how they can move. There are butterflies and peacocks and pirates, and even some interesting interpretations of a dairymaid. Truly, I can't imagine a grander affair than this one.

My eyes are drawn to the man in black on the far side of the room. Devereaux is devastating in the fine black trousers and trim black shirt, a matching black mask covering most of his face. The only spot of color is the yellow cravat tied around his neck that perfectly matches my dress. His head comes up, and he scans the room, spotting me in seconds. I drop into a curtsy, the golden skirt pooling around me.

He immediately starts making his way across the ballroom to me. The crush of the crowd and the number of people who recognize him hamper his progress, making every inch a battle.

Seeing the necks crane to locate the source of the prince's interest, I duck behind a large group of people chatting, hoping to find anonymity in numbers. I work my way toward Devereaux, staying by the walls until our paths finally meet. He's even more striking up close. The black clothing adds a dangerous edge to his already forceful personality. Devereaux's black mask flares up at the corners, giving the impression of wicked horns. He looks like a creature from the underworld ready to lure you into darkness with whispered promises and wicked deeds.

He takes my hand and bows over it. "At last, I see my beauty tames the beast."

"Tame?" I shake my head. "Never. But perhaps I could enchant my beast for an evening."

"Dancing is usually the best way to do that. Shall we?" Devereaux places his hand on my waist and sends us spinning through the crowd.

The hours fly by as we whirl around the dancefloor, our eyes locked on each other. I drink in the sight of him, memorizing every detail, every touch. Devereaux is a peerless partner, guiding me through the steps with ease and seamlessly covering for any I've forgotten. The crowd fades away until it feels like we're alone in the ballroom.

At the end of the current set, Devereaux deftly steers us out the door and onto the shadowy balcony. We're alone in the moonlight, the faint sound of the ball coming through the closed door. I tug him into a dark corner where we won't be easily spotted and kiss him until we're both breathless.

"Are you sure you know who you're enchanting?" he teases.

"My beast, obviously. However else can I hope to tame him?" I tug on his cravat, letting the silky fabric run between my fingers. "But perhaps you're mistaken about your maiden. I could be anyone under this mask."

"There's only one stubborn woman who makes me feel like this." He leans closer, his breath tickling my ear. "I told you I would know you the moment you entered the room. You kept me waiting far too long."

"Beauty takes time." I wrap my arms around his neck and brush my lips along his jawline. "I'll make it up to you."

"I've been thinking about that."

I lift an eyebrow and grin. "Rather presumptive of you, but I guess I can't expect better from a beast."

"Come to Charistel with me." He presses my hands to his chest. "I know we haven't figured out how our lives will fit together, but we will. If we stay together, we'll find our way. But not if we're scattered across different kingdoms."

"Devereaux, don't make me be the villain here." Tears sting my eyes. "Nothing's changed. I can't keep holding my breath, waiting for you to find a few minutes for me. Having my heart break every time I think I'm going to see you and then you're pulled away for something else." I grip his hand tightly. "I don't blame you, but I also can't go on like this. I'm leaving in the morning, like we discussed." I bite down hard on my lip, muffling a sob.

"I'm sorry. I know. I—I just don't want to accept it." He cradles my face in his hands, kissing away my tears.

"Neither do I. I hate it! I don't want to leave you." My chest feels hollow. "Devereaux, I—"

I spot the glint too late. The knife flies through the darkness with deadly accuracy. Even as I shove Devereaux down, I know it won't be enough. I'm too slow. There's a sickening, wet thump before we hit the ground.

My scream shatters the night.

28

I prowl the upper hallways of the palace, unable to face anyone or stay within the hateful walls of my room. *I should've chased the attacker. There were plenty of people to help Devereaux. Why didn't I pursue them instead of clinging to him and sobbing like a helpless damsel in some bad romance novel? Useless. Worthless. How could I let this happen? By completely abandoning my duty. I was too busy kissing him to protect him. I should have sent for a replacement as soon as the pass opened. Someone who could actually do the job, since I'm a miserable failure.* The self-recriminations fly around my mind, each one landing a solid blow to my bruised and battered spirit.

Devereaux has been in seclusion with no visitors, though the healer from the village assures everyone repeatedly he'll be fine. The knife wound in Devereaux's arm caused a lot of blood loss and pain, and he'll need months of rest for it to heal properly. *No permanent damage. Except a scar and the trauma from being injured during an attack. One I could've prevented if I wasn't playing princess.*

Despite my best efforts, I keep getting drawn back to the hallways around Devereaux's rooms, hungry for any news. The sight of Lady Isabeau's cronies standing around gossiping, acting like it's a party instead of something devastating, fills me with rage. My fists clench and I grind my teeth to keep from screaming at them. The next moment I'm hollow, unable to muster the energy to move away.

An arm wraps around my shoulders. Papa watches me with a worried look. "It'll be all right, my dear. Lord Devereaux's young and strong. His wound wasn't that serious. He'll be fine."

"I know, I just—I need to see him." No matter how many times I hear it, I can't quite believe he'll recover until I see him with my own eyes.

A flurry of high-pitched voices sounds at the end of the hall. The crowd gathers around Lady Isabeau as she dabs her cheeks with a handkerchief, murmuring to the people around her. I inch closer, straining to hear her over the chatter.

"You!" Lady Isabeau's red-rimmed eyes lash out at me, condemning me. "How could you? Is this what you wanted?"

I can only stand mutely as her tirade continues.

"This is why you rescinded your contract, isn't it? You knew an attack was coming. You thought you couldn't be held responsible if you quit before it happened. Did you plan this?" Her fury hammers against me, each accusation a punch to my chest. "Who are you working with? Who did this to my brother?"

My father jumps between us. "Now, see here. I don't care who you are, you can't accuse my daughter of having any part of this evil plan. She returned your money because we were leaving the next day, and she didn't feel right about being paid since she hadn't identified Lord Devereaux's enemy, even though that wasn't part of her contract. If that doesn't prove her character, then I don't know what will."

Lady Isabeau stares him down. "If she's so honorable, why was she alone on the balcony with him? Why would she let the assassin get so close?"

"She saved his life!"

"She almost got him killed!"

They glare at each other, their anger radiating off the walls.

She points down the hallway. "Get out. If I ever see either of you again, I'll have you locked up and leave you to rot."

I gently pull Papa away and steer him toward the exit. "As he said, we were planning on leaving, anyway. Please send Lord Devereaux our wishes for a speedy recovery." My voice is flat. *No wonder she suspects me. I can't even manage to sound worried.*

On the walk back, Papa opens his mouth several times, then closes it without saying anything. When we come to the intersection that separates our rooms, he squeezes my hand, then hurries away to finish packing. I trudge the rest of the way with my eyes locked to the ground, numb to the glares being thrown at me. When I open the door to my room and find my bags already packed, I'm too deadened to register any surprise.

I drag my luggage out to the stable. Nobody is in sight, but Henri's saddled and waiting for me next to my father's horse. I wrap my arms around the stallion's thick neck and press my face against his coat. *I can't cry. If I cry, I'll never put myself together again. Don't cry. Papa needs me. I have to hold the tears in until I can break properly. Until then,*

Henri twists to rub his cheek against my shoulder, then *whumphs* into my hair. I give his nose a grateful pat, then attach my belongings to his saddle, my hands working mindlessly.

"Julietta."

I spin at the prince's voice, my heart pounding. "Devereaux."

My eyes race over him, looking for signs of his injury. His face is paler than normal and a sling supports his left arm, but otherwise he seems back to his old self. Every hair is impeccably groomed, his clothing perfectly pressed. Even that commanding aura around him is at full force.

Tears flood my eyes. I rush toward him, then falter, the cold look in his eyes bringing my feet to a stumbling halt. "What's wrong?"

His eyes narrow. "I've been trying to figure out how I missed all the signs. How you deceived me so easily."

Panic threatens to overwhelm the numbness that's holding me together. "Wh—what are you talking about?"

Devereaux holds up a handful of documents clenched in his fist. "You're the spy."

"I found them in your room. Or rather, Helene did, and brought them to me." He shakes the papers. When I don't react, he spits out, "The treaties I've been working on all winter."

My eyes widen and ice trickles into my stomach. "I didn't take them. I've never even read them."

"Stop it!" he shouts. "Don't lie to me."

"I'm not, I—"

"You're the only one who knew where I hid the real ones. And you said it yourself. Helene would never betray me. But you—" he steps closer, shoving the papers at me. "You did. It all makes sense now. This is why you were holding yourself back. Why you kept insisting you couldn't come to Charistel. It was all an act."

I didn't know it was possible to feel worse. Every word is a knife plunged into my chest. It's impossible to believe he could think I was fooling him about my feelings all these months. "No! Devereaux, no. I've never lied to you about anything, especially about how I feel about you."

"You told everyone you were my matchmaker."

"That's different and you know it!" I reach out to touch his arm, then flinch at his withering look and drop my hand. "You've always known the truth about why I was here."

"The perfect reason to move all over the palace without suspicion. You're clever, I'll give you that." He shakes his head. "That night in the library when you pretended to see someone at the door and chased them. Planting that fake coin with the symbols in the hallway to throw any suspicion off you. Setting traps in the desk. Pretending to search the palace day after day, acting frustrated. Yes, you're very clever to cover your tracks and point me elsewhere."

"It wasn't an act. There's a spy, but it's not me. I'm being set up."

"How long were you hiding in Charistel? Getting in and out of the castle there must've been simple with your skills. You probably seduced the guards to let you in and out of my rooms. I bet Isabeau never even hired you."

I reel back, anger bubbling up at his accusations. "How dare you! I've never been to Charistel. If you care, there are people in Cassia who can vouch that I was there for over a year before I took this assignment."

He waves his hand. "People you've paid off. It has to be you. Nobody else knew where the treaties were, or that the ones in my desk were fake. You were planning to leave even before Isabeau confronted you outside my room. You would've gotten away with everything if Helene hadn't found the copies you made." His eyes narrow. "You thought you'd hidden them so well."

A roaring fills my ears. *What can I say to make him believe me? If I was standing in his shoes, I'd believe I was guilty too. How can I convince him?* "You've accused me of being a spy before. You were wrong then, and you're wrong now. After everything we've shared, everything we've felt for each other, can't you trust me?"

"I have to believe the evidence." His eyes are stones.

I'm falling, with nothing to grasp but air and only emptiness where my heart beat moments ago. The growing lump in my throat makes it hard to swallow. "I don't know what I can say, except it wasn't me. I haven't lied to you about my feelings for you, or anything else. If you can truly think that I would do something like that—that I could be that deceptive about something so important, for so long— then you don't know me. You never did."

"I don't think I do." He straightens, his hand dropping to his side. "Leave Fallian Province. Immediately. In two days, you're going to be declared a traitor. If you ever set foot back here, your life will be forfeit."

I nod, the lump in my throat choking me. *Don't cry. I can't cry. Papa needs me. Hold it together for just a little longer.*

He turns away. "Goodbye, Julietta."

When Papa arrives in the stable, I've pushed down the shock and betrayal enough to finish tying on Henri's saddlebags. I hope my expression resembles a smile more than a grimace, but it's hard to tell. We set out at a brisk trot, eager to be away.

My father talks about all the things we can do after we get home, sending the occasional worried glance at my monotone replies. I haven't told him about Devereaux's threat. That someone I love thinks I could be capable of such cold manipulation is too much to bear.

Papa holds a hand over his eyes as he peers at the sky, his brow furrowed. "Do you think we can make it through the pass before dark?"

I rouse myself out of my fog enough to glance at the sun's position. "I don't think so. But we should be able to travel well enough with the moonlight."

He shoots me an incredulous look. "In the winter, when a storm could blow up at any minute? Julietta, no. We'll spend the night at the village and try for the pass tomorrow if the weather holds."

"You're right." *Can we make it out of Fallian Province before Devereaux's deadline?* I mentally shrug. *What does it matter ...*

I give myself a mental slap. *What am I doing? Having Devereaux think I betrayed him is terrible, yes, but it's not the end of the world. I'm hurt—all right, I'm devastated—but I'll recover with time. I can mourn the loss of what we were and what we could have had, but I need to keep myself together for me. I deserve to be happy and to find someone who'll trust me. Someone who knows I'd never be so malicious to hurt another person like that. If Devereaux's willing to declare me a traitor over planted treaties, I can only imagine what would've happened if I went to Charistel and people were constantly plotting against me.*

As we approach the outer wall, I can't help but take one last look back at the palace where it sits shining on the horizon, the light reflecting off its white walls. When I arrived, I thought it was cold and lifeless. But now I'm leaving my home. Despite the tragic ending, I'll never regret a moment of my time here. I finally know I can love someone.

I sit up straighter in the saddle and give Papa my first genuine smile in days. "I haven't been to the village yet, but I hear they have a wonderful inn."

30

A broad man with beefy arms waves to me from behind the bar. "Welcome to The Clock and the Candlestick. What can I help you with tonight, milady?"

I search back through the stories the Lacee and the other staff told me about the village. "Are you Remi?"

The innkeeper's forehead wrinkles. "Have you heard of me?"

"You and your sourdough bread. You're famous."

He rocks back on his heels, a grin lighting his face. "Well then, the first loaf is on me."

I return his smile. "That's very kind of you. I'd like to get rooms for myself and my father for the night, stabling for our two horses, and any advice you have about whether we can get across the pass tomorrow."

"I'll let you know about that last bit in the morning. Storms blow in quickly in these parts." He reaches beneath the bar for the room keys. "The rooms come with supper included. You can purchase breakfast from me, or there's a bakery in the village."

I lift an eyebrow. "Sending customers away? That's very neighborly of you."

He winks. "My wife runs the bakery."

I chuckle. "Ah, enterprising and clever. We'll need to buy some supplies for our journey, so we'll be visiting your wife shortly in either case."

"She'll be happy to help you. We've had a lot more travelers coming through with the pass open so early in the season."

The innkeeper hands over the keys with instructions on how to find our rooms and his wife's shop. I help Papa bring in our saddlebags after seeing that the horses are settled in their stalls. We decide to use the last of the sunlight to tour the village since we hope to get an early start in the morning.

Everything about it reminds me of home, except the roofs are shingled against the snow instead of thatched. People go about their business with friendly nods and greetings. The main road holds the inn and the few shops, the rest of the residences set out in a haphazard pattern. The innkeeper's wife is just as friendly as he was, setting us up with dried beef strips, apples that have wintered over, and the promise of two fresh-baked nut loaves to be delivered in the morning before we depart.

We return to the inn after sunset and settle at a trestle table for supper. Rosemarie's grudging praise of the food here was well-deserved. There's a thick lentil soup loaded with hearty root vegetables and a side of the famous sourdough bread. For dessert, we have a buttery cake topped with blueberry preserves and fluffy whipped cream. A lovely pear cider provides a perfect accompaniment to the meal. Even deep in winter, everything tastes fresh and delicious. My appetite is lacking, but I force myself to eat a good portion of the tasty food.

After the meal, we sip our drinks and enjoy the music from the local lute player strumming in the corner. Papa suggests we turn in early, and I'm about to agree when I spot a familiar face in the crowd.

"I'll be up in a minute. I want to finish my cider." I kiss him on the cheek, waiting until he's disappeared from the top of the stairs before making my way over to the table in the corner.

Marcel watches my approach with hooded eyes. His blond hair is slicked back, his large black hat and leather gloves set on the table beside him. He's traded in his favorite blue jacket for a green one with black buttons. "Julietta, join me." He gestures to the seat across from him.

I settle in the chair, swallowing hard. *Not a single 'poppet' or 'darling'. This is bad.* "I'm glad to see you here. I had to leave before my replacement arrived at La Sailles."

"They've been dispatched. I'll babysit the princeling until they arrive."

Devereaux and Marcel? They'll tear each other apart before a day has passed. Imagining them trading barbs, Devereaux with his forthright manner and Marcel with his lazy drawl, is almost enough to bring a smile to my face. "Then I'm leaving him in excellent hands. I'm tired and have a long journey ahead of me, so let's not waste time." I fix him with a look. "Go ahead. I know you can't let me leave until you deliver your news."

Marcel shifts in his chair. "The Guild has received word of your … exploits here."

I lean forward. I know what's coming, but it doesn't stop my stomach from twisting into knots. "Marcel, let me explain—"

He lifts his hand. "It doesn't matter what or what explanations you have. They've decided. You're blacklisted."

I close my eyes, absorbing the news. It could be worse. Papa and I have enough to get by comfortably for a long while. But my professional reputation will be in tatters for the rest of my life. The Guild's influence spreads to almost every kingdom, which is why they guard it so fiercely. Any hope I had of securing a long-term position with a noble household has vanished. And it could conceivably spill over and impact Papa on his next business deal.

But we'll find a way. We always do. "Thank you for bringing me the news personally. I know how you hate to travel into the country, especially in the cold." I stand and offer him my hand. "It's been a pleasure working with you. I'll understand if you can't acknowledge me as a friend after tonight."

Marcel studies me for a moment, then stands and takes my hand in both of his. "Good luck, poppet."

"Safe travels. And I hope you tell Ysabel how you feel. Love doesn't come along every day."

He winks before climbing the stairs to his room. I'm about to follow when I spot Remi wiping down the bar, and it reminds me of one last piece of business.

I touch his shoulder. "Sorry to bother you. Is Edmon around?"

"Edmon?" The innkeeper thinks it over for a moment, then shakes his head. "Nay, can't say I remember anyone by that name, and I know almost everyone around here."

An uneasiness creeps over my skin. I hold the bar in a white-knuckled grip, steadying myself. "The boy you have running errands to La Sailles and helping around here?" At his blank look, I add, "Young, freckles, green eyes, limbs too long for his body?"

His eyes light up with recognition. "Oh, I remember that lad. He visited here a month ago, and then today. Four gentlemen were in here earlier talking to him. I only remember because they were in such a hurry to leave, they almost forgot to pay their bill and I had to stop them at the door."

Fear slams into me, threatening to send the world spinning off its axis. Lacee told me she met Edmon when he was running errands for the innkeeper. He lied. He had no business being at the palace. *It's him. Edmon's the spy.*

Devereaux is in danger.

31

I barrel up the stairs, shouting at the top of my lungs for Marcel.

He bursts out of his room shirtless. "Poppet, why the racket?"

I shove him back through the door. "Get dressed. They're going after Devereaux."

To his credit, Marcel flies into action without question, yanking on his clothes while I rouse Papa and tell him what's happening. "Get the healer and anybody else you can think of, and get to the palace."

Marcel grabs my hand and we're flying down the stairs and out to the stable. The horses are saddled in minutes, then we're speeding down the road, the moonlight shining down on our path. I quickly fill him in on what I learned from the innkeeper and my suspicions.

"I think Edmon was spying and going through Devereaux's papers. He might even be the same spy from Charistel, or mayhap it was one of those men with him tonight. But the five of them together, leaving in a rush right when Devereaux's unguarded, can't be good."

He nods grimly. "They have too big of a head start. We'll never catch them. Our only chance is if they traveled slowly, or are waiting until the palace quiets down for the night to make their move."

The rocks in my stomach grind together as I weigh the odds. *Not good.* "We have to try."

We both lean forward, encouraging the horses to greater speed. Their hooves fly over the snow. The weeks of warmer weather and heavier travel have made the road to the palace a muddy mess, but the stallions don't falter. Mile after mile passes and my dread grows. *What if we can't get to Devereaux in time? What are they planning?* My only hope is Devereaux is wary after exiling me this afternoon and has his guard up. I silently curse myself for being so distracted by Devereaux's injury that I forgot to carry my weapons today, of all days.

We make the turn for the palace as the moon begins its descent in the sky. A dark puddle in the road and a shadow in the ditch has me yanking Henri's reins, jumping off the horse before he's stopped.

"Devereaux?" I rush over, my heart in my throat.

Gently, I turn the man over. Edmon's boyish face is twisted in pain, his freckles standing out against his white skin. He groans, clutching his stomach as blood seeps between his fingers. Judging by the wound's location, and the stains on his clothes and surrounding snow, there's nothing to be done. It's only a matter of time.

"Edmon, where's Devereaux? What were you planning?"

He whimpers. "I never agreed to kill him. You have to believe me! I didn't think anyone would get hurt. My family needed the money. That's the only reason I agreed to any of this. They stabbed me, said they were done with me. They said nobody would get hurt, they just wanted some information, otherwise I wouldn't have agreed to help them. You believe me, don't you?"

I grip his shoulders, resisting the urge to shake him. "I believe you. Now tell me where they are. I have to stop them before they hurt Devereaux."

"They said the prince was getting in their way. Don't tell Lacee what I did. I didn't think anyone would get hurt. But they stabbed me." Edmon's eyes are dull, his lips blue. "The prince was chasing after you. Thought you were going through the pass tonight."

I'm running back to Henri before he finishes. Marcel kneels next to Edmon and whispers in his ear. The boy winces, then nods, trembling. I gallop past them as Marcel pulls his knife out. Knowing what comes next, I send a quick thought to the Fates to watch over Edmon, then turn my attention to the road ahead.

It's impossible to pick out Devereaux's tracks or those of the men following him among the hoofprints. But there's only one road to the pass and I have to believe they'll all stay on it.

Devereaux was coming after me. Did he change his mind about the two-day deadline ... or something else? Why did he give me two days instead of throwing me in the dungeon? I shove the thought out of my mind. I can't get my hopes up or be distracted, not while Devereaux's in danger. *If they left Edmon out in the open like that, they're in a hurry. Not worried about discovery. Sloppy. Unprofessional. Marcel and I just might have a chance to outfox them, even if we're outnumbered. But it also means they're planning to finish with Devereaux tonight and then race back into whatever slimy hole they crawled out of. They won't leave any unfinished business.*

Marcel's stallion is trailing somewhere behind me, but I don't slow down. Getting to Devereaux is the only thing that matters. It all depends on the timing: when Devereaux left the palace, when the men discovered his departure and followed, and how far we are behind them. If only the Fates could murmur in my ear where everyone is and if I'll get to him in time.

Poor Henri's tiring after a long day, but he pushes valiantly on. I keep up words of encouragement, knowing he's giving me his all. As we get deeper into the forest, the ground rises, marking the beginnings of the climb. A flash of a rider ahead of me. My pulse quickens, energy surging through me, every nerve alive. I stand in the stirrups and signal Marcel to be prepared.

A shadow drops from the tree above me, knocking me off my horse.

I go down in a tangle of legs and arms and snow. My back hits the ground, the air forced from my lungs, leaving me gasping. The man pins me down, his face a snarl. The blade flashes in the moonlight. Only instincts save me as my arm deflects the attack, the knife burying in my shoulder. I scream. My fist connects with his head, knocking him off me. I struggle to my feet, blood dripping into the snow as I yank out the blade.

We circle each other, looking for an opening, the dagger tight in my hand. My attacker tenses, then tumbles to the ground, Marcel's knife in his back.

The Guild member reins in next to me, but I shout at him to keep going. He takes off in a spray of snow. I warily approach the downed figure, but he doesn't move. I quickly dispatch him, then jump on his fresher horse. Clucking at Henri to follow, I race to catch up to Marcel. A hastily wrapped scrap of torn fabric staunches most of the bleeding from my shoulder, but a trickle seeps through, leaving a grisly trail glistening in the snow.

The nightmare ride stretches out as we catch glimpses of the riders ahead of us, but never seem to gain on them. There's only two of them, leaving me to worry where the third one has gotten to.

Minutes feel like hours. The riders know we're following, shooting frequent looks over their shoulders. The trees are thick as we wind our way toward the base of the mountain. Just when I think we're trapped in an endless chase from which we'll never break away, the horse ahead stumbles, bumbling into another. It's just enough to let us close the distance.

Marcel balances in his stirrups, his natural grace and hard-won skill clear as he hurls the dagger at the lead rider. The knife hits its mark and the man slumps over his horse. Marcel urges his stallion closer to the remaining rider, then performs a beautiful flying tackle, bringing the man to the ground.

I glance over my shoulder as I fly past, confirming Marcel's knife buried in the man's chest. He signals the all clear, yanking the blade out before scrambling to his feet.

Three down, one to go.

32

It feels like days drag by as we ride. Half of me is hoping Devereaux left so long ago it will be impossible for us or the remaining assassin to catch up to him, the other half hopes I'll find him safe and sound around every turn. Waves of dizziness leave me clutching at the stallion's mane, but I push on, determined to get to Devereaux.

We come to one of the rare patches of road where the trees fall away, leaving a long stretch visible. The moonlight shines on a lone figure walking his horse. My heart instantly recognizes Devereaux, though there's no way to see any details at this range. Relief floods my body, bringing on another surge of faintness as I call out to him.

Devereaux leaps on his horse and gallops back to me. We simultaneously dismount and I jump into his arms, tears streaming down my face. I murmur his name before his lips crash down on mine, capturing my mouth in a heart-stopping kiss. Trying to pull him even closer, I press myself against him, wrapping my arms around him. Too late, I remember his injury. I loosen my grip, but he pulls me in tighter.

I break away with a gasp. "Are you insane? You're hurt and you come out here in the middle of the night alone. What were you thinking?" I grab him and kiss him again, cutting off his response.

We finally break apart, both breathless. I clutch his shirt, trying to keep from attacking him again.

"Julietta, you're here." His hand grips my shoulder and I flinch back with a cry. "You're hurt!" His hand hovers helplessly over my hasty bandage, his eyes flashing. "Who did this? I'll kill them! What happened?"

"A run-in with the men chasing you." I quickly fill him in. "We have to get you to safety."

Marcel gallops up with a spare horse in tow. "You owe me a new coat."

Devereaux steps between me and Marcel, holding me back with his good arm. "Who are you?"

I shove around him. "Marcel, Devereaux. Devereaux, Marcel. Marcel's from the Guild. There, we're all acquainted. Now everyone get off the road."

Devereaux keeps a wary eye on Marcel, staying between us as I herd them over to the trees. Hidden in the darkness, we hold a quick whispered conversation.

I adjust the bandage on my shoulder, trying not to let the pain show on my face. "Our options are to make for the pass and hope can we reach the next town before the assassin catches up, turn around and try to sneak past him, or stay here and set up an ambush."

Marcel keeps watch on the road. "We don't know anything about the man, including where he is. We should hole up somewhere. Your father's raising the alarm in the village and they'll alert the palace. In a few hours, this place will be swarming with people and the attacker will run for the border."

"Or blend into the crowd and strike in the confusion if they're not concerned with surviving." I close my eyes against the flash of dizziness. "Hiding it is."

Devereaux huffs. "Don't I get a say?"

"Only if you have a better idea."

"We can't stay out here all night. We'll freeze. Not to mention hiding five horses would be difficult."

I turn on him. "You came out here knowing you could freeze to death? Stubborn, foolish —"

"I was coming to apologize! And I thought you were going to be out here. In danger. Again."

"That's no excuse for you to risk yourself, especially when you shouldn't even be out of bed."

"I'm perfectly fine to walk and ride a horse."

"Is that what—"

Marcel clears his throat. "I hate to break up this lovely reunion, but there's still someone out there with his sights set on your prince."

"Right, right." I stomp down my temper and try to focus on the problem. "Is there anywhere we can take shelter? A homestead? Cave?"

Devereaux starts to shrug, then stops. "There might be—"

"Shush." Marcel crouches against a tree, scanning the road.

I pull Devereaux down, listening. Horses. More than one. Cursing, I shove him flat on the ground and crouch over him, knife in hand. Marcel does an excellent impression of a rock, his eyes glittering in the darkness.

The riders blow past us, headed for the palace. Five men, heavily armed, light armor. My heart squeezes as our odds of surviving drop dramatically.

Marcel waits until the hoofbeats fade before saying, "We have thirty minutes before they find their friends."

"Can we outrun them?"

Marcel chuckles without humor. "It depends on how annoyed they are with your prince. Congratulations on that. Somebody is going to a lot of trouble to kill you."

I glare at him. "Not helping. Devereaux, what were you saying about a shelter?"

He shrugs. "Nothing, really. There are supposed to be some hunting nests in the trees, but I've never seen them."

"Then not something we can count on."

"There might be another path. There's a river that should be frozen over. It'll get us off the road."

I shake my head. "We'll still make better time on the road, and we don't know if the river can take the weight."

Marcel peers down the path. "They could have more friends on the way. I'd rather not run into them."

"Worth the risk. We'll use the spare horses as remounts, which will buy us a little more distance between us and them. Come daybreak, we can see where we are and decide our next move."

"What about cutting across the forest and going back to the palace?" Marcel paces deeper into the trees. "We won't be fast, but it'll be harder for them to track us if we stay away from the road. They have numbers on their side, and probably fresher horses."

"There's too much danger trying to go around them," I argue.

Devereaux frowns. "There's really no good option. We just have to pick one and hope the heavens are on our side."

Marcel snorts. "Never trust to luck when a skill will do.

But you're right. They're all equally bad. What about—"

He wobbles, surprise lighting his face. The ground disappears from under his feet. I reach out to Marcel, but too late—he falls into the darkness.

33

"Marcel!" I lunge forward, relieved to see the hole is only about eight feet deep. "Marcel, are you all right?"

He groans, throwing an arm across his eyes. "Leave me alone. I'm done playing with you and I'm going back to bed."

I give a shaky laugh. "Not yet, my friend. After Devereaux's safe and sound, I'll make sure you're given the royal treatment. But until then, on your feet."

"That might be a problem. I twisted my knee on the way down." Marcel grumbles as he sits up. He winces, holding his left leg. "That's unfortunate."

"Hold on. We'll find something to pull you out."

"Splendid plan, darling. Not that I couldn't make it, but I'd hate to dirty my boots."

Glancing at his head-to-toe layer of mud, I snort. "Can't have that."

Devereaux and I haul Marcel out of the hole using reins cut from a bridle. It's a painful, grueling process for all of us. We collapse on the ground, nursing our injuries. Marcel's knee swelled to the size of a melon in the time it took to pull him out. It's apparent he isn't going to handle a cross-country trek, or even a hard ride to the pass. Devereaux's face is pale and a sheen of sweat shines on his face despite the frigid temperature. I'm sure I look just as battered with all the tumbles I've taken tonight and the blood once again leaking from my shoulder wound.

We're in no shape for a fight, but if Devereaux's right—and he usually is about this kind of thing, much to my annoyance—staying hidden in the forest means we'll slowly freeze to death.

There's only one way out, but Devereaux's not going to like it ...

Marcel struggles to his feet, his leg causing him obvious pain, but he doesn't utter a single complaint as he tests his weight on it. He shakes his head. "Are you sure you don't want to rethink leaving me? I'm going to slow you down."

"You're not getting off that easy. I'll still get some use out of you, no matter how much you try to wiggle out of it." I turn to Devereaux, knowing he's the one I have to convince. "One of us needs to lead them away, and it has to be me." When he protests, I press a finger to his lips. "Marcel's too badly hurt and you're the target. I can trick them into following me, then lose them in the forest. I'll be fine. If they get close enough to realize you're not with me, they'll abandon the chase and retrace their steps to search for you. Remember, they're after you, not me."

Marcel frowns at me, but I give him the barest shake of my head. I don't want Devereaux to realize that killing me and making my body disappear would be the perfect coverup for the assassins. Everyone already suspects me after the masquerade. This would be the clincher. Our attackers have probably been setting me up for weeks, planning for this night. Only they didn't expect Helene to find the planted treaties so soon, or me and Devereaux to leave the palace before they got there.

I stare into the prince's beautiful eyes, my heart thundering in my ears, ready to leap off the cliff. "Devereaux, I love you."

Devereaux sucks in a breath as Marcel mutters, "This is awkward." The Guild member discreetly slips away as fast as his injured leg allows.

I take Devereaux's hand, holding it to my chest with both of mine. "I tried so hard not to love you, but you're my weakness. I've never met anyone like you. I love every stubborn, annoying, honest, gentle, and generous thing about you. My heart always belonged to you, I just didn't know it."

The joy on his face makes my heart twist. "Julietta, my love. You know you captured me long ago."

His kiss steals my breath. It's beyond painful knowing I'm leaving him, that we're being forced apart before we've had a chance. I can only hope he can't feel the harsh desperation churning through me. I close my eyes against the dizziness as his lips brush against my forehead.

Devereaux pulls back, his mouth set in a firm line. "I'm coming with you."

I press my hand over his heart. "This is bigger than both of us. You're the prince. If something happens to you, the kingdom would be in chaos." I step closer, staring determinedly into his eyes. "I'm going. You know I can do this and I have the best chance. Trust me."

Devereaux frowns, but nods reluctantly. "We'll meet back at La Sailles."

Marcel hobbles back over. "No, the village. They'll

expect us to go back to the palace. There might be an ambush waiting for us."

I nod. "Good point. We'll meet at the bakery. It's less obvious than the inn. Wait until you see them go past, then ride for the village."

I whisper to Henri to take good care of Devereaux and Marcel, giving him one last pat on the nose. He's given me his all tonight. The ride back to the village will be hard on him, but safer than what I'm about to do. Devereaux leads him deeper into the woods with his and Marcel's stallions, leaving me alone with Marcel for a moment.

We slowly walk over to the two horses captured from the assassins. I lend Marcel my shoulder for support and lower my voice. "Keep him safe, whatever it takes. After … tell him I'm sorry."

He nods, sympathy in his eyes. "I'll make sure he understands, poppet."

"Thanks, Marcel." I kiss him on the cheek. "And I meant what I said about Ysabel."

When Devereaux returns, Marcel limps away to work on the decoy, giving us a moment of privacy.

The prince cups my cheek, his thumb gently tracing across my skin. His eyes are dark pools, drawing me in. "I don't like this."

I close my eyes, savoring his touch. "I know, but it's our best chance." *He'll be all right, that's all that matters. Marcel will protect him.* "Now give me a kiss for luck, and I'll see you at the village in a few hours."

"If you insist."

I kiss him, with all the emotions coursing through me flooding to the surface, trying to pour all my love and passion and everything I can't say into this kiss. There's an urgency to his touch, a consciousness of the danger I'll be in, even if he doesn't know the ending in store for me.

I break away gently, knowing our stolen time is running out. That this moment, this kiss, will never be enough, no matter how long I linger here.

He presses his forehead to mine and gives me a stern look. "Come directly to the bakery. Don't stop for tea on the way there."

I slide my hand around his neck, letting my fingers toy with his hair. "But what if they have chocolate cremes?"

"You can have platters of chocolate cremes at every meal for the rest of your life."

"Even at breakfast?"

"Whatever you desire, my love. Just … come back to me." His smile can't hide the worry in his eyes.

"I love you." I drink him in, trying to memorize every feature so I can carry him with me for what's coming. I give him a quick kiss on the cheek, then turn and stride away, not wanting my courage to fail in front of him. *Goodbye, Devereaux. Please forgive me.*

Marcel is waiting with the captured horses. He hands over the reins on the lead stallion, giving my hand a squeeze as we silently say goodbye.

My steps are light, my eyes clear as I lead the horses onto the road. Knowing I'm saving my love banishes any sorrow or regret. I'm distilled down to one purpose now: give Marcel and Devereaux as much time as I can.

Marcel did a good job of dummying up a decoy rider for the second horse, considering the short time he had to work with. From a distance, in the darkness, the tree branches covered with a cloak should be enough to fool the men chasing us. I sent a quick prayer up to the Fates that the captured horses have another long ride in them.

At the road, I mount up, orienting myself. We're closer to the valley than I realized, which means Devereaux and Marcel should reach the village in a few hours if the weather holds. I point my horse toward the pass, checking that the trailing stallion's lead rope is tied tightly to my saddle with a slipknot for quick release if needed. Verifying everything is in place, I keep my head down and my hood tight as I spur the horses into the night.

# 34

It doesn't take long for the men to find me.

They burst from the forest, shouting to each other, whipping their horses into a frenzy as they give chase. Their mounts are tired from the earlier climb through the pass, putting us on even footing. Hooves pound a relentless beat behind me, pursuing, always there. I glance over my shoulder once to confirm all five are following, then keep my gaze locked forward. Everything around me is a blur as I hunch over the horse's neck, trying to squeeze out every bit of speed. I know how this chase is going to end. Until then, every second I keep them following me is another gained for Devereaux and Marcel.

A patch of ice slows my horse for a moment, giving up a precious few feet to our pursuers. Fear threatens to break through my numbness, but I shove it away. Devereaux and Marcel are counting on me. I will not fail. I can't.

Time stands still in this eternal struggle; neither of us can gain a decisive advantage over the other. My borrowed horse is past his limits, but I beg him to keep going just a little longer. The moonlit road twists and turns, rises and falls, preventing arrows and knives from bringing things to an end before the Fates are done with us.

The horse stumbles with a shrill scream. I fly off, the world spinning around me. The world goes black for a moment as I slam to the ground. My injured shoulder warms with the sticky heat of blood. I ignore the burning pain. No time to check the horse for injuries. The second horse's tether broke free, and he's running down the road, out of reach. I struggle to my feet and stagger through the trees, forcing air into my lungs.

There's only room for one thought in my mind: *keep them away from Devereaux.*

The men crash through the forest behind me, gaining on me. Closer, closer they come. It feels like they'll reach out and grab me at any moment. I keep running. Over rocks, through bushes, slipping on ice. Always forward. My legs shriek for relief and my shoulder screams, but I can't stop. Everything narrows to the next step. Keep. Keep leading them away. It'll be over soon, but I'm going to fight with everything I have until that last breath. For Devereaux. Any pain is worth it if it means saving him.

The ground rises. My senses tell me I'm still heading toward the pass, although I can't tell how close I am. Up, up, up, I climb, the incline getting steeper as I go. My wound makes me clumsy, but I refuse to slip. I cling to the mountain, dislodging as many stones as I can as I go. My efforts are met with muffled curses, and I grin. The ascent abruptly ends and I slide down the backside in a barely controlled descent, bouncing off rocks and other forest debris littering the hillside. A hard jounce sends me tumbling sideways, curling in a ball to protect my head. I sprawl at the bottom, lightheaded and covered in dirt. *Keep going. Save Devereaux. Move.*

My hazardous descent bought me a few minutes. The men are swearing loudly as they pick their way down. A loud *thump, thump,* followed by a scream that abruptly cuts off. I'm not sure what happened, but it's a safe bet there's one less man following me. The knowledge gives my legs an extra spurt of energy.

If I can stall my hunters a little longer, lead them farther away, Devereaux and Marcel will be out of reach soon. I keep to as straight a line as I can, making no attempt to cover my trail. My aching feet pound against the ground, my straining muscles earning every inch. But the long night and cold have taken their toll. My legs are unsteady, my head woozy. The queasiness is a minor annoyance I ignore as my lungs labor to suck in air.

A wide, shining silver ribbon spreads out before me. Sending a prayer up to the Fates, I slide out onto the ice. My feet slip and slide as I scrabble across the frozen river. The ice creaks and groans under me, the dark water visible beneath the surface. Cracks spread beneath my boot. I throw myself forward, sliding on my knees. I crawl as fast as I can, my skin sticking to the ice, my boots scrabbling for grip on the slick surface.

When I'm mere feet from the riverbank, my remaining pursuers reach the water. Without hesitation, they run after me, their boots pounding on the surface. I haul myself up, leaping for the side as a loud snap breaks the night air. One man plunges into the river with a scream, disappearing beneath the surface. More cracking and breaking ice sounds. I don't wait to see if the water will claim anyone else, diving into the trees as the men yell and run for the riverbank.

Branches whip by, scratching my face. My airways burn. Every step feels like it'll be my last, but I keep going. I stumble and smash to the ground. The rocks open gashes on my palms. My shoulder is in agony. I scramble up and keep running, needing to keep them away from Devereaux and Marcel as long as I can.

I burst into a small meadow, a huge rock wall rising in front of me. Before I can disappear into the trees again, snaps and crashes echo around me. My pursuers are closing in from all sides. They'll be on me in moments.

I stumble across the clearing. *If I can move my legs, I can climb. Now GO!* My numb fingers wedge into the first crevice. My shoulder howls in protest. Every muscle is shaking. I grit my teeth and force myself up the icy surface. Shouts sound behind me.

Nausea and dizziness flood my senses. My foot slips. The weight is too much for my damaged shoulder, tearing muscle as I scramble to hold on. I tumble through the air, hitting the frozen ground on my injured side. I strangle the scream in my throat. Blinded by pain, I try to stand, but my body has finally given up.

A thought works its way in through the red haze: *don't be taken alive.*

I draw my dagger, bracing to carry out one last duty. The man is on me before I can lift the knife to my throat. He stomps on my wrist, pinning it in place as he pulls the weapon from my grasp.

The other two are behind him, moving as though everything was choreographed ahead of time. The second man stands within striking distance, watching us, while the third scans the trees surrounding the clearing. *Coordinated. Some training, used to working in teams. Not experts or the third one would have stayed hidden.* I can't help cataloguing the information, even though I know it won't do any good.

The man grabs my coat collar and drags me up to my knees. *Local coloring and features.* Brown hair, brown eyes. His skin is weathered, but so are most people who work outside. Up close, there's nothing to call attention to him or mark him in a crowd. The only thing that would make you look twice is the chilling smile that freezes the blood in your veins.

"Look what we caught." He studies me for a moment, his grin widening nastily. "You're the foreigner the little rat told us about. The one the prince fancies."

No accent. There's no reason to disguise it now if he has one. "You're mistaking me for someone else. I'm just a lost traveler on my way home."

He runs the blade down my cheek with a leer. "Nice try. You're lucky we're in a hurry or else I would enjoy spending more time with you." With one clean slice, he opens a gash in my coat and presses the blade's tip over my heart. "Where's the prince?"

I laugh thickly. "Beyond your reach."

"I don't have to hurt you, but it's one perk of the job." His hand flashes through the air, backhanding my cheek with a sharp *crack.* "Now, one more time. Where's the prince?"

The blow brings tears to my eyes. My cheek throbs with every heartbeat. I glare defiantly at the man, rage the only thing keeping me conscious.

He shrugs. "No matter. There's only so far he can get before we catch him. But your body will be a wonderful diversion for the people at the palace."

I'm torn between relief he's going to make this quick, and wishing to prolong the exchange to buy Devereaux a few more seconds. But I'd rather Devereaux not be forced to deal with my broken remains showing up in his front yard. Fates know he'll blame himself enough without it. "You're wasting your time. They'll know I'm not responsible for any of this."

"Will they? Perhaps, in time. But it'll create enough doubt and confusion to serve our purposes." He leans forward, his sour breath brushing my face. "Goodbye, little girl."

A snowball explodes against the man's head. He turns his head, distracted. I grab the knife and reverse it, stabbing the would-be assassin through the eye. Before the body hits the ground, I've yanked the blade out and thrown it at the closest target. He collapses to his knees, his hands gripping the blade buried in his throat. Devereaux bursts from the tree line with a roar, attacking the last man with a thick branch. A wet *thump*, then the man crumples in the snow.

"Devereaux," I sob. "No! Why are you here? You're not supposed to be here." I struggle to stand as he runs over to me, crushing me against his chest. His arms tighten to an uncomfortable degree, but I don't protest, needing the same reassurance.

"Julietta!" He buries his face in my hair, his body shuddering. "Are you hurt?" He pulls back long enough to quickly look me over, eyes widening in horror at the blood soaking my slashed clothes.

"Not mine," I reassure him. "Are you really here? I'm not dreaming?" My hand presses against his cheek, needing to feel him, to know he's real and not some hallucination of the afterlife.

He pulls me tight against him, his head resting on mine. "I'm fine, we're fine. Marcel's behind me somewhere. We couldn't leave you out here on your own." Devereaux half supports, half carries me back toward the trees and away from the bodies cooling in the snow.

"Your timing is perfect, but why did you come after me? Are you all right? What happened? Is Henri hurt? Why didn't you go to the village?"

"Yes, hm." He gives me a mischievous grin. "Well, after you left, I remembered you said your partner usually handled the fighting side of the job. And then I realized you didn't have a partner to help you, so I thought I would come offer my services."

I try to scowl at him. "The whole point was to keep you out of their hands."

"Plans change. You're the one that taught me to be more flexible. So really, this is all your fault. And if I was in the village, then I couldn't do this."

Everything melts away as he pulls me closer. I throw myself into the kiss with total abandon, joy pouring through me. My heart feels like it might burst from happiness.

I break away. "Don't think that's going to make me forgive you."

"Then I'll have to try again."

His lips crush against mine. Just when I'm about to dissolve into a puddle, he pulls away, leaving me breathless.

"Now?" He raises an eyebrow, a slow, tender smiles spreading across his face.

I press against him. "I'm starting to see your point of view, but I need more convincing."

"I'd be happy to oblige, but let's get you out of the cold first."

"Spoilsport. You always use that excuse."

"One of us has to make sure you keep all your toes."

Marcel hobbles into view, leaning on a long stick. "Looks like I missed all the fun. You couldn't even save one for me after all I've done for you, poppet?"

I glare at him. "You were supposed to keep Devereaux away from them."

He refuses to look guilty. "Apparently he's stubborn."

Devereaux grins. "I figured if they were following you, they wouldn't notice us following them."

"That's terrible logic!"

"Yes, but I was coming after you, no matter what. Having a flimsy excuse made Marcel feel better."

"You're both idiots." A wave of dizziness and exhaustion hits me like a hammer, my vision going black around the edges. My legs collapse.

Devereaux catches me before I hit the ground, his face panicked. "Julietta, what's wrong?"

"Just tired," I mumble. "I'm still annoyed at you."

Marcel peels back what's left of my coat to look at my injured shoulder, then shares a sharp look with the prince. "I'll get the horses." He disappears into the trees.

Devereaux cradles me in his arms, his steady heartbeat lulling me to oblivion. He kisses the top of my head. "Rest, love. Everything will be all right. I've got you."

35

It takes a moment for the room to come into focus, and another to recognize it as my bedroom in the palace.

Lady Isabeau smiles from the chair next to the bed. Her honey-colored hair is arranged in a simple twist, with a few ringlets framing her face, her cream gown impeccable. "You're finally awake. Good. Before you worry, Devereaux's fine. He wanted to be here when you woke, but I sent him off to get a few hours of sleep. You may have noticed my brother sometimes lacks common sense, so I have to impose it on him."

I try to gather my muddled thoughts together, hampered by the cotton in my brain. "Marcel and my father?" My tongue feels thick.

"Fine, as well. Your father brought most of the village with him last night. Your friend is resting comfortably and has already charmed half the ladies in the palace. The doctor said his leg will be fine. And your horse is in the stable, being pampered by the stableboys."

"Thank you." My thoughts keep scattering. "Did … Is

everyone …" I put a hand to my head. "I can't think."

She nods to a large pitcher on the nightstand. "Probably the herbs they've been ladling down your throat. They smell ghastly. We're still sorting everything out, but your friend claims all the enemies were disposed of and things should be safe for now. A storm struck last night, which should stop any more unexpected visitors. Regardless, we have trusted people watching all your rooms."

Devereaux's sister seems confident there's nothing to worry about, and I'm too befuddled to question it. I watch her as my mind drifts in a haze, thoughts dissolving into puffs of clouds before I can grasp them.

"Here, take a sip." She lifts a cup to my lips.

I shudder as it burns down my throat, making me gag. A detached fog drifts over me.

Lady Isabeau leans forward, her brown eyes calculating. "I promised I would fetch Devereaux when you were awake, but I wanted to discuss some sisterly business first."

A faint warning bell tries to shake me from my stupor, but my brain can't banish the mistiness that's taken over. "Could we later? I don't think I'll talk good now."

"No, I think now is the perfect time." She gives me a dazzling smile that does nothing to set me at ease. "Why did you come back?"

"Dev'row was in trouble." My lips feel funny.

"How did you know?"

"Figured it out." I tap my forehead, then get distracted by my fingers. They're shorter than I remember. I move them, fascinated, as they make shapes in the air.

"Are you a spy?"

"Nope."

She narrows her eyes. "My brother cares about you.

Does he love you?"

I squirm back into my pillows, avoiding her eyes.

"Here, have another sip." She holds the cup up to my mouth.

This time I barely taste it. I press my finger to my nose, wigging it back and forth with a frown. "I can't feel my face."

"You'll be fine. Now, about my brother. Does he love you?"

I grin at the ceiling, Devereaux's face swimming into focus. "Yes."

"And you love him?"

"So much! He's so sweet and han'some and when— when—when he kisses me …" I sigh.

"Then why did you leave?"

I puzzle over her question. Finally, "You told me to? Or he did?" My eyelids grow heavy and I yawn.

"But if you love him, why not stay and fight for him?"

"Doomed." I snuggle down in the bed, wrapping my arms around the pillow.

Lady Isabeau curses, muttering something about doctors and wine. She shakes my shoulder. "Julietta! Why are you doomed?"

I mutter, "Teacups," my mind already falling into the beckoning darkness.

I crack my eye open, wincing at the pain in my head. My throat is as dry as the Sulomi desert in summer. I struggle to sit up, tugging at the cocoon of blankets wrapped around my legs and waist.

Devereaux captures my hands. "Careful with your shoulder."

I drink in the sight of him, my body relaxing at his touch. "You're here."

He gives me a glass of cider. I keep hold of his hand as I gulp thirstily, the pain in my head retreating.

Devereaux squeezes my fingers. "I would've visited you sooner, but Marcel's been guarding your room like a dragon watching his hoard, insisting you need rest. Isa had to distract him so I could sneak in here. She's the only one around here with more charm than him."

"You don't give yourself enough credit. You're very persuasive when you want to be."

"True, I managed to bewitch you." He dimples.

I nod seriously. "It was the arrogance. I'm helpless against a man who keeps walking into all my booby-traps repeatedly."

"And here I thought you were using me for Rosemarie's chocolate cremes."

"Those too." I wince at the pain in my cheek, my fingers gently probing the cuts covering my face. "I must look ghastly."

"You've never been more beautiful."

My heart flutters. "You're lying, but I appreciate it."

"I'm not. You're here, alive." Devereaux's face turns serious. "You thought you were going to die when you led those men away."

I tighten my grip on his hand as the nightmarish events flare through my mind. My shoulder throbs. "It doesn't matter now. What's important is we're all fine."

He glares at me. "It matters to me."

I cast around for something to distract him. "Do you know who sent them?"

"Some minor rabble-rouser I've never heard of who was convinced I was plotting against him. Marcel's dealing with it. Don't change the subject. Why, Julietta?"

My stomach lurches, remembering how close I came to losing him. "Because it's my job." I try to tug my hand away, but he won't release his grip.

"You made me think you were going to be fine. That nothing would happen to you." Devereaux runs a hand through his hair, a haunted expression in his brown eyes that I long to soothe away. "I wasn't naive enough to think it wasn't dangerous, but I thought you had a plan."

"I did."

He glares at me. "Dying is not a plan."

"It is when all that matters is keeping you alive." I twist up to my knees, putting myself at eye level with him. "Devereaux, I love you. I would do anything to keep you safe."

"Don't you think I feel the same way?" He moves from the chair to the bed, settling next to me. "Julietta, you mean more to me than anything or anyone. I love you. If you had … If I …" He shakes his head, his eyes glistening. "Promise me you won't try to sacrifice yourself for me ever again."

My heart aches at his obvious anguish. I rest my hand against his cheek. "Can you promise me the same thing?"

He presses his lips together. "That's different."

"Not to me. And not to your kingdom."

"I don't care about the burning kingdom, or anything else!" He carefully wraps me in his arms, his head resting on mine. "You can't make me choose, because there's no choice. All I care about is you.”

“Oh, Devereaux.” A lump grows in my throat and tears spring to my eyes. I bury my face in his shirt, clutching the fabric as my tears soak into it.

“Blast it, I didn’t mean to make you cry.” He fumbles for a handkerchief.

“It’s a good cry.” I manage a soggy giggle as I dry my eyes. “I’m going to Charistel with you.”

“You are?” He breaks out into a beautiful smile, which quickly changes into a frown. “But what about all your reasons? What’s changed?”

I shrug, wincing as the movement pulls at the stitches in my shoulder. “Being hunted by assassins together really puts things into perspective.” The smile fades from my face as I nestle closer to his side, reassured by his presence.

“I almost lost you. I can’t go through that again. You were right that we need more time to figure things out. We’re both still learning how we can fit into each other’s lives. I thought I was giving up too much by going to Charistel without a plan, but really, this could be exactly what I wanted. I was looking for a new start after this contract, a new adventure, and that’s wherever you are. And since you can’t come to me, I’ll go to you. Just because we don’t know how it’ll work doesn’t mean we can’t find a way. It’ll be hard, but look at everything we’ve already overcome.”

I fix him with a stern look. “But things will have to change. You’re wonderful at the big gestures, but I need to know you’re there for me every day, not just when things go awry. People will try to tear us apart, so we need to trust each other. And I’m not going to beg for scraps of your time. I’ll make a place for myself there somehow, and we’ll make room for each other. A real partnership. And that starts with me going to Charistel, and helping you find people you can trust to take over some of your duties."

Devereaux makes a face.

I laugh. "I know, but if you try to do everything yourself, you'll go mad. You need people you can trust around you. People who will help you when you become king. It's understandable that you have misgivings about your father's advisors. So, hire your own. It'll take time, but I'll help you find them. They can manage the smaller tasks and research, and you can focus on the important things, like me." I wink.

"I'll hire you. Then you'll be at my beck and call and have to do everything I say." He kisses the inside of my wrist, his lips lingering on my skin, making my heart stutter.

"I'm happy to work *with* you, but I'll never work *for* you. You're already an arrogant beast. I can only imagine all the wicked things you'd think up to torture me if I you could actually order me around."

A roguish gleam lights his eyes. "I don't know. It sounds like a great idea to me."

I give him a mischievous grin. "I have other ideas about what to do when we're alone together."

He kisses the soft skin behind my ear, making my breath catch. "I look forward to hearing every one of those ideas. And I know you'll love Charistel. You already have one friend at court. Isa said you convinced her you weren't involved with the assassination attempts. She also said you had some very interesting thoughts about me and our relationship." He grins.

What is he ... Snatches from her visit float up to the surface. "Oh. Oh, no!" I groan, covering my eyes. "Your sister must think I have wool for brains."

"She was laughing when she told me, but you still impressed her." He pulls a folded parchment sealed with wax out of his pocket and dangles it just out of reach. "Isa has a proposal for you. A job offer."

I shake my head. "That's kind of her, but I'm not going to accept any more Guild contracts. I'll figure out something else to do while you're busy in council meetings and all the other tasks you refuse to give until I knock some sense into you."

He chuckles. "It's not that kind of job. I think you'll like what she has to say."

"We'll see." I hold out my hand.

"First, promise you'll accept it."

I snort. "There's no way I'm agreeing to that."

"Even if it solves all your problems?" He looks too pleased with himself.

"That's what I thought about this contract and look at the mess we landed in."

His eyes darken, sending a thrill through me. "It had some advantages." Devereaux leans toward me, his eyes intent on my lips, then shakes his head and straightens. "Isa wants to offer you a consulting job. I know she doesn't have my dazzling wit or unending patience, but she can be charming when she wants to be. Besides, there's no point in refusing because she always gets her way in the end."

I frown. "I'm not much of a party planner."

"She's thinking ambassador duties and treaties. Her way of being more involved in the kingdom's affairs, like our parents want, without putting in any actual effort." He gently pulls me into his lap. "Of course, I would need to work with you on them. Lots of intense one-on-one time."

I wrap my good arm around him and look up at him

through my lashes. "That sounds terrible."

"It gets worse." He nuzzles my neck. "We'd be based in Charistel, but we'd have to spend a few months here every year. For research."

Heat blazes across my skin everywhere his skin touches mine. "This is the better library. And you know I love to research things."

"We'll have to make sure we don't accidentally get snowed in, of course." He presses kisses down my jaw, gently nibbling as he goes. "Otherwise, we would be trapped here for months. Alone. Together."

"Of course," I say breathlessly. "We definitely want to avoid that."

"And there will be a few trips to other kingdoms as we negotiate a treaty or try to build goodwill. I'll need your help on those, too."

"I am the only one who could help you with things like that." My mind struggles to process the offer while Devereaux does an exemplary job of chasing every thought out of my head with his lips. *Everything I wanted. Papa can move with me or visit me whenever he wants. Something I could do that makes a real difference and still be with Devereaux ...*

I bury my fingers in his hair, trying desperately to keep my thoughts focused. "I don't want to spend all our time discussing treaty terms, no matter how much you love them."

His soft laugh against my neck makes me shiver. "You might distract me for a few minutes here and there."

"There'll be rumors."

"Good. I plan to give them plenty to talk about. And given how stubborn you are, I suspect you're going to insist on having all these helpers trained and in place before I can convince you to marry me.”

My heart beats impossibly faster. “Is that so? And how are you going to persuade everyone else—including your parents—to let you? They may have an Irelish princess picked out for you.”

“I’ve been told by someone very smart and perceptive that I’m stubborn.”

“Don’t forget arrogant,” I murmur in his ear.

“That reminds me.” He reaches for something on the floor. “There’s one last thing we need to do before you decide.”

Snow trickles down my back, making me shriek. He chuckles as I curse, writhing to get the icy slush away from my skin.

“Could have been a knife.” He winks.

I swat his arm, laughing. “I’m going to make you pay for that.” I tug him closer, brushing my lips across his.

Devereaux presses his forehead to mine, his eyes full of mischief. “I look forward to it.”

***

Note from the Author: Word of mouth is crucial for any new author. If you enjoyed the book, please leave a review on Amazon, Goodreads, or your favorite review site. Even a few words make a huge difference and are greatly appreciated!

Thank You!

Amanda Kaye

Want more Julietta and Devereaux? Sign up for my newsletter to get an exclusive BONUS EPILOGUE for more banter and steamy kisses: https://www.amandakayebooks.com/beasts-blades-subscribe/

ALSO BY AMANDA KAYE

To hear about the next exciting release from Amanda Kaye,
sign up for her newsletter at:
AmandaKayeBooks.com/subscribe-now/

<u>Blades Series</u>

Cinders & Blades (short story)

Briars & Blades

Wolves & Blades

Beasts & Blades

Sirens & Blades

Trails & Blades

<u>Other Short Stories</u>

An Oath of Fire

Slithers & Swords

Restless Tides

ABOUT THE AUTHOR

Amanda Kaye loves plotting new ways to torture her characters and throw them into danger. Nothing makes her happier than reading an amazing book with an awesome character arc; her favorite authors include Mercedes Lackey, Robin McKinley, and Patricia Briggs. She can always find an excuse to buy sparkly nail polishes and chocolate chip cupcakes. Amanda lives in sunny California with her two mini-monsters masquerading as kittens.

Her stories remind you that there's always a silver lining no matter how dark the night. She'd love to chat with you about your favorite books at:
https://www.amandakayebooks.com/subscribe-now/

www.ingramcontent.com/pod-product-compliance
Lightning Source LLC
Chambersburg PA
CBHW030806210726
48290CB00002B/450